JANET PYWELL

Faking Game

A Mikky dos Santos Thriller

First edition

ISBN: 978-1-9998537-2-3

This book was professionally typeset on Reedsy.
Find out more at reedsy.com

Foreword

FAKING GAME - A Mikky dos Santos Thriller

THEY DID THE WORST THING YOU CAN DO TO A WOMAN ...

And only sweet, sweet revenge will do in Janet Pywell's fourth Mikky dos Santos thriller.

Ever rebellious, the reformed European art thief takes on two assailants who stole a gem from her more precious than any work of art – leading her hot on their tails in **an international mystery that blends Eastern European intrigue with page-turning psychological suspense.**

Mikky dos Santos is a changed woman. The ex-forger has traded her life of crime for domestic bliss – these days she's an aspiring portrait photographer and a mom-to-be, expecting a baby girl with her love Eduardo. If it weren't for the vibrant tattoo of Edvard Munch's *The Scream* prominently displayed on her forearm, she'd be downright domesticated.

But at a birthday celebration in an idyllic Spanish villa, tragedy strikes. Lulled by her newfound domestic happiness, Mikky wanders into the villa kitchen for a midnight snack (for the baby, not her) and unwittingly walks in on two thieves stealing the multimillion-euro birthday gift. In the ensuing fray, **the most tragic theft isn't that of the priceless work of art –**

Wracked with guilt and despair, Mikky is devastated. **And she just can't seem to shake the feeling that she knows one of her assailants ...**

After a grief-stricken Eduardo leaves her, **she decides her only course of action is revenge: Find the men who killed her daughter and left her life irrevocably destroyed. Mikky embarks on a one-woman quest of vigilante justice,** tracking the thieves through Spain, Poland, and Estonia, and enlisting help from her past life in the European underworld – much to the delight of armchair travellers and fans of fierce female sleuths, alike. But **it's not long before she realises the art thieves aren't at all who they'd seemed** – and her vendetta becomes unimaginably dangerous.

Fans of female sleuths from the YA series HEIST SOCIETY right up to Kinsey Millhone will fall for this vulnerable, kick-ass adventuress. She has more than tattoos in common with the protagonist of Stieg Larsson's MILLENNIUM series, and she's an irresistible treat for readers who love the complex plots and sly sophistication of movies like OCEAN'S 8 and shows like GOOD GIRLS.

Set in Spain (Barcelona), Poland (Wrocław), and Estonia (Tallinn), this exciting novel will keep you hooked. You won't want to stop turning the pages. A promise is a promise ...

Acknowledgement

Many thanks to all my friends and family who have supported me in writing this novel.

Grateful thanks to sculptor and artist Tracey Falcon, fellow international crime author Tim Heath, motorbike enthusiast Robert Mienes, Paula Mathews and Louise Hickmott.

And, especially to Amanda Gerrard who gives me roots and wings.

Golden Icon - The Prequel

Golden Icon – The Prequel

Josephine Lavelle, a once-famous opera singer, has one last opportunity to resurrect her career and earn the right to perform again on the world's most prestigious and celebrated stages.

But her fight for the future she craves is derailed when her ex-husband forces her to take possession of a solid gold icon, part of a secret hoard of art treasures stolen by the Nazis, that dangerous men are prepared to kill for.

As well as determining the fate of the Golden Icon, Josephine must come to terms with her past, and fight for her own life. If only her choices were simple ...

For your FREE copy subscribe to my newsletter: https://www.subscribepage.com/janetpywell

Chapter 1

"Every block of stone has a statue inside it and it is the task of the sculptor to discover it."
Michelangelo

I take Eduardo's hand as we weave our way through the crowds toward the red-carpeted steps of the Arte Moderno Museo Barcelona.

Suspended over our heads, twelve metres high, by invisible taut wires, Umberto Palladino's latest masterpiece, *Los Globos* – three balloon-shaped sculptures over four meters in diameter – sway deliberately and precariously on the mid-summer breeze.

'My goodness,' Eduardo whispers in awe. 'How could someone think of this?'

'Isn't it magnificent?' I reply. 'And, it's all made of paper.'

At the cordoned-off area, uniformed staff smile professionally, while vigilant security guards with dark glasses eye up the guests, matching them with the list in their hands.

Eduardo pulls our invitations from the inside pocket of his jacket while I gaze in awe at the glass, titanium, and limestone curved exterior of the museum. We're only five minutes from Las Ramblas, one of Barcelona's most famous and busiest streets. The iconic song, 'Barcelona', sung by Freddie Mercury and operatic soprano Montserrat Caballé, blares out from gigantic speakers, creating a festive atmosphere, and a light show illuminates the sky in multicoloured bursts of magic.

I recognise a Spanish Premier League footballer, a German supermodel, and a few American actors looking groomed and gorgeous behind designer sunglasses. Standing in the shade, Glorietta Bareldo and Josephine Lavelle, two of the world's most famous sopranos, are holding court to a multitude of fans. Their partners, Bruno and Simon, stand to one side, deep in conversation.

A ripple of excitement flutters through me, and I squeeze Eduardo's fingers. I'm always delighted to see my birth mother. When Josephine catches sight of us, she smiles and separates herself from the group, and I'm drawn into her embrace, inhaling her familiar exotic perfume.

'Hello, my darling.'

'Hi, Josephine,' I whisper.

Glorietta turns to me. 'You look radiant, Mikky. Pregnancy suits you.'

'I'm over three months, and there's barely a bump,' I complain, stroking my stomach.

Simon's eyes crinkle in greeting. He shakes Eduardo's hand and kisses me. 'You look very beautiful, Mikky.'

'Perhaps you'll have twins,' Bruno suggests, winking.

'No, the scan's been done and there's only one,' Eduardo says with confidence, and I'm conscious of his arm around my waist. I lean against his shoulder, aware of the love that surrounds me, and I know that I'm the happiest I've ever been in my entire life.

This is my family.

'I'm so pleased you're here, Mikky. We're so looking forward to Glorietta's birthday party tomorrow – all of us together again at last.' Josephine links her arm with mine. 'Have you seen the sculpture? Isn't it amazing?'

'Stunning, but what does it all mean?' Eduardo replies, and Josephine turns away, distracted by another conversation.

I nudge him. 'You're a philistine, my angel.' Then I explain, 'Each of the three globes – the balloons – represent our world, planet Earth.'

'They're massive.' His voice is filled with admiration.

'The first globe' – I point – 'is made from all types of paper since printing began. It represents the creation of mankind and the recorded word. It's also indicative of how communication influenced two global wars. If you look carefully, there are burnt images – war scenes and distressed faces – scorched onto the globe ...'

Eduardo pushes blond hair from his eyes. 'How do you scorch images onto paper? The faces are so lifelike and harrowing.'

'The tragedy of war is reflected in their eyes,' I agree. 'Umberto used newspapers from archives and presumably it took years to source them. There's a lot of controversy about him using them for a project like this.'

'You mean burning pictures onto them?'

'The scorched war scenes show the destruction and devastation, but it's a contradiction in terms. Critics argue that Umberto has also caused destruction, and they're dismayed he used old and valuable newspapers for a project like this. That's why it's so political and controversial.'

I squeeze Eduardo's hand and point to the second globe, pleased he is as affected by its dramatic impact as I was the

3

first time I saw it, a few days ago.

'The second one is made of newspapers that represent fake news in our current society – the world in which we live now. It questions us, forcing us to face the truth. How can we trust what is said, what is read, and what is meant? What is real, and what is fake? This globe is made from news reports and stories in all languages from around the world. The pages are all taken from fake news that creates fear, chaos, and uncertainty.'

'Are things really that bad?' he asks.

I shrug. 'It represents our daily struggle to understand and decipher the complicated truth from all the information that bombards us on a regular basis through social media. You see there, the images burnt on the second globe are psychological portraits of despair. See the faces? Confusion, agony, fear, and pain.'

One of the images scorched onto the paper is similar to Edvard Munch's *The Scream*.It's a masterpiece that is familiar to me because I have an exact replica tattooed in vibrant colours on my forearm.

I wait for Eduardo to digest this information before continuing with my explanation of the third globe.

'And the last one,' I add, 'represents the planet of the future. It's made of foreign banknotes from around the world, and shows how mankind has valued money, power, and greed over humility and kindness.'

'It looks out of shape, and it's much larger than the other two,' Eduardo says frowning.

'It's engorged. It's a world that has stuffed itself on money, power, avarice, lies, and greed, and it's about to explode.'

'So, is that genuine money, glued and rolled up?'

'Yes.'

'It must have cost a fortune – is it legal?'

'He's done it,' I say with a shrug. 'More controversy. More attention.'

Eduardo stares at me. 'Is this supposed to be controversial or artistic?'

'That's the beauty of art. It's how we interpret it. In this sculpture, Umberto Palladino wants to demonstrate that man has effectively learned nothing from history. We've ceased to help others and, in doing nothing kind or loving, we have allowed our vices to take over, and we effectively destroy ourselves.'

'That's depressing.'

'I guess so,' I say with a smile.

'And it's all made of paper? How did he make them?'

'It's a technique that he's learned over time and I think it's part of their charm or illusion – not to know how he does it.'

'It's very clever,' says Eduardo. 'It looks like they've just evolved in the air without any effort, like spacecrafts. They're massively impressive.'

'I'm sure there's a YouTube video or podcast on how to create things like this on a smaller scale, but to craft something on this level is incredible,' I agree.

'You wouldn't want one of them to fall on you. They must weigh a ton.'

'Or more.'

'Do Josephine and Glorietta like this guy's work?'

'Umberto Palladino is probably one of the most well-known sculptors in the world, up there with Jeff Koons, Antony Gormley, Kiki Smith, and Rachael Whiteread.'

Eduardo looks blankly at me, and I nudge him and laugh. 'Try to pretend you know who they are.'

Over the next half an hour, we're introduced to the various people invited to the official launch of *Los Globos*. There are curators, artists, agents, local business people, and dignitaries. The atmosphere is exciting and fun, and when Glorietta slips her arm around a short man with a bulbous nose, thick lips, and a deeply wrinkled forehead, I'm curious, and I realise I'd like to take his photograph.

'Umberto Palladino is the creator of *Los Globos*,' Glorietta announces proudly.

I'm surprised the sculptor's hand is as soft as a child's. He leaves a wet kiss on my cheeks, and I discreetly wipe away his spittle.

He shakes Eduardo's hand, and it gives me time to study his profile; bulging eyes, sagging jaw, and hairy ears. He wears a yellow bandana at his neck, and although he's clean-shaven, an open shirt reveals thick grey chest hair. His crumpled, baggy jeans drag on the floor next to overworn leather sandals, his toes are gnarled, and his nails are dirty and chipped. He doesn't seem to bear any resemblance to the groomed man in the article from *El Pais* last weekend, and I wonder at the use of airbrushing under the dramatic headline:

Umberto Palladino – A Genius of Our Time?

Umberto appears nervous and unsettled, and he is quickly whisked away to be introduced to another group of people; business people in suits, probably investors or bankers, or someone else far more impressive than Eduardo and I.

'He's a wonderful man,' Glorietta says, smiling at a young-looking, attractive blonde woman with a group of well-dressed teenagers. 'And he's a loving husband and father to four wonderful boys.'

I touch my bump.

We'll be a proper family. My child will have roots. It will be our family. Will she have Eduardo's blond hair or will she be dark like me?

After fleeing from New York a few months ago, after my disastrous art exhibition, I'd had time to think. I'd also realised I was having a baby. I hadn't planned on getting pregnant, but I was overjoyed, and I'd rushed back to Eduardo in Mallorca. Since then, we haven't been apart. Now, as we walk to our secluded positions for the official opening, under the sculptures of *Los Globos* – hailed as the most successful piece of artwork created by the master of all sculptors Umberto Palladino – the only thing on my mind is the growing baby inside my womb.

Josephine whispers in my ear, 'Isn't Umberto a genius? You'd never think it to look at him, would you? Bruno has commissioned a sculpture of Umberto's for Glorietta's birthday present. *The Bull* – it's absolutely amazing.'

'Have you seen it?'

'Only briefly, Bruno will reveal it tomorrow at her birthday party. It's amazing, Mikky. You'll never believe it.'

'Why?'

'It's made of sheet music,' she whispers, and then falls silent as the city's mayor is introduced to the crowd. He takes the stand and taps the microphone, and there's spontaneous applause.

I'm happy in my silent thoughts, gazing at the vapour trails overhead in the cloudless blue sky, counting the remaining months of my pregnancy. My daughter is due at the end of October. I know she's a girl. I haven't had it confirmed by doctors, but I just know in my heart. When I lay my hands on my stomach, I know I'm touching my baby daughter.

I glance at Josephine, and we share a small smile. This is my chance to start again. This is our family, my daughter – and no one is being given away this time.

The mayor of the city is speaking. His dull voice is flat and boring, and it drones at a monotone level. I suppress a yawn and stretch my neck, easing the aching pains creeping into my skull, tilting my neck from side to side. I'm tired, and I could do with sitting down. I've been awake most of the night with indigestion. I stand on one foot and lean against Eduardo for support, and he smiles at my growing impatience.

'Stop fidgeting,' he whispers.

The dull noise seems to grow louder and more monotone, reminiscent of an annoyingly loud wasp. The speech is droning on, and I glance up, squinting behind my sunglasses, turning my head and scanning the sky. I recognise that sound.

Eduardo smiles indulgently at me. He doesn't seem to have heard anything, but I've heard it many times. I've used drones to track thieves and murderers, but also more pleasurably, I've used them to film Eduardo kitesurfing and skiing.

'Do you hear that?' I whisper.

He follows my gaze and a few other people standing near us also begin to look up at the sky.

'They must be filming the event,' I say.

The drone appears to be one of the more professional ones, frequently used for the inspection of wind turbines, roads, bridges, and forestry or agriculture. These unmanned aerial devices are now also used to deliver mail by Amazon and to film terrorists in war zones. I imagine the view the controller will see from the drone's camera; a crowd of over two hundred people and three massive paper globes.

I search the crowds to spot the ground-based controller,

but they could be kilometres away – these drones have an incredible range.

Josephine shades her eyes dramatically under her floppy summer hat. At her side, Gloria smiles irritably. She's hanging on every word the mayor is saying about Umberto's work, but the drone's insistent aria grows louder.

Umberto pulls the bandana from his neck and dabs the perspiration at his temples while faces begin to turn upward, looking for the source of the high whine. This drone has a camera, but there's also a small package clipped to its under-belly, and instead of circling overhead, the drone appears to be heading right for the sculpture, and at a tremendous speed.

Someone screams, a man shouts, a security guard runs.

'Oh my God!' I grip Eduardo's arm. 'It's going to hit the—'

The explosion is deafening.

The paper worlds above us explode. Shattering, igniting instantly, flames burst into the sky – a multitude of bright oranges, reds, and blues. The flaming exhibits hang precariously, swinging, suspended by the invisible wire over the crowd, who collectively seem to suddenly realise that this isn't part of the planned opening performance.

A cloud of black smoke descends, and I duck as the sparks rip and ricochet around us. The fumes are toxic, and in the confusion, I lose Eduardo's hand. I cough and choke, and covering my face and streaming eyes, I run. I'm trampled on and pushed aside by people panicking; running blindly, I can't identify anyone. Bodies are falling, hands are pushing, and people are surging in all directions. I stumble down the steps, falling to my knees. A burning ball crashes to the ground and rolls along the flaming red carpet, coming toward me, expelling notes, foreign currencies that float free, burning in the air. The heat and toxic smoke are overpowering. I jump to one side as it crashes down the steps and comes to a halt at the barrier, smouldering and burning brightly.

I run to a safe distance, where the air is pure, and catch my breath. Eduardo finds me and pulls me to him. 'I couldn't see you.'

At my feet, Umberto collapses onto the pavement, choking tears and coughing.

The second globe sways and then smashes to the floor, bouncing down the steps and onto the pavement, crashing into the cement fountain. The screaming crowd disperses, scattering in all directions; running and covering their heads with their hands, sheltering from the flying debris.

The remaining ball dangles and swings from the invisible wires. Fanned by the fierce flames and poisonous gases, the newspapers catch fire easily. The globe sways and smoulders, and the anguished faces on the sculpture, now seem to have long flickering fiery tongues. The stench of burning newspaper and noxious fumes is overwhelming, and bits of newspaper float on the breeze toward us like flaming arrows.

I'm shaking, but Eduardo pulls me closer, and I'm wrapped in his arms unable to speak, gazing at the raging fires.

'Are you alright?' he whispers.

I nod, watching the medley of tumbling burning paper in dreaded fascination, and I'm shocked as a reporter shoves a microphone in Umberto's face. A photographer snaps images of the scene, but a security guard appears beside the mayor and pushes them roughly away.

Beside us, Josephine holds onto Simon's arm, and Bruno stands protectively at Glorietta's side.

Originally here to report on the exhibition, TV and newspaper reporters are now taking advantage to film the shocking drama and broadcast the event live to the world.

Around us, a handful of uniformed police are speaking on radios, clearing the area, and in the distance, the wail of sirens fills the air, coming louder, closer with screeching urgency. The audience that was only a few minutes ago so majestic and self-contained, are now distressed and hurrying away.

Security guards arrange transport and many people leave; the glamorous and the celebrities are the first to escape. Umberto's wife and children climb into a waiting car, but I can't take my eyes from Umberto's face and the silent tears cascading down his cheeks.

Selfishly, I wish I had my camera. I'd like to capture his look of terror, disbelief, and disappointment.

The stench is overpowering, and I assume it's the glue that flares and flashes, blue and white streaks that give off the nauseating aroma. I cover my nose with a tissue, detached with curious interest, watching the burnt newspaper falling to the floor and the debris settling on the pavement.

'Terrorists?' the mayor shouts into his phone, and with a uniformed guard, he hurries toward an unmarked police car. 'ISIS?'

'Anyone hurt?' asks a Guardia Civil officer.

We sit in the shade a safe distance from the fire engines, watching scores of people surge out of the museum in a state of urgency and fear. It seems heartless to walk away as many have done, and I regard the scene with morbid fascination, focusing on faces and expressions of despair and worry.

Simon says, 'I thought the drone was part of the display.'

'I thought it was taking pictures,' adds Eduardo.

A warning is shouted by the fire crew, and we all watch as the last globe wrestles free from its restraints and falls to the floor with an explosive thud. There's a gasp from the remaining crowd, but this time the fire crew deftly extinguishes the flames until the sculpture has been totally destroyed.

I exhale calmly and hold my tummy.

My baby is safe. My family is safe.

'Should we say something?' Eduardo nods at Umberto, who remains motionless, surrounded by people who I assume are students and friends from his studio. Perhaps they helped him with this incredible project that now lies in ruins.

'What can we say?' I reply.

Simon guides Josephine, Glorietta, and Bruno to the waiting taxi. 'Come with us?' he says.

I link my arm through Eduardo's and shake my head. 'I need to walk beside the sea. We'll see you back at the villa later.'

We watch their car navigate its way into the congested traffic, where hooters honk, and sirens fill the streets. It's as if all the emergency services have been galvanised into action.

'Was it a terrorist attack?' whispers Eduardo.

'I don't know, but there was a bomb attached to the drone,' I reply.

'Is that possible?'

'ISIS regularly attach bombs to spy drones in Iraq and Syria.'

'Do you think you should tell the police?' He nods at the sea of Guardia Civil uniforms spilling from a black van.

I shrug, but I'm casting my eyes everywhere. I know the controller won't be far away. I imagine they'd want to witness the damage and devastation they'd caused.

'But why bomb this exhibit?' I think aloud.

'Who would want to destroy Umberto's sculpture?'

'Good question, Eduardo. Who and why?'

* * *

The following evening, there are fifty important guests for one amazing birthday celebration. I glide along the terrace of Glorietta and Bruno's villa like a ghost, between clinking glasses, laughter, and whispered conversations. Moonlight glistens on the illuminated vineyard below, where rows of neat vines radiate out like long fingers, spreading from the finca and over the hills, pointing toward the half-moon and the infinite darkness.

I glance down over the balustrade to where couples are dancing beside an illuminated kidney-shaped swimming pool. A fifteen-piece band, singing Nina Simone's, 'My Baby Just Cares for Me', drowns out the sound of laughter. I'm happy to stand alone in a quieter part of the terrace with the clicking cicadas, and where sweet jasmine, and *dama de noche* – lady of the night – fill my senses with a heady scent.

I'm having a baby.

The June breeze fills the Catalan hills, and I think I can smell the salty Mediterranean from twenty kilometres away. Sant Sadurní d'Anoia, in Alt Penedès, is only forty minutes from Barcelona, and home to the well-known Spanish sparkling wine known as Cava.

Glorietta and Bruno's villa, on a vast and industrious estate, is minutes from the beautiful bodegas of Freixenet and Codorníu. I've spent a restful week relaxing here – until yesterday – and the shock of the exhibition and the destruction of Umberto Palladino's famous sculpture, *Los Globos*.

The event made headlines around the world. Umberto's tearful face was splattered across news channels, and he hasn't appeared tonight at Glorietta's birthday party. She had thought of cancelling the celebration, but after speaking to him, he had insisted she go ahead with her party. Interestingly, he also told her that no terrorist group had taken responsibility for the attack, and until forensics returned with a more solid conclusion, it might even be regarded as an accident – a stray drone operated probably by an irresponsible teenager.

An accident?

'Well, if drones can close airports,' says one guest.

'Look what happened at Gatwick,' replies another.

I'm sure a bomb was attached to the drone. If there's camera footage taken from one of the guests or television crews who were watching the opening of the exhibit, then that might verify my story, but I've promised Eduardo I won't get involved. We're on holiday, I'm pregnant, and as he pointed out – I have to leave it to the professionals.

I wander along the terrace, happy to be alone with my thoughts as I listen to snatches of conversation. The refurbishment of the property since Bruno invested here has been remarkable. His dream is to make a sparkling wine to rival some of the best in the world, and we have spent most evenings teasing him about the quality of his bodega. Even though I'm not drinking alcohol, I've taken a sip, and teasingly declared my preference for a rival wine.

The vast terrace covers three sides of the villa, and entering at the side through bifold doors, I'm inside and standing in the reception, where a group have gathered to admire Bruno's birthday present to Glorietta. Unveiled earlier in the evening to an appreciative crowd, Umberto's unique creation, *The Bull*, is in the centre of a large mahogany table. The proud fighting bull stands on a plinth, forty centimetres high and eighty centimetres long. Nose to tail, it's a third of the size of a Spanish fighting bull – *toro de lidia* – a specially selected bull chosen for its stamina, strength, energy, and aggression.

'The woven paper is specially crafted using sheet music,' Glorietta explains to the guests around her. 'The paper has been treated and dyed red and black to give a shiny effect on the bull's coat.'

'Is it from the opera *Carmen*?' asks Olivia, an attractive woman who was once Glorietta's personal bodyguard. As she leans forward to study *The Bull*, her long auburn hair falls over her shoulders. She holds her locks to her cheek and peers closely to read the twisted notes on the bull's flank, before smiling triumphantly.

'It's definitely *Carmen*.'

'I love it. I love the fact that it's in motion – charging with his head down – and you can see the ripped muscles and strength in his neck and shoulders.'

'It's so wild and full of fire and passion and energy.'

'Just like in the opera.'

'Glorietta's favourite opera,' exclaims Jeff.

Olivia's husband is shaped like a banana. As if he's embarrassed to be tall, and there's a restlessness in his watchful gaze that I've often seen in men.

'We saw Glorietta in *Carmen* in Seville, didn't we, darling?' he adds.

'It's a fluke.' Filippa, Glorietta's cousin, speaks in heavily accented Italian. She wears Gucci's latest creation. It's an orange and turquoise evening dress that compliments her brown eyes and olive skin.

'Not fluke – you mean a fake.' Her husband, Antonio, must be pushing seventy, thirty years her senior. He flips a white silk scarf over his hunched shoulders that hides a withering Adam's apple. His protruding neck reminds me of an ageing tortoise. 'You mean it's a fake, Filippa. You're talking nonsense again. It isn't a fake!'

'Fluke, fake …' Filippa slurs, and waves her hand in dismissal. 'It's not a real bull,' she insists, helping herself to more Cava from the waiter's tray.

Antonio shakes his head in annoyance. 'Don't drink any more.'

'Umberto came and installed it personally,' Bruno says.

'Poor Umberto,' whispers Glorietta. 'He absolutely wouldn't come tonight. He said he couldn't face anyone, not even his friends. He's devastated.'

'What a shock,' adds Dolores, my friend and ex-art teacher, who runs an art gallery in Mallorca. 'It was all over the press. I saw it on the news.' She sells replicas of famous paintings. She tells her buyers they are not forgeries – but copies – and explains the subtle difference. Her dark hair is scraped severely into a bun, and she holds an unlit cigarette like a conductor waving a baton.

'Poor Umberto,' adds Josephine. 'It must be a shock.'

'It's good publicity for him,' says Antonio.

'It's not the sort of publicity anyone would crave,' I reply. 'Not after all that hard work.'

Antonio sticks out his tortoise neck. 'It will add value to the crap he churns out.'

'You can't call it crap!' Filippa flashes an angry frown at her husband. Her glass tilts and a few drops spill onto the floor, but she doesn't seem to notice. 'Umberto is above criticism. He's untouchable.'

'As you think you are, too,' Antonio retorts.

'It was a frightening experience for everyone.' Josephine

16

ignores their bickering. Four years ago, she was shot on stage, and the bullet wound effectively ended her comeback in the role of *Tosca*. 'It was terrifying. You wouldn't expect or want that sort of attention – ever – believe me; I know from first-hand experience. No publicity is ever that important.'

I marvel at her physical recovery and her strong spirit. It was after that near-death experience that she came to find me in London.

'I can't see the attraction in his work,' complains Antonio. 'I know you won't agree with me, but I think he's extremely overrated.'

'Art is supposed to be personal, isn't it?' Olivia smiles at Glorietta and shakes her head, as if in despair. 'That's the point of it all. We're allowed to have different opinions and tastes.'

'He didn't cut all that paper up by himself. There's a whole team of designers and workers in his studio.' Antonio sways his tortoise neck as he speaks. '*Los Globos* was ridiculous. An insult to mankind. He was just trying to rile everyone – to provoke a reaction. Politics has no place in art.'

'Did you see it?' Olivia asks him.

'I didn't need to. It was all over the papers.'

'It was spectacular.' Then Josephine adds under her breath, 'Such a shame it went up in flames.'

'Umberto is a genius. He's extremely talented, and he deserves the recognition and fame.' Dolores waves her cigarette in the air. 'He's original and unique. It will be a very long time until someone like him comes along again. Probably not in our lifetimes.'

'He's the modern-day Michelangelo,' slurs Filippa.

Antonio grunts.

Olivia slips her arm through Jeff's, but he moves away to inspect the bull's eyes and twisted paper horns.

Dolores continues, 'It was such a waste, a tragic waste – a year-long project – to be destroyed like that. So utterly pointless. What would anyone gain from destroying it?'

'Does anyone have any idea who's behind it?' Simon asks. 'Or who would want to obliterate it in such a dramatic way?'

'I've spoken to the police.' Bruno moves closer to the group. 'They're pursuing all angles. They think that it could be politically motivated, especially due to the content and theme. *Los Globos* probably wasn't to everyone's taste.'

'You've got to be careful, making political statements like that. People don't want art used as political statements,' Antonio grumbles.

'But it was stunning,' says Josephine.

I say, 'It was impressive watching them hanging in the air, but then the drone appeared and ...'

'You saw it?' asks Olivia.

'I assumed it was taking photographs. You know, how they put film up on YouTube and social media. I assumed it would circle above us, but it didn't.'

'It crashed into the middle globe, and the whole thing exploded,' adds Eduardo, resplendent in his white dinner jacket. 'Like a fireball.'

'A couple of people had burns, and one had to go to the hospital,' Bruno says.

'It was lucky no one was seriously injured,' adds Josephine.

'Think of the cost.' Antonio grins, but no one else smiles. 'All that investment up in flames. Ironically, he'll be even more popular now.'

'You mean his work will go up in value?' asks Eduardo.

'Of course,' Antonio replies. 'That's what happens. A surge in sales.'

Jeff removes his glasses and studies *The Bull.* 'I'd expect no less of you, Glorietta, than to have something so gloriously original – it's like nothing I've ever seen.'

'It suits this villa, Glorietta, and it gives the reception a ... how would you say? A look of understated opulence,' chimes in Filippa. 'Spanish charm.'

Josephine's laugh echoes in the large hall, and – like her voice once used to ring out on the world stage – its tone is rich and husky, reminding me she was once one of the world's famous opera stars. You would imagine that there would be rivalry and jealousy between Glorietta and Josephine, but they are best friends. They are closer than sisters, and I watch them share a whispered comment and smile.

I place my hands on my swelling stomach. I'm secretly proud that Josephine is my mother and will be grandmother to my daughter. We have talked through the difficult issues of our separate lives until she came to find me three years ago, when I had been on the verge of stealing Vermeer's masterpiece, *The Concert.* Josephine had been determined to save me from a life of crime and theft.

Eduardo leans over and whispers in my ear, 'Don't ever think of putting crap like that in our home.'

I giggle and pull him gently away and out of earshot.

'You're a philistine, my angel. You have no artistic appreciation. Anyway, don't worry, art is personal, and the important thing is that Glorietta and Bruno like it. You don't have to. In two days' time, we will be at home, looking for a place of our own to buy and deciding on baby clothes.'

'I'm not having a paper bull in our home,' he grumbles.

'There are worse sculptures,' I say with a smile.

'It reminds me of Jeff Koons's lobster,' Antonio announces loudly to the crowd. He appears to like an audience. 'It's ridiculous. Animals are taking over the art world.'

Eduardo rolls his eyes and leans toward my ear. 'Don't tell me, really – a lobster?'

I laugh more at his exaggerated reaction and reply quietly, 'Yes – it's a giant red lobster, and he's also sculpted a massive balloon dog and – would you believe it – gaudy tulips ...'

'Why would he do that?'

'It's art.'

'And probably worth a fortune, is it?'

'Christie's sold *Orange Balloon Dog* in 2013 for fifty-eight million dollars.'

'*Madre mia,*' Eduardo mutters, and pushes his hand through his tousled, bleached blond hair.

'*The Tulips* sold for thirty-three million. I bet you'd want those in our home?'

'Only to sell on to someone else,' Eduardo says with a smile.

After two years with me, Eduardo still has no real appreciation of the value of art or the ridiculous sums of money people pay for it, or even the extreme lengths collectors will go to own it.

'I believe it's one of several sculptures,' Dolores whispers, standing beside us. 'All specialist pieces designed with a theme – that's what adds to their value.'

'Imagine the cost of making it,' Eduardo comments, shaking his head.

'It's not the cost of production that influences the value of artwork,' Dolores explains quietly. 'It's the reputation of the sculptor, the originality, and the craftsmanship. It's the commercial side of the art world that decides these things – unfortunately – and it can detract from the beauty or originality of the artwork itself.'

'It can be inflated?' Eduardo asks.

'It's actually about what someone – anyone – is prepared to pay for it. If buyers and collectors get into a price war, then it can soar incredibly. Commercially, selling artwork is an absolute nightmare,' Dolores replies with authority.

'It's the best birthday present – ever,' Glorietta announces, oblivious to the comments around her. She claps her hands in delight. The priceless diamonds on her fingers glisten in the light, radiating from the overhead crystal chandelier. 'Now, this is supposed to be a party, let's dance!'

* * *

Outside on the verandah, the purple sky is bathed in studded stars, and a bright moon lingers on the horizon. The lead singer begins a sultry version of Elvis Presley's 'Fever', and I sway to the rhythm, studying the musical group: a pianist, lead guitarist, bass and rhythm, drummer, trumpet, sax, horn, and clarinet. Eduardo orders champagne.

'Juice?' he asks me.

'Thank you.' Luckily, I don't want to drink alcohol. Now I've passed the early morning sickness stage, I'm prone to increasing heartburn that is both painful and uncomfortable. It's after the buffet and well past midnight when the three-tiered chocolate cake is wheeled out onto the patio. The band strikes up and we all sing 'Happy Birthday', and Glorietta blows out two candles – representing four and five – on her birthday cake. Afterwards, the guests drift onto the dance floor and, leaning over the terrace, Eduardo and I watch the scene below.

'Look at Maria. She's growing up so quickly,' Eduardo complains.

Amongst the medley of dancing bodies, Maria – Dolores's daughter – is dancing with a handsome young man, who is wearing a black dinner jacket and bow tie. She's grown up, even in the six months since New York, when I held my disastrous art exhibition. Her hair is now dyed purple, and she is wearing heavy eye-make-up that makes her appear older than her seventeen years.

'She seems to have grown from a child to a woman in just a few months,' I agree, watching her negotiate the dance steps, swirling, twisting, and jiving. 'She'll be eighteen soon ...'

'And probably falling in love,' Eduardo says with a smile.

'She deserves someone special. If our daughter is half as beautiful as Maria, then I'll be happy.'

'Daughter? I thought I was having a son.'

'You, my darling, are not having anything. It's me who's giving birth.'

'I'd like a boy.'

'Next time, my angel. It's better this way. Families are softer if the eldest child is a girl.'

Eduardo splutters and wipes his mouth with the back of his hand. 'What?'

'It's true. Older boys don't have the gentleness of girls. They're much rougher.'

'Bullshit.'

'It's true.'

'You're reading the wrong parenting books, Mikky.'

Maria catches sight of us looking down at her, and she waves back.

'Who is she dancing with?' I ask.

'Lorenzo, Filippa and Antonio's son.'

'He has his mother's good looks, but I hope he doesn't take after his grumpy father.'

'Dolores will have to keep an eye on her.' Eduardo nods in the direction of Maria's mother on the far corner of the terrace, currently sucking on a long cheroot and exhaling a stream of smoke. Dolores is debating with a small group of art experts that I had spoken to earlier, but I'd become quickly bored. That was my past life when I was an artist and forger. Now, I'm looking to the future. It's all about what's ahead. I'm going to become a mother. I pass my hand over the small bump of my stomach. I'm so excited.

My daughter is just over three months old, and I carry the first blurry image of her in my bag.

My baby.

Josephine and Simon wander out onto the terrace and Josephine takes Eduardo's arm. 'Come on, let's dance to this – 'Mustang Sally'. It's one of my favourite songs.'

I watch them negotiate the few steps down to the dance floor beside the swimming pool.

'I still like rock music, but I now also like opera, jazz, and blues – who would have thought? Am I getting old?' I ask Simon, as I lean on the balustrade and swallow the bile rising in my throat, trying to resist the pain of rising heartburn creeping into my stomach while watching the dancers below.

'Not old, but you'll have to look after yourself now, Mikky. No more charging around the world and getting into trouble,' Simon replies.

'Me? As if ...' I feign innocence and he smiles.

'Are you still painting?'

'Not after the last disastrous exhibition. I've decided I'm going to focus on photography.'

'Taking pictures for museums?'

'No, that's my past. I'm through with painting and working for other people. I'm going to do my own thing, maybe an exhibition – you know, portraits in black and white. I'm becoming obsessed with faces and the stories of people's lives reflected in their eyes.'

I think briefly of Umberto Palladino and the pain I saw in his face as *Los Globos* smouldered and burned at his feet.

'Is there a theme?'

'Life – pain, joy. I haven't decided yet.'

He nods in understanding. That's why I've always liked Simon. He listens, but more importantly, he doesn't assume or pretend he knows everything.

'Where will you display them – will you have an exhibition?'

'I don't know.' I smile and hold my tummy. 'I'm taking each day as it comes.'

'You're going to settle down in Mallorca?'

'I could live anywhere, but it's Eduardo's home, and he loves his job, so it would seem crazy to move anywhere else at the moment.'

I glance over Simon's shoulder; the banana-shaped figure of Jeff Harrison walks toward us, defeated, like an exhausted balloon.

'Isn't he Olivia's husband?' I ask.

Simon glances over his shoulder. 'Yes.'

'She was Glorietta's bodyguard?'

'Presumably, Olivia was assigned to the protection force, and in her capacity as bodyguard to Glorietta, they became good friends,' he replies.

'Why do so many women marry ugly, older men?'

Simon is laughing as Jeff joins us.

'I've never been to anywhere so utterly splendid,' Jeff comments with a smile.

'It is beautiful,' Simon agrees.

'Do you know Spain?' I ask him.

'We have an apartment just north of the city. We spend most of the year here now.' His smile is crooked. 'It allows me to play lots of golf, and now that Olivia is retired, too, it's very convenient for us. We love it.' He turns to gaze over his shoulder, and his eyes darken, and I wish I knew the reason for the sudden change. I'd like to snap Jeff Harrison's portrait and his unfathomable expression. He nods to a gangly lad walking across the terrace, carrying a couple of wine glasses down the steps to the dance floor. 'That's Martin, our son. He's at university here, studying Languages. He's a good friend of Lorenzo's ...'

I suppress a yawn and glance at my watch. It's almost two o'clock in the morning and although my back aches, I am happy. I rest my hands on my stomach. I am loved. My daughter will be loved, too.

Beside me, Simon is talking about his home in Canterbury, and Jeff is talking about his jewellery business in Covent Garden. He doesn't look like a shop owner or a jeweller, but it makes sense. Olivia is dripping in gold; rings and bangles adorn her hands and wrists. She looks like an Egyptian goddess, and I wonder if he worships her as such.

Bruno stands beside me and surveys the scene below. He's like the brother I never had; reliable, sensible, and caring. He hooks his arm casually over my shoulder.

'That man of yours can dance,' he says,

'He can almost keep up with Josephine,' I agree.

I wrap my arm around his waist and lean against his shoulder, feeling the first stages of heartburn gripping my chest.

'So?' he asks. 'Are you still not interested in getting married?'

'When Eduardo proposed to me in New York, I was shocked. I didn't expect him to propose.'

'Eduardo is good for you.'

'I know, but sometimes ... if I tell you the truth, I honestly don't know what he sees in me.'

Bruno squeezes my shoulders. 'Sometimes, there's no rhyme nor reason. Look at Glorietta and me. No one would have thought we'd still be together, but we can't be apart. It's called love, Mikky. You have to go with the flow and see where it takes you.'

'Ummm.'

He laughs. 'I never figured you for a coward.'

'Nah, I'm just cautious.'

He kisses my forehead just as Eduardo and Josephine come up the steps. Although I smile, Eduardo immediately knows that I'm in pain.

'Heartburn?' he whispers.

'I'd like to go to bed, but you can stay up if you like. I don't mind.'

'I'd prefer to snuggle up with you,' he whispers. 'Besides, a lot of people are leaving. That was the last song. The party's over.'

It takes a while to say goodnight to the other guests, and inside the villa, the caterers are finishing cleaning; carrying chairs and makeshift tables to vans outside the front door.

They look weary and tired, and as they slam the van doors closed, we wave goodnight, then pause in the reception to look at *The Bull*.

'It is incredible,' Eduardo mutters eventually.

'I agree,' I reply, and he laughs at my deliberate misunderstanding.

* * *

I can't sleep.

It's not heartburn that disturbs me but hunger – and it's not me that's hungry, it's my daughter. Well, that's what I tell myself. Eduardo is snoring peacefully, and I roll his hot body away from me, removing his arm that is lying across my breasts. He doesn't stir, so I slide out of bed and search for a dressing gown to cover my naked body.

A stream of light shines through the slatted shutters. It's not quite morning – not yet; the horizon hasn't yet cracked open, but there's the hint of a magnificent glow to a beautiful dawn.

I pull the gown over my shoulders, covering the assorted artwork tattooed on my skin; *The Scream* on my arm and the severed, bloody head of St John the Baptist across my breasts.

What will my daughter make of me?

How will I explain my life to her?

My stomach growls and I hold my small swollen belly. Only the truth will do. There will be nothing but love between us: no secrets, no lies – just love, trust, and security.

'I'll get us something to eat, sweetie, hold on,' I whisper. I creep quietly from the bedroom and close the door. The corridor is silent. The party is over. The doors to the other bedrooms are closed. Everyone is asleep, and I'm excited to be alone in the silent darkness.

I glance along the corridor, where I know Glorietta and Bruno's room is at the far end of the corridor. Josephine and Simon have a room opposite ours, and somewhere along the corridor are Filippa and Antonio.

Their son Lorenzo is sleeping in one of the guest cottages, and Maria and Dolores are in the second cottage. I believe the other guests have either returned to their homes in Barcelona or are in hotels nearby.

My feet are bare, and I welcome the cool marble on my soles. I pad quietly, enjoying the peace and solitude, and at the top of the sweeping staircase, I pause briefly. Then I continue holding onto the rail and step carefully downstairs.

In the reception hall, *The Bull* is exquisite. I lean forward and tilt my head to read the notes of the sheet music, but then my stomach rumbles and I'm distracted.

Alright, my darling, I'll find us something to eat. I wander along the corridor to the kitchen. The caterers have cleaned up, and the surfaces are spotless. I open the fridge and rummage through covered plates of food, cutting a slice of queso manchego and nibbling on thin slices of jamon jabugo. I eat quietly, standing at the kitchen island and helping myself to rich black olives, staring out of the window into the dark landscape, chewing slowly and spitting the pips into my palm.

'It will soon be daylight,' I whisper. 'The start of a lovely new day.'

I turn at a sound from the hallway. I wait, expecting the kitchen door to open, but no one appears. I'm not used to the night sounds of the villa like I am in our home in Mallorca, but I'm happy talking quietly with my daughter.

'Still hungry?'

There's a small thud, and I turn. My heart begins to race. The olives are strong, and I belch quietly, eat slowly, and cut another slice of cheese to take with me. I wipe down the surface and check everything is clean before heading into the cool and quiet corridor. There's a muffled sound ahead of me, and I falter, swallowing my last mouthful. Perhaps someone else is hungry?

I expect to see Josephine – who, like me, is a light sleeper – roaming the corridor, looking for food, but as I turn the corner into the reception hall, a strange and eerie glow is reflected on the walls.

It takes me seconds to assess the situation: two black-clad figures are huddled over *The Bull*. One lifts it, and the other is kneeling, holding open a bag. It takes me a few seconds to realise they're stealing Glorietta's sculpture – her birthday present.

It's a few strides to the staircase, and I move quickly, screaming and shouting.

'Bruno! Eduardo! Help!'

I'm running toward the wide staircase, my dressing gown flying open, billowing, revealing my bare legs. I have my foot on the first step when a hand grabs my ankle, and I'm yanked down the steps. I fall, hurting my wrist and hitting my cheek on the marble. I cry out.

The figure bends over me and grabs the back of my head. I lash out at the black hood, throwing wild punches, but in a few swift movements, I'm smacked against the floor like a helpless rag doll, and pain shoots through the back of my skull. Breathlessly, I stare up at the two slits in the hood, and for a brief second our eyes meet.

A voice shouts. It's an urgent whisper across the room, 'I have it. Leave her.'

I scramble to my feet, preparing to leap at my attacker, but they lean back and raise their foot.

'No! Not my baby!'

It's a martial art move, and I'm lifted into the air, falling and crashing awkwardly. The pain causes me to roll onto my side, my hands protecting my baby's bump, but the assailant won't leave me alone. I cry out as a heavy boot connects with my fingers, then my world goes black.

* * *

It's all a blur. Screaming. Shouting. Voices. Then it's a white-out. My head is filled with noisy electricity, and when I open my eyes, I realise I'm not in Mallorca. I'm not at home. I'm in Glorietta and Bruno's villa, lying on the cold, marble floor. Eduardo is beside me, looking oddly confused and concerned.

The excruciating pain in my stomach makes me light-headed and sick. There's a cold compress against my forehead, and Josephine holds water to my lips.

'You're going to be alright,' she says.

'My baby ...?'

A cool hand touches my fingers. 'It's alright. I'm here,' Eduardo says, leaning over me. 'Everything is alright.'

'And our baby?'

'Everything is okay,' he whispers, but there's an emotional catch in his voice. I try to sit up, but he holds my shoulder firmly. 'You might have concussion, Mikky. Stay still. Your cheek is bruised, and you've got a nasty cut on your head.'

My head is throbbing, and my throat is dry. I sip the water.

'Did they get away?'

'Yes.' Josephine holds my shaking hand.

'Did you hear me shouting?' I ask.

'Bruno and Simon rushed after them, but they were gone. Glorietta has phoned a doctor. He's on his way.'

Josephine does not take her worried eyes from my face, and she presses the cold, damp towel to my forehead.

Eduardo pushes his hair from his face and kneels beside me. 'I heard you scream. If only I'd reacted quicker.' He looks wretched, like he hasn't slept, and I want to reach out to him and tell him it's alright. I want to reassure him. I want to tell him our daughter loves us both, but I'm overwhelmed with emotion and my eyes well up with tears.

Bruno paces the floor beside the table where *The Bull* had been displayed. 'Where are the police? I called them ages ago? First *Los Globos* and now this. I can't believe it!'

'You think it's related?' Josephine's eyes widen in surprise.

An excruciating pain shoots through my body and rips at my stomach.

'Oh God! No!'

Liquid is seeping between my legs, and my gown is turning crimson – a river of red blood. Eduardo pulls my dressing gown apart. I can't stop my sobbing tears – or the raw stabbing pain attacking my unborn child. 'My baby. Oh, my baby. Please God, not my baby ... not my daughter,' I sob, and a savage pain seizes my womb.

* * *

In the private hospital room, I have plenty of time to think. I'm sedated and deciding between the two conflicting worlds in my head; the happy world of yesterday and the naked sorrow of today.

I have lost my daughter.

I cannot speak. I can only cry silent tears. I'm vaguely aware of visitors and stilted and random conversations. Glorietta is filled with guilt, and when she holds my hand, I pull away. I know it's not her fault, but I don't want any human contact. I don't want to feel. I don't want to think. I don't want to be comforted. I don't want anyone.

I don't want to see sadness and pain reflected in her eyes as she stands at my bedside, not knowing what to say. I've burdened her by losing my baby, and I'm pleased she has to leave the country – she is booked to perform in Tokyo.

'I can cancel it, Mikky.'

I shake my head. 'You must go.'

'I don't know what to say, Mikky. Only that I love you.' She kisses my forehead, but I turn away. I don't want her to see my tears. It isn't her guilt to carry. It's mine. I'm responsible. She was my unborn daughter.

Josephine sits quietly beside me, overflowing with pity but unable to help or to do anything. It's all too late, and I'm sure neither of us misses the irony of my birth and subsequent adoption and now the loss of my unborn daughter. There are no words.

Josephine stays silent beside me, but I'm happy to have her close, as it bridges the awkward conversation between Eduardo and me.

He stands stoically with silent heartbreak, unblinking and close to tears. As an intensive care nurse, he is used to coping with life and loss, but this is personal. He loves me, and I see him struggling to cope with his emotions and my barricade of silence. Standing at the window, he looks down into the street for answers – or distraction – but I can't handle his loss – his grief – their grief – only my own.

I don't want them near me.

I don't want their pity, but I'm not strong enough to let them go. I'm weak and pathetic. I can't be the strong person that Eduardo begs me to be with his watchful, silent eyes. I know he wants his outspoken, rebellious, fiery girlfriend back, but I've disappeared inside myself. The prospect of motherhood had softened me. I've changed. I was happy with the new me, but now I don't know what to feel or what to think. I don't know who I am. I only know one thing – *I am not a mother.*

As I sit propped up against pillows on the bed, there's growing anger inside me. It stems from the core of my womb, gathering momentum like an evil monster breathing fire and fury, unfurling a cold, icy, solid resolution of ultimate stubbornness and defiance.

They didn't just steal a sculpture – *they stole my child.*

I am monosyllabic and uncommunicative. When they think I'm not looking, I watch Josephine and Eduardo swap silent glances, and I see their blinking acknowledgement of despair.

They don't know what to say.

Sometimes, Josephine is compassionate and calm, and at other times cajoling and upbeat, sounding resolutely cheerful and making suggestions and plans for the coming months ahead. She plans theatre trips to Milan and even suggests we join Glorietta on her tour of Japan, but I turn my head or close my eyes.

It's easier not to speak.

Eduardo and I are struggling. We know our lives must resume, but I cannot make arrangements to go home. I can't think about our apartment in Mallorca or returning to our island. There are too many happy memories associated with our life there.

We were planning to move out of Eduardo's apartment and to buy our own home with a garden for our daughter. We were looking at baby clothes, planning decorations and gifts for our newborn child. We had been planning our lives – our family – our future, but now there is nothing, just a hollow emptiness that hurts like a dull, persistent throb. The pain is permanent. It has settled around me, numbing my senses, my rationality, and my reasoning. My life has no meaning, and I am filled with solitary grief. In the loneliness of the dark hospital bed, after everyone has gone, I remember Eduardo's rejected face at his offer to stay the night with me in hospital.

I need to be alone.

I don't want anyone.

It's all my fault.

And finally, when the nurse gives me more sedatives, I'm grateful. I can finally embrace the world of darkness – alone – and my only wish is that it could last forever.

* * *

Josephine was never with me as a child, but now, in compensation, she hates to leave my side. She came with me to the hospital, where I've spent the rest of the night and morning. She's determined to be the mother that she could never be during the first thirty years of my life, and although I love her, I'm weary. I want to be alone.

'I'll be fine,' I say repeatedly.

They all tell me the theft of *The Bull* is not important. They don't care about it. They only want me to get well. Time and grief and other opportunities are mentioned, but I have switched off from their kindness and love. It's awkward, and I divert their questions about me to the theft of *The Bull*.

Simon tells me the police are following up on the investigation. They are following the normal procedures, and I mustn't worry. His words are a blur, and I'm not registering or even listening. It's a reminder that I have lost my daughter, and a priceless sculpture has been stolen – *The Bull*.

Later, I'm interviewed by an overweight policewoman with short blonde hair. She writes everything down, but my statement creates no reaction. It would be quicker for me to use my computer and write it all out for her, but then she'd have nothing to do. So, we go through the performance of her obvious questions several times over, with me repeating the same details.

Why did I go downstairs? My daughter was hungry.

No, I didn't notice anything strange on my way into the kitchen.

No, I didn't hear anything.

No, I didn't know them.

And no, I wouldn't recognise them.

Although, that's a lie.

I don't admit it to the policewoman or Simon or Josephine, but I know I'd know them immediately.

Instinct.

When Eduardo comes to visit me after lunch, I'm sitting in the chair beside the bed – alone. We are supposed to be flying home tonight, but I'm not interested in leaving the clinic. I want to stay cocooned in my silent world, protected from reality, but I can tell he has something on his mind. He can't stand still and, after kissing me on the cheek, he walks to the window.

'I don't mind you leaving,' I say, trying to make it easier for him. 'I know you have to return to work. Bruno says I can stay at the villa.'

'It's my job to help people, Mikky, but I'm struggling with you,' he replies. He's an intensive care nurse who once helped save my life. Back then, I'd almost died. I'd survived a burning building and scarring on my forehead. I didn't care if I lived.

This time, I already know, it's not going to be as easy or as straightforward. This time, I have lost my daughter – our child. I have returned to the dark world that I thought I had left behind forever. It's a world of thieves and evil people who have broken into our lives and stolen the most precious thing to me in the whole world. They have ripped my daughter from me. She hadn't stood a chance.

How could a small baby survive that violence and cruelty?

Being with Eduardo and pregnant with our child had given me hope, but more importantly, it had finally given me love and security. I'd put my old life aside. I would have had everything I'd always dreamed of, a loving man at my side and a beautiful child – we were going to be a family, but now it's over. I'm vulnerable, lost, and my empty soul is filling with hate and loathing. I watch Eduardo moving restlessly from the window. Eventually, he grips his hands together and sits beside me on the bed, as if in prayer.

'The thieves spray-painted two of the CCTV cameras at the villa, but they missed one at the gate and one from inside the reception,' he says. 'Bruno has a tape.'

I can't take my eyes away from his and I realise I'm hardly breathing, and that my mouth is incredibly dry.

'There are pictures of what happened?'

He nods seriously. 'A videotape.'

'And you can see what they did to me?'

'Yes.'

'Oh my God! Has Bruno shown it to the police?' I sit up straighter.

'Of course.'

'Then they'll catch them.' My heart is beating rapidly, but the thought of the thug who kicked me, facing the courts for justice, confuses me. On the one hand, it makes me happy, but on the other, it takes retaliation out of my control. It makes me feel useless, as if I'm waiting for someone else to do my job for me.

I stand up, but I'm weak, and my stomach hurts. I move slowly to the window and stare outside at the ordinary lives of people coming to and from the clinic. Beyond the parking, below the main road, cars are whizzing past, and I'm wondering how my assailants made their escape from the villa.

They can be found.

'Mikky?' I turn to find Eduardo staring at me. 'Aren't you listening to me?'

'Yes,' I lie.

He takes a deep breath. 'They've gone – they've disappeared. They could be anywhere. Bruno and Simon weren't fast enough, and they got away. So, unless there's news in the next day or so, the trail will go cold. The police are already hinting that they don't have the resources, especially after what happened this week with Umberto's sculpture at the museum.'

'Do they think the two incidents are related?'

'They thought the drone bombing of *Los Globos* was politically motivated, and now they are considering the possibility that the two incidents might be linked. But it's only a possibility.'

'Are they investigating it?'

'Without any solid leads or information to go on, they'll soon lose interest. Even you know that.'

'But they have evidence. The CCTV will incriminate them. Can they identify them?'

Eduardo shakes his head. 'Their faces are covered, and the quality of the images isn't good.'

'But they may be known criminals. The sculpture may have been stolen to order. These things very often are and—'

'Mikky, stop!' Eduardo holds up his palm. He looks defeated and exhausted.

'Are there any fingerprints?' I insist.

Eduardo shakes his head. 'They've done all the forensics. They're waiting for the results, but judging from the CCTV, the thieves were wearing gloves.'

'There are no traces of fibres? How did they get into the villa?'

'I don't know.'

'Was the door locked?'

He shrugs.

'Have the police got any leads at all?'

'Look, Mikky, it doesn't matter, does it?!' he shouts, and stands up angrily.

'What? Of course it matters. Of course it bloody matters! What are you thinking?'

'What I mean is, it's nothing to do with us, Mikky. We're not getting involved.'

'But we are involved – aren't we?' I eyeball him, but he

won't look at me, so I lower my voice and whisper, 'I'm involved. I've just lost our baby, so please don't tell me that I'm not involved.'

The anger is burning, bubbling, and churning like a massive cauldron inside me, and I'm unable to subdue the hatred growing, growing in the place where my daughter should be.

'Mikky ...'

'I can't let them get away with it, Eduardo. Don't ask me just to forget it and walk away. Don't ask me not to be involved.'

He looks at the floor, so that I can't see his dark eyes and the pain he's trying to hide. He, too, has lost his daughter, but I cannot look after him and, at the same time, do what I have to do.

'I want to see the tape.'

'Why?'

'Because I want to know what they did.'

'You know what they did.'

'I might find evidence.'

'Don't be crazy. Come home with me.'

'I can't. Not now.'

'What?'

'I'm staying here.'

'You can't.'

'I can.'

'Why?'

'I need to think,' I lie easily, and stand at the window and stare at him. I'm back to my old tricks, falling back to my old way of life, where deceit comes naturally.

'I have to go back to work in the morning,' he replies. His voice is cracking. 'Don't do this, Mikky. Please, I lost a daughter, too. We can heal together.'

'But you know it was my fault. That's why you can't look at me. You blame me, don't you?'

He doesn't reply, and he continues to stare at his hands.

'I see it in your eyes, Eduardo,' I continue. 'Every time you come here, you're angry, and now you've seen the video of what happened – you think it's my fault, don't you?'

'No ...'

'You think that I'm to blame and that it's my fault I lost our daughter – I know you do!'

'No.'

'Tell me the truth!' I shout. 'You think I should have done something. Run. Hide. Maybe not go downstairs – maybe not be hungry. For Christ's sake, Eduardo, don't lie.' I flinch at the irony of my words.

He turns away. 'It's not true.'

'You might not want it to be true, but you can't help it. I know you're lying. I see it in your eyes and the way you look at me.' I turn away, feeling the blame and guilt of the unspoken anguish etched on his face.

I leave the silence to grow between us, and then he says quietly, 'I don't know what happened, Mikky. I don't know what you were thinking. They were masked – dangerous. You didn't even know if they were armed. They might have had weapons – a gun or a knife. You might have been killed.'

'But I wasn't,' I whisper. 'Our daughter died instead.' The words lodge in my throat.

'One was a martial arts specialist. The one who kicked you!' His eyes are troubled, and he can barely look at me. 'Why do you have to be so bloody heroic all the time?'

'What?'

'Why? That's all I'm asking. Why could you not – just for

once in your life – do something sensible? Why couldn't you just have turned away – hidden – said nothing – crept back into the kitchen?'

'How could I?!' I shout. 'They were stealing and ...'

But Eduardo raises his voice and shouts over me, 'It's always about you – and your stupid bloody ideas!' he retorts. 'You had no awareness for our baby. You never even considered her – or me. You think you can sort everyone and everything out. The poor little tough girl who had a rough and troubled life – well, it's never enough. You've no idea what it's like living with you and the danger that you constantly seek. It's an adrenaline rush, for you. It's this constant need for excitement. This constant feeding of your ego and your bloody-minded attitude. You have this amazing capability to think you're invincible, like a super-hero, and that you're different from everyone else. But you're not a hero. You think you're special and that you'll never get hurt – but you do. You just don't think of the danger or of the consequences that you bring on yourself – or on us and now on our baby.'

'But ...'

'You're not normal, Mikky.'

'Normal?'

'What mother would risk her child's life for a bloody paper sculpture?'

'Is that what you think?' I ask softly.

He runs his hand through his hair and flops into the chair. 'I don't know what to think anymore. I thought this was all over. You know – living life on the edge, almost getting killed or beaten up. I won't always be there to save you – and I don't want to lead that kind of life. Don't you understand? I help save lives, Mikky, and this is just – just crap!'

He turns away, unable to hide his grief.

'But we can still be together, can't we?'

He shakes his head and coughs to clear his throat. He doesn't look at me, and I feel despair and anger rising inside me like a giant tidal wave. It's overwhelming, and I'm suddenly so weak that I sit on the edge of the bed. I know he blames me, but it wasn't my fault.

'Well, that's cleared the air between us,' I whisper.

He still doesn't reply, so I say, 'I didn't ask them to break into the villa and steal *The Bull*. I didn't ask them to take the fecking sculpture.'

'I know that,' he says quietly.

He's accused me of putting our daughter in danger before she was even born. I want to shake him and scream.

It wasn't my fault!

But he's forced me to confront my own fear, the nagging sense of betrayal and a lack of responsibility toward my daughter, and all the other nightmares going through my head.

What sort of mother am I?

'So, where does that leave us?' I ask.

'I don't know.'

'I'm going after them.'

That's when he looks at me, and I know that I have his full attention.

'You're what?'

'I'm going to find the bastards who killed my daughter.'

He stares at me for what seems a very long time, then he shakes his head and pushes his hand roughly through his hair. 'You're nuts! You think you're a law unto yourself and you can go around taking revenge. What sort of person are you, Mikky?

What sort of mother talks like that? You're irresponsible and quite frankly—'

'Quite frankly what?' I challenge him. 'What am I? Inept at relationships? A useless mother? A disgraceful, irresponsible piece of shit who only wants revenge? Well, that's true, Eduardo. I do want revenge. Too right, I do. I want to kill them. I want to rip out their hearts with my own bare hands.'

Chapter 2

"A sculptor is a person obsessed with the form and shape of things."
Henry Moore

Eduardo's angry words hang in the room like pointed daggers. He doesn't kiss me, and I don't watch him leave. It's over between us, and I know the hospital door, slammed in his wake, will never reopen.

There is nothing left of me to give. I have no more love, only growing anger. I'm consumed with angry revenge, swelling and unfurling, stretching like a dormant and hungry dragon wanting to kill.

I stand gazing out of the window, looking down into the familiar landscape of the car park and garden, but I don't see Eduardo. There's no friendly or familiar face looking up at the window, searching for me, wondering if I'll call out, but it doesn't matter. I don't want anyone. I have closed down my emotions, just like I did as a child. The softness Eduardo brought out of me, that melted my cold heart, has now disappeared. My soul has solidified and hardened, and I recognise the old familiar me, the me who doesn't need anyone. I need to be on my own. I'm cold inside, like an ice sculpture; crisp and sharp, and I have a sudden urgency to get out of the hospital and go back to the villa. I have a job to do, and I have a purpose.

I have a reason to live.

In two strides and two minutes, I've ripped off my hospital gown and I'm dressed. I walk out of the hospital without a backward glance.

I'd arrived in hospital at six in the morning, and now it's five in the afternoon – twelve hours and my life has irrevocably changed.

* * *

The taxi drops me at the villa, beside the stables. The doors are wide open, and as I climb out of the car, snorting horses – in their individual stalls – stare back at me, munching contentedly. A black and white stallion eyes me curiously while it chomps methodically, and a grey mare whinnies and pokes its head over the stable door, and I'm transfixed by its large black eyes.

Turning back to the villa, I'm calmed by the ochre colour, subdued and bathed in glorious golden evening sunlight. I remember another time and place, when the sultry air was restful and peaceful.

It appears deserted, but I know a team of workers are tending the vines, looking after the horses, and organising the bodega below in the cellar.

I walk purposefully around the swimming pool, where the air is filled with wild herbs – thyme, rosemary, and garlic. I venture inside the villa through the kitchen door, and pause in the cool interior, where another me happily ate cheese and talked to her unborn daughter.

I'm unprepared for the wave of crushing emotion that engulfs me. I grab a stool at the breakfast bar to regain my balance, and wait until my breathing is under control and my hands are no longer shaking. Then I take a deep breath. I wipe my eyes, conscious of my hollow footsteps echoing on the marble floor, remembering how my assailants were lurking in the shadows. I pause at the foot of the winding staircase. The step where I was attacked shows no sign of my struggle, so I turn my attention to the empty mahogany table where *The Bull* had occupied the central location, ten metres from the front door.

I move closer, inspecting the floor to look for clues – fingerprints, or perhaps something more obvious like a mobile phone with the thieves' details – but I'm being unrealistic. The area has been examined. Forensics have already been collected, photographs have been taken, and the area has been wiped and polished clean.

Everything has changed. The Happy Birthday atmosphere has been replaced by one of cold grief and solitude. I no longer carry my daughter inside me, and I bear the physical and mental pain as punishment for letting her down and for not protecting her. I didn't do what a proper mother should do, and this is the burden I shall carry with me, throughout my life – forever. But as I lay my hand on my flat stomach, I make a simple vow: I will avenge my daughter's death, and I will make the murderers pay.

I promise, my angel.

I gaze at the step, looking at the spot where I fell and hit my head, and touch the tender bruise on my skull, but the pain is nothing compared to what I feel inside. Closing my eyes, I re-imagine what happened that night – the noises, sounds, and words.

Did they say anything?

With long, confident strides, I move quickly along the corridor and push open the door to Bruno's office without knocking.

He stands up from his desk at the window, clearly surprised. 'Mikky, I didn't know you were coming out of hospital.' He walks toward me, and I let him kiss my cheeks in greeting. 'Does Josephine know?'

I shake my head.

'You've just missed her. She's taken Dolores and Maria to the airport. How are you feeling?'

I had forgotten.

'Eduardo told me that you showed him the tape.' I dump my rucksack on the floor. The bag that Eduardo had packed quickly in the early hours of this morning.

'The tape?'

'Don't try and fob me off, Bruno. I want to see the CCTV footage that you showed to Eduardo. Even if you've given it to the police, you must have kept a copy. Did you?'

'You look very pale, Mikky. Please sit down. Can I get you something to drink? Water?'

'I want to see it, Bruno. Please.'

'Mikky,' he says with a sigh. 'You really want to ...?'

'Yes.'

'Very well. Sit down and I'll bring it over.' He indicates for me to sit on the sofa in the middle of the room, while he leans over a large Apple computer and taps at the keyboard.

I sit on one of the two red leather sofas, at right angles to a low wooden coffee table covered with an assortment of glossy magazines – covering a range of subjects from horses, interiors, music – and I'm reminded of a waiting room in a private doctor's or dentist's practice.

A large Andy Warhol print of *Orange Prince* covers the far wall, but I cannot focus on the painting. My head is thumping, and I feel sick. I take a deep breath to control my shaking hands, and stare out of the slatted blinds at the rows of vines, like tramlines over the hillside.

Bruno speaks on his mobile phone. 'Hi, are you busy? Do you want to come to my study? I have something to show you.'

I close my eyes, hoping to block out the pain and wondering who Bruno was talking to, but I don't have to wait long to find out, as a few minutes later the door opens and Simon Fuller walks in. He's holding a book, as if he's been sleeping on a sunlounger and has woken suddenly. He smiles when he sees me.

'I didn't realise you were back, Mikky. Josephine will be delighted. How are you feeling?' He kisses me, and I'm aware of his penetrating stare, and I know I can't lie.

'Angry,' I reply.

'Ummm.' Simon strokes his goatee and regards me carefully.

'I'm very, very angry.'

'Take a seat.' Bruno indicates for Simon to sit beside me on the red sofa, and his gaze rests on me as he speaks. 'I haven't had a chance to show this to Simon yet, so it will be good for you both to see what happened. The footage is quite grainy. It's not good quality. They blacked out two of the cameras with spray paint, but at least we have something from the other cameras.'

'Four cameras?' Simon raises his eyebrows. As an expert on

valuable, ancient manuscripts, texts, and books, he's aware of the need for security.

Bruno squeezes onto the couch beside me, smelling of expensive aftershave, and places his iPad on my lap so that we can all study the screen together.

'Two at the gate, one at the front door, and one inside the villa. Okay, here it is. Are you sure you're alright with this, Mikky?'

'Yes,' I lie.

He points to the screen. 'I've edited some of it, and we can fast forward other bits. This was earlier in the evening, when we were all together looking at *The Bull.*'

I lean forward to stare at the dark images of a group of people standing in the foyer of the villa. It doesn't take me long to realise we had all been filmed earlier in the day. The hidden security camera must be in the ceiling, and it has recorded everyone. All of our movements have been captured on film.

'My goodness,' Simon mutters.

'Did you show this to the police?' I ask.

'Yes. Keep watching. I'll fast forward the unimportant bits.'

I watch the scene unfold in rapid action. It's like a bad black and white silent movie, where characters move quickly, even comically, but I'm not laughing. I remember fragments of conversations. Someone said it was a fake, someone said it was a fluke. Eduardo and I leave arm in arm, and I remember him telling me not to buy crap like that for our home.

And I had laughed.

Now the foyer is empty, then several guests come and go; the fleet of catering staff can occasionally be seen in the top-right corner as they carry things to the van at the front of the villa. Fast forward, and Eduardo and I are going to bed. We

49

linger to look at *The Bull* and wave goodnight to the catering crew as they close the front door.

Fast forward again, and Josephine and Simon climb the stairs to bed. Then Filippa and Antonio, and finally Jeff and Olivia. A young man appears, and I frown at the screen, recognising Lorenzo – Filippa and Antonio's son – and see that he's holding Maria's hand. She flicks her dyed hair over her shoulder and smiles coyly. He says something, and she laughs and for some reason taps *The Bull*'s head. They kiss on the lips for rather a long time before moving out of the picture, and fleetingly I wonder if they spent the night in the beds allocated to them or if they had been together.

Bruno and Glorietta are the last ones in the reception hall. Hand in hand, they admire the sculpture, and Bruno checks the front door before heading upstairs. The time in the bottom corner of the screen shows 3.20 a.m.

Fast forward, and it's 3.28 a.m.

Unaware that I was being filmed, I walk slowly down the staircase. I pause to look at the sculpture, gazing for a while to study *The Bull*, and then I disappear from view, bottom left, into the kitchen.

3.35 a.m. The front door opens. They are inside the villa in seconds. They cross the reception hall. The smaller one stands beside *The Bull*, his back to the camera. The tall one places the holdall on the floor but drops the torch he's holding.

'I heard a thud when I was in the kitchen,' I mumble.

The shorter one walks around the reception, as if admiring the location and position of the sculpture. The taller one is kneeling on the floor with the open holdall, waiting for his accomplice to lift *The Bull* into the bag. They both turn as I appear, bottom left, and I'm holding my stomach.

I was pregnant then.

Bruno squeezes my hand. 'I know this is difficult for you,' he whispers.

I watch myself deliberating.

Run or hide?

Was Eduardo right?

The stairs are a few metres away. I run. I was determined to get up them, but my assailant moves in a flash. There is no sound, but I know I'm screaming. I remember my fear and panic. The smaller one grabs my foot, and my dressing gown flies open. His hand is around my ankle, and my head smacks on the marble step. Stunned, I crawl and roll away, but then a flying kick to my stomach sends me reeling backwards. I curl into a foetal position, clutching my stomach, cushioning my unborn child. My attacker kicks me with the toe of his boot. He turns and lowers *The Bull* into the bag, and then they're gone.

'Can you replay it?' I ask Bruno.

'Wait a moment,' he replies.

I'm lying on the stairs. Eduardo appears, and he leans over me. I remember regaining consciousness and seeing the distress and panic in his eyes. The front door is open, and Bruno and Simon chase outside while Glorietta sits beside me. She is already on her phone. Within seconds, Josephine runs down the stairs and sits beside me on the stairs.

It's 3.39.

'That was quick,' I mumble. 'It's all over.'

The Bull is gone, and so is my baby daughter.

'Goodness.' Simon rubs his chin.

'They knew what they wanted. They knew what they were doing,' Bruno says quietly.

'They didn't take any other artwork or anything else in the house?' I ask.

'Nothing.'

'Any pictures?' asks Simon. 'From the other cameras?'

'They sprayed the camera at the front door and one at the gate that was easy to spot. But the second camera at the gate caught this.' Bruno switches screens to show images of the gate. It's early evening, and the bright glare of the sunlight blocks half of the image. 'This was taken earlier in the evening by one of the cameras.' The second catering van is arriving and when the gates swing open, another vehicle can be seen. 'Look! There's a white transit van parked in the street.'

The faces of the two occupants in the front seat are shaded by peaked caps.

'Did you show this to the police?' Simon asks.

'Yes, but we've agreed not to speak about this publicly. We don't want to reveal it to the press. We want to keep this as low-key as possible.'

'Why?' I ask.

'Do they think the two incidents are related?' Simon asks.

'It's early days, but they're looking into it.' Bruno's normally laughing eyes are serious. He looks tired and worried.

'I suppose it's hardly a coincidence that a drone bomb flew into Umberto's masterpiece a few days ago and now thieves have stolen *The Bull*,' I say.

It's Simon who replies, 'Normally, the police want to tell everyone – the public, collectors, curators – and also the Art Loss Register, so it deters people from buying it on the black market.'

'The more publicity, the better,' I agree.

'Glorietta doesn't want publicity,' argues Bruno. 'She

doesn't want to be known for her collections. She's very private. Singing is her passion, and she doesn't want to be known for the price tags on the artworks in her home.'

'Based on the assumption they took nothing else, they already knew what they wanted. So, did they steal it for themselves, or has it been stolen to order?' I ask, thinking aloud.

My previous experience as an art forger in the underworld tells me that priceless works of art are very often stolen specifically. They fund drug cartels, human trafficking, and other similar illegal activities. Most often, they're traded and used as currency on the black market, and very often their original value isn't recognised. I also know that they can end up in a collection belonging to some gangster in Eastern Europe, Russia, or even as far away as China, and never be seen again. I glance at Simon, who like me understands the cruel reality of stolen and priceless artworks.

'So, who are these guys?' Simon leans back, stretches his long legs, and looks thoughtful.

'Who knew *The Bull* was here?' I add.

Bruno shakes his head. 'Umberto Palladino studied with the famous Giacometti – he's originally from Milan, but now he lives here in Barcelona with his wife. He's a leading sculptor – very well known and revered in all the right circles. His work has been bought by kings, princes, sultans, and presidents around the globe. He's just been commissioned to create a piece for a public square in Moscow, and he's also exhibiting next year in Paris.' Bruno clasps his hands together and leans forward. 'Palladino made *The Bull* especially for Glorietta. It was my birthday gift to her.'

'Why him?'

'Our families are friends from way back.'

'Why *The Bull*?'

'Because of the sheet music. When I first met Glorietta, I saw her in La Scala opera house in Milan. She was in *Carmen*. Afterwards, I was lucky enough to be invited backstage, and I told her that her voice was more exquisite than the most beautiful nightingale. She laughed and said that it was the male nightingales who sang and not the females.' He smiles at the memory. 'And that broke the ice between us. It was a very special moment, and I knew then that I wanted to marry her. *The Bull* was symbolic of the bullring in Seville where she performed – the night I asked her to marry me.'

'Let me take another look at the film.' Simon takes Bruno's iPad, and as he scrolls through the images, I walk to the window, trying to ignore the burning pain in my stomach and the sickness rushing through my veins.

They killed my daughter.

Anger is swelling in me, and I know I must concentrate on the logistics of the theft before plotting my revenge and making them pay.

'It doesn't make sense,' I say, turning to look at Bruno. 'Look at the artwork on the walls. You have a Monet and a Degas hanging in your salon. Why didn't they take those instead of *The Bull*?'

'The thieves knew exactly what they were doing. They knew what they wanted,' he replies.

Simon asks, 'What about security? They came in through the front door – how did they do that?'

Bruno rubs a hand across his cheek. His usually happy face is creased in concern and frustration, and he breathes heavily, as if expelling the devil from his soul. 'I didn't set all the alarms.

Knowing we had guests and so many people staying in the house, we didn't think it necessary.' He waves his arms as he paces the room. 'Before the party, we were the only ones here – Glorietta, me, and then Mikky, you, and Josephine flew in a few days early and, as you know, I arranged for Umberto to install the sculpture as a surprise. I never expected for one minute that this would happen and it would be stolen.'

'Who knew about it?' I ask.

He shrugs in typical Mediterranean fashion, something Eduardo also does often. 'That is what I keep asking myself. Not only who knew about it, but what do they want with it?'

'A collector?' I guess, glancing at Simon.

'This is one of five animals that Umberto has sculptured in this collection, so it's a possibility,' Bruno says, frowning.

'Five?' Simon looks up.

'Do you know who owns the others?' I ask.

'No.'

'Umberto would know,' I say.

'He won't reveal his clients.' Bruno shakes his head.

'Maybe *The Bull* is somewhere nearby? Maybe they haven't taken it very far and, if they want money, they will ask for a ransom,' I suggest. 'What about roadblocks or police cameras?'

'There were no roadblocks set up. By the time Simon and I had rushed downstairs, they had jumped into the van, and they were gone. I called the police immediately, but their resources were limited – they're busy looking for terrorist activities in the area ...'

'We're so near the Spanish border, and they could be any-where by now. They could have gone south to Morocco or Algiers, north through France to Scandinavia, or east to

Russia,' I say.

'They were very clever. It's an ordinary white van. One that you see all over the place in every country.' Simon frowns at the screen. 'There are millions of them all over Europe.'

'Can you see the registration on the film?' I ask.

'Not clearly.'

'What are you going to do, Bruno?' I lean over Simon's shoulder and study the screen. On the replay, I study the images of two people watching the villa from the safety of their van. Their faces are hidden.

'How did they get in? Did they have a key?' I ask. 'I'm guessing they knew the code to the gate.'

'It's quite a sophisticated alarm system, and the police think they used a mobile phone to block out the circuit.'

'I don't understand modern technology,' complains Simon. 'How can they do that?'

Bruno shrugs. 'It's possible.'

'What about the insurance company?' I ask. 'Have you contacted them? They'll get someone onto this straightaway. They'll investigate it.'

Bruno looks uncomfortable and won't meet my gaze. Eventually, he replies, '*The Bull* is worth twenty-five million euros. The problem is, the insurance company is telling me that because I didn't set all the alarms, then it isn't insured.'

Simon whistles and I gasp.

Bruno adds, 'I've broken their contractual agreement, and they want nothing to do with it.'

'What do you mean?!' I cry. 'Not insured? That's crazy.'

'Insurance companies can tie you up for months – if not years – because of something like this,' Simon says.

'Couldn't you have set all the alarms?' I ask.

Bruno holds up the palm of his hand, as if he's pushing away the devil himself. 'I know, Mikky! Don't tell me! Glorietta will be furious when I tell her, and I don't need you to tell me I'm a fool, too.'

Instead of the laughing crow's feet at the corner of his eyes, his forehead is creased in worry and anger. He has never looked so anxious. He moves around the room with loping steps, not caring that his shirt is hanging out of his trousers and that his hair is dishevelled, as if he hasn't slept all night.

'So, what's the plan?' I ask.

'Plan?'

'Where do we start?'

'We?'

'That's what you want, isn't it?'

Bruno looks at me, and there's a flicker of surprise in his eyes. 'No ... I ... You can't get involved, Mikky.'

'We're family, aren't we?' I bite my lip in silent determination, so they won't see the murderous anger that inhibits my heart.

'Yes, we are, but—'

'But what?'

'You've just lost your ...'

'I know, Bruno. I know I've lost my baby, but that's all the more reason to get involved. My daughter is gone, but let's try and save something – let's try and get *The Bull* back. We're not going to let them get away with it, are we?'

'Mikky,' Bruno says softly. 'I understand – we understand what you've been through, but you're emotionally distraught.' He places a hand on my arm, but I pull away. 'You need to relax and recover.'

'Bruno is right,' Simon adds. 'You need to look after yourself,

Mikky. It's too soon. Your body has been through a shock, and you need to rest.'

'If you don't want to help me then I'll do it on my own. Come on, Simon. I know you have contacts. It will save time if you help me, but if you don't, then I'll find them anyway. I promise you. Even if I have to spend the rest of my life searching for them, I'll find them. I've made a promise.'

'You can't, Mikky,' says Bruno. 'Please – no. What would Glorietta say if any further harm came to you? She feels bad enough as it is. She wanted to cancel her tour. She didn't want to go to Japan. You know she considers you her daughter, Mikky. She loves you. She wouldn't want you to get involved in this ... mess.'

I turn my back on Bruno and glare at Simon. 'Watch me do it alone or help me, Simon. What's it to be?'

* * *

Simon blows out his cheeks and scratches his chin. He sits for a few minutes with his head in his hands, thinking, and I wait, staring at the top of his head.

'Okay.' He looks up. 'You win.'

'Come on, Simon!' Bruno shouts angrily. 'You can't! Where's your sense of loyalty? Josephine will kill me – and you – if Mikky gets involved.'

'She doesn't have to know, does she?' I reply, feeling a small sense of triumph.

Simon says, 'Mikky, you know more about the underworld and theft of artworks than anyone I've ever met. You're an artist and a forger. You know how it all works, and I'm sure you'll know someone who—'

'But not *this* sort of artwork.' I sit beside Simon on the sofa. 'Not sculptures like *The Bull*. I don't know much about Umberto, either.'

The three of us sit in silence. Outside, the whirling of a grass-cutting machine shrills loudly, and I imagine the swimming pool in the sunshine. I remember times I had dreamed of making memories with my daughter – swimming, walking, laughing, talking – and a heaviness falls over me that I think might crush my weak body.

'Well, I might know of someone ...' Simon says.

'Really?' Bruno's face lights up. 'Could they help?'

'I don't know – probably. You know I can't do anything. My hands are tied. I'm lecturing tomorrow in Geneva, but I think we could ask Olivia – Glorietta's friend. She's ex-police – the London Met. She might be able to tell us where to begin our search. She only retired a couple of years ago, but she should still have a good idea about procedures or where to start looking.'

'I'll go and visit her in London,' I say.

Bruno says, 'She's still here. They have an apartment north of the city, and I think they're here for another month or so.'

'Then I'll go and see her first thing in the morning. Text me her address.'

'Let's not tell anyone,' Bruno says. He looks pale, as if he's swallowed something awful and he's about to be sick. 'Don't mention it over dinner to Josephine.'

I reach for my rucksack and take out my computer. 'Let's start with the basics. You'd better tell me exactly who knew about *The Bull*. Who knew you had commissioned it? And, you'd better give me the guest list. Who was at the birthday party?'

59

'The party? It wouldn't be a guest who stole it,' Bruno argues, looking suddenly forlorn.

'Let's not discount anyone. We have to be methodical and thorough. We need a list, and we must hurry. We must find them before they disappear forever.'

I've made my promise. The only thing against me is time.

* * *

After dinner, Josephine comes into my bedroom. I've showered, and I'm sitting up in bed with my iPad, about to check the guest list for the third time. I'm also researching more background information on Umberto Palladino.

Could the bombing of his exhibit and the theft of The Bull *be related?*

'You look very pale, Mikky,' Josephine says. 'This must be so hard for you – you know, staying here in the villa ...' She casts her hand around as if she wants to add, *in this room without Eduardo.*

'I'll be fine.'

'I know you will be. I'm just saying, it's not easy, but I'm here for you.'

'Thank you.'

We sit in silence for a few moments until I say, 'He blames me.'

'He doesn't mean it. He's upset.'

'I know that, but he still blames me. He thinks it's my fault.'

'Give him time.'

'It's over.'

She shakes her head, and when she doesn't respond, I ask, 'Do you?'

'What?'

'Blame me?'

'No!' She looks genuinely surprised. 'Of course not. This wasn't your fault, Mikky.'

I can't tell her about the CCTV. 'He thinks I should have run back to the kitchen before they saw me. He thinks I'm irresponsible, and that I had no regard for my daughter.' I brush tears from my cheeks, and suddenly Josephine is pulling me into her arms. I push her away and grind my jaw together.

I will not cry tears of self-pity.

'It's okay to let go, Mikky. It's okay to cry.'

I shake my head and stare resolutely away from the directness of her stare. 'What are your plans now?' I ask.

'Simon is leaving early tomorrow for Geneva, and I was going to go with him, but I can stay here ...' her voice drifts off hopefully. 'If you need me—'

'I'll be fine.'

'What will you do?'

'I'm not going back to Mallorca.'

She sighs. 'What about your car and all the things in his flat?'

'He can keep the car and box up my stuff – he can send it up to Dolores. She'll keep it for me.'

'Don't you want to see him again?'

'Would you – if he'd accused you of killing your daughter?'

'Things are often said at a time when we're tired, anxious, upset, or vulnerable. I'm sure he didn't mean it. He loves you. Try to think kindly about him – he's going through a lot, too.'

'He isn't the victim, Josephine,' I reply tersely. 'I am – and so was my child.' *And I've made a promise*, I add silently.

* * *

Olivia and Jeff's apartment block is situated in a gated residential complex in Diagonal Mar, an expensive leafy suburb with parking. The trees provide shade from the early morning sunshine. I lock Bruno's borrowed Audi with a firm clunk, and it echoes the dull pain banging in my heart.

Bruno telephoned ahead to make sure Olivia would be at home. By the time I've strolled through her luxurious and palatial home, with its bifolding doors which lead onto a massive terrace and admired the sea view, she's already placed freshly brewed coffee on the glass table.

We sit companionably on the wicker sofas overlooking the Mediterranean, watching tilted yachts racing in the breeze, making small talk, comparing Spanish and English lifestyles. The coffee is excellent. Had the circumstances been different, I'd have appreciated the magnificent view and Olivia's interesting company more.

In her mid-forties, she has long auburn hair and green eyes. Gold bangles and rings adorn her hands, and I find it hard to believe she was once Glorietta's bodyguard. She speaks openly and with ease about how she retired early last year.

'I became bored protecting people, does that sound crazy?' she asks with a laugh.

'Risking your life every day for someone else? Now that is crazy. I wouldn't do it,' I reply.

'It's not as bad as it sounds, and besides, I was very lucky.'

'It must have been tough?'

'I was in the Metropolitan Police for fifteen years and attached to police protection in London.'

'I can't imagine you confined to a police uniform,' I say, and she throws back her head and laughs. 'Is that when you met Glorietta?'

'About eight years ago, there was a threat to her life – an over enthusiastic fan – and they couldn't take any more chances. I was one of the crew detailed to protect her. You can spend a lot of time with those you protect, and with her it was special. We became friends, which is unusual. Over the years, she got to know my family. Martin was younger then; he must have been thirteen or fourteen.'

'Isn't it unusual for a bodyguard to have a family?'

She seems to consider my question. 'Not really. Jeff was always very supportive, and we were invited to stay at her villa on Lake Como.'

'Lake Como is one of my favourite places.' I smile at the memory of my visit with Josephine just a few years ago, after I'd found out she was my birth mother. I'd almost lost my life, and I'd been invited to Glorietta's villa to recuperate.

'Many years ago, we were staying at Glorietta's villa, and Filippa's family were visiting. We all got on really well. Over the years, their son Lorenzo and our son Martin have become great friends. In fact, Lorenzo is staying here with us now. His parents have returned to their home in Sardinia, but he wanted to stay on here. The boys tend to spend their holidays drifting between families – we share our sons,' she says with a laugh.

I remember the handsome Lorenzo dancing with Maria on the night of the party and the CCTV of them kissing at the foot of the stairs.

Olivia continues speaking, 'Martin is studying Languages at university here in Barcelona, but it's great as he also gets to practise his Italian with Lorenzo. They're like brothers.

There's a group of them who play soccer, and they go to the beach, that sort of thing. They have great fun.'

'What does Lorenzo study?'

'Sciences. He wants to be a vet. They're both going into their third year in October. Lorenzo studies in Milan, so he'll go back to Italy at the end of the summer.'

'It's great they speak so many languages,' I say.

'Your English is excellent. You're bilingual?'

I reply with a scant version of the truth. I tell her how I was adopted by an Irish mother and Spanish father. I don't tell her how awful they were, but I'm sure she can see the scar on the back of my hand, where my mother once tried to kill me. She doesn't see the colourful tattoos that cover my body in biblical defiance of my scarred childhood. Even *The Scream* tattoo on my arm is covered by my long-sleeved T-shirt.

'And, Josephine is your birth mother?' she asks.

I'm surprised by her directness. It's not a secret, but not many people know. I assume that Glorietta has confided in her former bodyguard at some stage. *Well, if she trusted her with her life, why not?*

Olivia pours more coffee. 'Jeff – my husband – loves golf. I'll be joining him later for lunch at the Club if you are free to join us, but perhaps you have other plans?'

Now is the perfect opportunity to explain my visit, so I take a deep breath and explain the situation in the best way possible. 'You already know what happened the night of Glorietta's birthday party?'

She nods, and her eyes grow serious. 'Martin and Lorenzo stayed in one of the guest cottages, but Jeff and I came back here in a taxi.'

'Well, I'd like to find out more information about the people who stole *The Bull*. You know the sort of thing: Did they steal it for themselves? Was it stolen to order? Who would want it? I'm sure I don't have to tell you about basic police procedures.'

She looks surprised and then frowns. 'You don't want to get involved.'

'Why not?'

'Look.' She places her china mug on the coffee table and leans forward, clasping her hands. 'I was really sorry to hear that you lost your baby, Mikky. You think no one will understand how you feel but, believe me, people do. Most people at certain times in their lives have been through personal losses and, after what's happened to you, your emotions must be quite raw. It's normal to want to feel revenge.'

'Am I that transparent.'

She shakes her head. 'No, but that's how I would feel.'

'I need professional help, Olivia. Where would you start to look?'

She blinks, leans back against the cushions, crosses her legs, and seems to consider my question. 'Do you think they were watching the villa?' she asks.

'They knew *The Bull* was there. It may be linked to Umberto Palladino.'

'You mean the bombing of Umberto's sculpture?'

It had been in the headlines of all the national newspapers. Although terrorism was suspected, many claimed the sculpture was a political statement and a violation of freedom. Some critics had even related it to Picasso's *Guernica*, and although no one had died, one person had reported burns to their skin. The bombing had unsettled the local population and, in particular, the art world. The assailant hadn't been caught. There were conflicting news reports, including a threat on the Guggenheim Museum in Bilbao, which is now under the watchful eye of the international terrorist police.

'All museums and galleries are on alert,' I say. 'But after the theft of *The Bull*, I believe that the thieves might have a vendetta toward Umberto.'

'Vendetta? You don't think it's terrorism?'

'Unlikely.'

'A coincidence?'

'I don't know, but if we find *The Bull*, we can find the link – if there is one.'

'Why would anyone steal the sculpture?'

'Sometimes, antiquities and artefacts are targeted, stolen to order. They can also be used as currency for drugs, or even for human trafficking. But the stolen artwork is rarely worth its true value on the black market. The problem is that it could end up in Russia, China, or just about anywhere in the world in a private collection,' I say with a sigh, and then pause for breath. 'I don't know who stole it, but I can't take a chance that it might disappear forever. We have to find *The Bull* quickly.'

'Ummm.' As she's thinking, she strokes her lower lip. Her eyes are framed by black lashes, and I can understand how men would find her very attractive. She stares thoughtfully out to sea. 'How did they get inside the villa?'

'Bruno said they somehow blocked the alarm, maybe using a mobile phone.' I don't tell her about the CCTV.

'That would take some planning, wouldn't it?'

'I don't know.'

Olivia raises her eyebrows. 'I don't think anyone from the party would steal it. I hope not.'

'Bruno says the police are going through the guest list.'

'You seem to know a lot of what is going on,' she says. 'Is there anything else?'

'Bruno has a tape, and we have it on film.'

'Ah, I did wonder if there were cameras.'

'There are images of the two thieves in black ski masks, and there are also a few shots of a white van they used for their escape. So, I'm wondering if there might be a possibility that the right person with the right technology could identify the number plate of the van. What do you think?'

She stares at me, registering this development, and her eyes widen in surprise. 'Wow! That's definitely a start.' Her quick smile is followed by a frown. 'But they've probably ditched the van by now. Do the police have a copy of the tape?'

'Yes, and only a handful of close family know about this film,' I emphasise. 'I trust you. We're not going to mention this to Glorietta or to Josephine.'

'Who is we?'

'Bruno, Simon, and me.'

'Why not?'

'Because they will only worry.'

'Worry about you?'

I don't get a chance to answer as the front door bangs open, and Martin and Lorenzo come crashing into the hallway in a barrage of deep voices and raucous laughter. They dump bags on the floor and from my position on the balcony, I have a chance to look at them before they see me. Lorenzo has film-star good looks, and Martin is taller and lankier. They greet us both with a kiss on each cheek, and I force a smile at the sincerity of their kind words. We stand awkwardly for a few minutes until I say to Lorenzo, 'I hope you won't break Maria's heart?'

His smile is charming and genuinely happy. 'I think that capability lies with her, Mikky. She's very headstrong and very, very lovely.'

'Will you see each other again?' Olivia asks him teasingly.

'She's asked me over to Mallorca later in the summer.' He glances at Martin, who has his father's banana-shaped body. 'Perhaps we'll both go.'

'Only if she has a beautiful girlfriend for me, otherwise you can go alone.'

'I'll take Antonio with me then,' Lorenzo says with a laugh.

'Well, if you took him, she'd never look at you again. If Antonio met her, you wouldn't stand a chance,' Martin teases.

'Antonio is the handsome one,' Lorenzo explains, leaving me to wonder how that could be remotely possible.

'Antonio will almost certainly flirt with her,' Olivia agrees.

'Nacho is the funniest,' Martin replies.

'Too much competition. I'll go on my own.' Lorenzo holds up his hands, and Martin explodes into laughter.

Olivia turns to me. 'The boys are gentlemen – believe me – Maria will be safe.'

'We're going into town,' Martin says. 'We'll throw the football kit in the machine.'

'I'm going to take a shower,' says Lorenzo.

'We're going out for lunch,' Martin explains.

'Jeff can't get them to play golf with him yet.' Olivia smiles, and the boys grin and raise their eyes to the ceiling, as if it's been a subject of discussion many times.

'The Old Town is only twenty minutes away on the bus and Barcelona is a fantastic playground for them,' Olivia says fondly, as they disappear laughing and joking down the corridor.

68

As a child, I used to know the city well, and I wonder how much it's changed and if the drug culture is under control. These boys have no idea of my former life and how I was treated as a child. They have privileged lives, and I wonder if that truly comes without its responsibilities.

'I love their company. I'm a golfing widow!'

'Is Jeff retired?'

'He has a jewellery shop in Covent Garden. He has a good manager who runs it. We divide our time now between Spain and England, but I try to avoid going with him. I must say, I love living here, and it takes a lot of persuading to get me to go back.'

'You're not bored?'

'Bored? I have no time to get bored, believe me, Mikky.' She laughs.

I'm ready to leave and, as if by some unspoken agreement, she escorts me to the front door. Fleetingly, I imagine her as a bodyguard, and I have an idea of how safe and reassured Glorietta must have felt. Olivia leans forward and kisses me. Then she opens the door. As an afterthought, she places her hand on my arm. 'Listen, I know a guy who might look at the film. It might be a start,' she whispers.

'Really?'

'I'll see if I can find him and I'll give you a call.'

'Thank you, Olivia. I'm not going to let them get away with it.'

'I understand.' Her voice is reassuring, and as I leave the building, I finally feel I have an ally on my side.

* * *

Umberto Palladino is Italian and still retains a studio in his home town of Milan, but his new studio is located in the centre of Barcelona. It's just off the main street of Las Ramblas and very close to the Arte Moderno Museo Barcelona, which is still reeling from the drone attack. Out of curiosity, I walk past the museum. The streets have been swept, and the debris of *Los Globos* has been cleared away. Police tape still cordons off one corner, near the steps where I fell, and there's an empty air of melancholy where the exhibit once hung. Queues of tourists line up outside. The incident appears to have done nothing to damage the popularity of the museum, and I wonder if the curator is frantically looking for another piece of artwork to be installed as a replacement.

Barcelona's Gothic Quarter hasn't changed in all the years I've been coming here. It's still exciting. Perhaps the bars or restaurants have changed hands, but essentially the streets are still the same: tapas bars, restaurants, and cosmopolitan cafés are filled with a vibrant mix of people from a variety of backgrounds and cultures.

Occasionally, I glance into a stranger's face and vaguely remember the idea for my last project, photographing expressions. Still, it's an idea from my past that's not associated with my life or my ambitions now. The compass of my life has swayed manically, and I'm on an irreversible track – to find the killers of my child.

I promise, I whisper. *I will find them.*

I am buzzed in through the traditional wrought iron front door via a muffled intercom. Inside the four-storey building, it's dark and dingy, but as I proceed up the stairs, I see skylights that have been strategically placed to allow the stairwell to be naturally illuminated. I stride forward quickly, my boots echoing on the marble, ignoring the pains in my injured body and my aching heart.

I will not be deterred.

A promise is a promise.

Bruno has phoned Umberto, and I guess he is expecting me. The iron door on the first floor is ajar, so I push it open to reveal a massive, untidy, and chaotic room with several work stations and benches. Each one contains art in various shapes and sizes. Works in progress. The strong smell of glue, oil, and burning metal causes my senses to reel and nausea rises in my throat. There are half-made models and sculptures in various stages of development. Paper drawings, plans, and stencils are laid out, folded, or rolled up. Some have even been balled up and tossed on the floor. It's an intriguing studio, and although I'd like to walk around it, I have a more important task on my mind.

'Hola?' I call out, moving cautiously into the hot and airless room. 'Umberto?'

At the far end of the room, a masked man is holding a blow torch, which explains the burning smell. He's moulding a piece of metal, but it's hard to see the design of his creation. He's wearing a grubby and stained grey boiler suit, and his back is toward me.

I raise my voice. 'Umberto?'

He turns around, switches off the torch, and raises his protective glasses. His hooked nose is overshadowed by deep brown eyes, and his face creases and twists angrily as he speaks. 'What do you want?'

'My name is Mikky dos—'

'I know who you are. Bruno told me you were coming, but I don't see the point. What do you want?'

I'm surprised by his hostility. 'I met you at the exhibition.'

'So?'

I step forward. 'Did Bruno tell you what happened at Glorietta's party?'

'Naturally.'

'I want to ask if you would have any idea who might have—'

'I have no idea. It's nothing to do with me.'

'But—'

He fires up the blow torch, and I regard the blue flame he points at me.

'Is *The Bull* a one-off design? Is it unique, or are there more in a collection?'

'All my work is unique.'

'I'm sure they all are. Are there other pieces in the collection? Maybe a collector ...' I let the sentence hang in the air.

His intense black eyes bore into me, and he lets the silence between us grow before eventually replying, 'I told Bruno what I know.'

'And what was that?'

'Nothing. I know nothing.'

He's a temperamental, an artistic Italian, and he reminds me of Raffaelle Pavelli, my art teacher from many years ago, but I'm not fazed. I've been used to dealing with creative and artistic people all my life.

'I want to find *The Bull*. It means a lot to Glorietta, and she is very upset that it's been stolen. Did anyone know that you were making it for her?'

'No.'

'Did anyone see you create it?'

He casts his arms wide. 'What do you think?'

'I think you're very unhelpful.'

'I work with many interns and students. They don't know everything, and I don't tell them all my secrets – they work *for* me.'

I glance around the massive space. 'Here?'

'And upstairs.' He points at an iron spiral staircase in the far corner of the room.

'Can you tell me who else works here?'

'Why?'

'In case they can help me.'

'They can't.'

'I won't know unless I ask them.'

'They are sworn to secrecy. Only the most brilliant students come here. This is not a place for the ordinary or the mundane.'

'What about thieves and liars?'

He turns his back on me and places the blow torch against the metal.

'How did you meet Bruno?' I call out.

He doesn't turn around, so I take a few paces forward and to his right. He glances up but continues to work as he replies, 'I've known his family for years. Anything else?'

'Did you make any more sculptures? Is there a collection of animals?'

I'm struggling to associate the delicate beauty of *The Bull* with the brutish attitude of the man beside me. He scowls and then contemplates the tip of the blow torch, as if he'd like to set me alight, then he returns his attention to his work. He circles the wooden bench in contemplation. The sculpture he's working on doesn't mean anything to me, but I'm interested in art, and when I step closer, he aims the torch like a gun to stop me.

I hold up my palms. 'I come in peace.'

He doesn't smile. '*The Bull* is one of five pieces. *The Bear* was the first, then *The Bee*, and after that *The Barn Owl* and *The Fox* and, before you ask, I designed *The Bull* especially for Glorietta because Bruno asked me to. I used sheet music from the opera *Carmen* because it has a special meaning for them.'

'And what about the other pieces? Were they personally commissioned?'

'I do not divulge the names of my clients.'

'Then tell me, why do they all sell for such huge prices?'

This is a shot in the dark. I have no idea of the prices, but after what Bruno told me *The Bull* was worth, then it's only reasonable to assume that the others would be of equal or similar value.

'That's not for me to say.'

I sigh. 'You're beginning to piss me off. Don't you care that *The Bull* has been stolen?'

'Of course, but artists can't be accountable for stolen artworks. It's not my responsibility.'

'You mean that once you get paid, you don't care?'

He takes a step forward and the blow torch flares. I step back.

'It's not my problem,' he hisses.

There's a loud thud from overhead, and I follow his gaze to the spiral staircase in the corner of the room.

'Who is up there?' I ask.

'Students.'

'Can I meet them?'

'No.'

I wonder whether to make a run for the staircase, but after my last unsuccessful attempt at dashing up some stairs, I'm not brave enough to risk it. The memory of my attack makes my stomach heave and pain swells across my abdomen, making me feel sick. I clutch the bench, willing the pain to pass, hoping I won't pass out and that the electric buzzing in my head will stop. My forehead breaks into a sweat. My breathing is shallow, and I swallow at the iron taste in my mouth as heartburn grips my chest and bile rises in my throat. When I glance up, Umberto is watching me. He doesn't move.

'Do you think the theft was related to the incident last week?' I ask.

'No.'

'Who would want to bomb *Los Globos*?'

'I have no idea.'

'Do you have any enemies?'

'No.'

I know he's lying. 'We all have enemies.' I turn to leave. I'm going to be sick. 'By the way – thank you.'

'For what?'

'For absolutely nothing. You should be ashamed to call yourself a friend of Bruno's.'

* * *

A small but welcome breeze wafts up the shady stairwell, and I'm hoping I won't throw up when Umberto calls out.

I pause, trying to ignore the pain in my body.

Umberto picks up a sculpture and follows me into the corridor. He holds it close to his chest like a small child, then very slowly he holds it out to me. His hands are small and delicate, and our fingers touch; his skin is soft.

It's a fox, and it's made of paper.

'It's life-size,' I say.

He frowns. 'Yes.'

'*The Bull* was one third of the original size.'

'They are all one third apart from this one and *The Bee*. It is three times bigger than its life-size form.'

When I take *The Fox*, I'm surprised by the weight of the paper. I turn it in my hands, trying to decipher the pictures and articles taken from glossy magazines in various languages. Unlike *The Bull*, *The Fox* is sculptured onto a plinth. Its neck and head are dipped, as if it's stalking prey, and his left paw hangs in the air, in a hunting pose. It's unfinished but still remarkable.

He takes it from my hands and turns it upside down so that I can see the fox's underbelly. 'Look! See here.'

I can't see anything, and so he tilts it toward the light.

'I burn my initials into the raised paw – or claw.'

The garlic on his breath sets off a wave of nausea in me. It attacks my stomach and pain spreads along the veins of my body. I clutch the door handle to keep myself upright, searching for his initials. Between the paw pads are the singed, entwined letters *UP*.

'Did you sign *The Bull*?' Sweat breaks out on my forehead.

'Yes.'

Outside the building, I throw up until my stomach is empty. Perspiration runs down my spine, and afterwards, my mouth is dry and sour-tasting. The sunlight dazzles me, and I stagger into the nearest bar and sit at the table in the window. I wait for the nausea to subside and for the air conditioning to cool my temperature. I order water and black coffee, and my head is in my hands when the waiter returns a few minutes later.

'Estas bien?'

'Sí, gracias,' I reply.

76

Why did Umberto call me back to tell me about his signature? Did he say it was just this collection he signed? Who has commissioned *The Fox*?

My head is buzzing. I miss talking to my daughter.

The pain in my back and chest subsides, and I check my phone. There are two missed calls from Josephine and a voicemail. She wants to know where I am – nothing from Olivia. I toss the phone on the table and sip my water, relishing the cold liquid as it slides down my throat.

From my vantage point in the window, I can't see the door to Umberto's studio; it's around the corner, off the main street, and I look at the faces of people in the street, thinking about Umberto. He didn't seem to be upset by the theft of *The Bull*, and he didn't admit to having any enemies.

Perhaps that's normal. He probably saw me as an interfering friend – a meddler – so I can hardly blame him. But I'm no further forward with my investigation.

I make a couple of phone calls to old contacts: Marina in Bruges, who has helped me since her father retired. She promises that if she hears anything about the sale of *The Bull* on the black market, then she'll let me know. I phone a contact in Madrid and another guy I worked with in Paris, and finally a friend in London.

'It might be worth checking his studio in Milan,' says Alex, my friend in Knightsbridge. 'There might be some jealousy or rivalry amongst students – that can happen.'

'I can't imagine him having an affair ...'

Alex chuckles. 'Can't you? It happens everywhere, Mikky. You of all people should know.'

He's right, of course, and as I hang up, I think of my lovely friend Carmen, who was the curator of a museum in Málaga. If only she was alive – she would help me. Her death still affects me, and I spend a few minutes thinking of her with a mixture of nostalgia and regret.

I know I must eat something, so I order tapas; chicken pinchos, manchego cheese, breadsticks, and a glass of red wine.

I have a great view of the people in the street – mostly sightseeing tourists – and as I eat, I play *guess their nationality*; English, Dutch, German, then the Asians: Chinese, Korean, Japanese.

I study their faces, looking for signs of stress, sadness, anger, and laughter. Each one is original and unique. It keeps me focused while my subconscious whirls, processing my conversations with Olivia and Umberto while deliberately ignoring memories of Eduardo.

I've finished eating, and it's almost three o'clock when I see two familiar faces. Lorenzo is strolling through the street, hands in his pockets, sunglasses on, T-shirt open at the neck. He looks like a Hollywood star. Martin, by comparison, although well dressed in a turquoise T-shirt and navy chinos, lacks the natural swagger. His tall body is already stooped, as if apologising for his height, in a genetic banana shape.

They are accompanied by a third guy, who is smaller, and has a cheeky smile. He wears a FC Barcelona T-shirt and carries a football that he spins periodically into the air on the tip of his index finger. Nacho or Antonio?

They don't notice me sitting in the window. They're lost in conversation, laughing, and I understand how happy Olivia must be to have them around. Their youth and carefree attitude are refreshing, and I feel a tinge of envy. The only time I have ever felt that way was a few weeks ago, when I was pregnant and in love with Eduardo.

So, how has that all changed?

Where does love disappear to?

Where has my love for Eduardo gone?

Where did my youth go?

How can I feel old at thirty-three?

The boys disappear along the thoroughfare and feeling sad and suddenly alone, I pay the bill and leave.

I stand outside Umberto's studio and stare at the wrought iron door. I don't know what I'm hoping for – a revelation or a clue? I'm willing it to open, hoping for inspiration, but nothing happens. It's just a closed door.

I check my phone.

There's another message from Josephine but still nothing from Olivia. I return it to my pocket, and I'm suddenly conscious of a shadow falling over me. He's about fifty, with deep-set, intelligent eyes and short pepper-grey hair.

'Hola, Mikky,' he says. 'Mucho tiempo.'

I don't recall who he is. He's not a threat, but I don't feel at ease.

'Hola,' I reply automatically.

'Te recuerdas de mi?' he asks. His crumpled cream shirt is open at the neck. His brown chinos and worn loafers give him a casual air of someone who is very comfortable with themselves. He's not dressed to impress.

'Do I remember you? No, but I have a positive feeling about you.'

His laugh is a spontaneous chuckle. 'That's a good sign.' He holds out his hand. 'Joachin García Abascal.' His grip is firm but not aggressive, and I feel a vague memory stirring. 'The last time we met, you were in hospital in Palma. You had survived a fire, but someone had just scored a nasty name into your forehead.'

'T–H–I–E–F,' I spell out the letters, aware of a returning memory. Not many people know about my past. 'You're a policeman, aren't you?'

'I'm a friend of Josephine's. She asked me to speak to you, and we arranged to repatriate Vermeer's *The Concert* that you had very generously tracked down for us. It was a very generous act of yours, and it enabled us to return it to the museum in America – in Boston – from where it was stolen.'

'Yes.'

Did he say generous?

'You were sedated at the time, but we did speak briefly,' he continues. 'You did hand me the painting yourself. You insisted on it.'

His version of the truth is reassuring. Josephine had lied on my behalf so that I would not go to prison or ruin my life. She had given him a different version of events and twisted my actions into a positive light, while at the same time insisting that I return Vermeer's masterpiece. Stealing it had almost cost me my life. It was going to be my financial insurance against the world. But Josephine had found me. She had tracked me down after thirty years. She had saved me. Ironically, that was also when I'd met Eduardo – my intensive care nurse.

I don't believe in coincidences, and I also don't believe Joachin García Abascal is here to arrest me or to drag up any illegal mistakes of my past.

'Are you still a policeman?'

'Sort of – do you have time for a coffee?'

I'm not sure what he wants, but I've never had a strong

affinity for the police force. It was never there to protect me, nor has it ever saved me. In fact, my ex-lover was a policeman. He'd killed my friend Carmen, and I'd been next on his list. I wasn't about to trust another man in uniform – or in Joachin's case, out of uniform but nevertheless still a policeman.

'I'm sorry. I have a meeting,' I lie.

He glances toward the door of Umberto's studio and nods. 'With Umberto?'

I shake my head in denial, and he tilts his head to one side. I give him a cheeky grin. He doesn't trust me, and I'm sure he knows I'm lying.

'I'm sorry about your baby,' he says softly.

The smile drains from my face. I want to slap him. I want to kick him and punch him, but nausea cascades into my heart, filling the empty hole that's gaping wide in grief, and I feel my knees buckle.

He takes my elbow, and I let him steer me to the terrace of the nearest bar, where he pulls out a seat for me. I lean on the table, cursing myself for not feeling stronger, waiting as he orders two brandies from the waitress.

I will not be weak. I promise.

I wait for the nausea to pass, and the waitress places our drinks on the table. He nudges the bulbous glass toward me, so I take a deep slug of the harsh liquid, welcoming the burning sensation on the back of my throat. I cough and wipe away my tears.

'Are you okay?' he asks softly.

I nod.

'You have more colour in your cheeks now.'

I nod.

'Are you still in pain?'

'Mentally or physically?' I stare defiantly.

This time, he smiles briefly. 'The police have taken witness statements from all the guests at Glorietta and Bruno's party. It's standard procedure. They're interviewing everyone – as they did you. It will be a long job to sift through everyone who was there: guests, catering staff, the band.' He crosses his legs. 'The Guardia Civil are also working on the CCTV video, but these things take time, and as you probably know, resources are always a problem. The theft of an expensive statue is not as important as rape, drugs, and more recently, the threat of terrorism.' He sips his brandy and clears his throat. 'Of course, they're not sure if the two incidents are linked or if the attack on *Los Globos* is related to terrorism. The investigation could go on for a long time and the longer it takes, the colder the trail will become, and the chances of us finding *The Bull* will be substantially reduced.'

'Do you think the theft is related to the bombing of Umberto's sculpture?'

'There is no evidence—'

'I don't want them to get away; to go underground and disappear.'

'Josephine called me. She's worried about you.'

'She wants you to keep an eye on me,' I reply.

'Probably.' His smile is disarming. There's a wedding band on his finger, and I wonder what his wife is like and if he has children.

'Are you with the Guardia Civil?'

He shakes his head. 'Not anymore. I transferred several years ago to the International Crime Squad at Europol. You know the sort of thing – fighting international crime syndicates, human trafficking, money laundering, cybercrime, drugs—'

'Terrorism?'

'I specialise in stolen antiquities in Europe. That's how we met the last time.' He smiles. 'I, and officers like me, use our experience and criminal intelligence to work closely with all the European police forces. In our capacity, we can't arrest anyone or carry out investigations without the approval of each country's authorities.'

'Isn't that restrictive?'

'Not really, but it is important for us to have the logistical help and support that the free trade agreement for cross-border policies allows.'

'What rank do you hold?'

'Inspector.'

I'm impressed, but I don't tell him. I'm still mulling over the fact that Josephine called him. Has she done it to support me or to keep an eye on me?

'So, what do you want?' I ask.

'Well, let's keep it simple, Mikky. Is there anything you can tell me at all?'

I shrug. 'Me?'

'Have you spoken to anyone?' he insists.

'Like?'

'Umberto Palladino?'

'He's arrogant and self-important.'

Joachin smiles and drains his glass. 'Well, I'm on my way to find out.'

'Good luck with that, then.'

'Anything else?' I try to look innocent, so he asks again, 'Have you spoken to anyone else?'

'No.' I'm not going to mention Olivia, not until I know

exactly what Josephine has told him, and besides, I may never hear from her again.

'I know that you have lots of contacts on the black market, Mikky. It would be helpful if we could—'

'Don't you mean, in the art world?'

'Of course. If you hear anything, will you please let me know?'

'Of course,' I lie.

He signals to the waiter for the bill and places a note on the table. 'What are your plans now, Mikky?'

'I'm going back to the villa.'

He nods. 'Good.'

'I don't appreciate being followed and spied upon, with every action of mine being noted by a policeman who thinks that because he's been promoted to an international force, he has the right to intimidate me,' I say.

He doesn't seem shocked by my outburst. Instead, his brown eyes soften, and he sighs.

'Look, I understand that you want to be involved, Mikky, but I don't think it's a good idea for you to go looking for these guys on your own. It could be dangerous. We don't want you to get hurt. They could be professional. They're certainly skilled, and you've been through enough.'

I assume he's referring to the injuries I received in Mallorca.

'I'm not frightened of them.'

'I know, but I insist you leave the investigation to us.'

'Us? How many are there in your team?'

'It depends. I have resources. We know what we're doing.' He leaves change on the saucer for a generous tip. 'We'll find them – and *The Bull* – and you must build up your strength and get well.'

I lean across the table. 'Who would bomb Umberto's sculpture in such a spectacular fashion – when the whole art world was watching – and then a few days later steal *The Bull* from Glorietta Bareldo's villa?'

'We're not sure that the two incidents are connected.'

'Okay, so why bomb the sculpture?'

'To get noticed.'

'Exactly. To make a statement.' I tap the table with my finger. 'They want to damage Umberto.'

'But it could have the opposite effect. It could have brought more attention to his work. It could be an advantage for him. The price of his artwork might increase,' he argues.

'Forever remembered,' I add.

'Yes, maybe.' He toys with his wedding band, sliding it around his finger. 'And he broke into the villa and stole *The Bull*? Is that why he didn't go to Glorietta's party as he intended, because he planned to return later that night as a thief?'

'You're making fun of me.'

His smile disappears. 'We'll all feel happier if you look after yourself, Mikky. Leave the investigation to us.'

'That's what Josephine wants.'

'It's what we all want.'

But I'm determined. I will find them even if I have to do it alone.

Justice will be mine.

I've made a promise.

* * *

I drive back to the villa, tired and irritable. I'm also in pain. I

85

pull into the drive, slowing down at the gates to look for the CCTV cameras mounted on the wall. One is hidden, at an angle, behind a tree, and I guess that's the one that caught the images. The other is on the wall of the gate. It looks clean, and I guess it's filming me as I get out of the car and check the positioning of the white van. It would have been parked opposite the gate, on the grassy verge.

How long had they been watching the villa?

If they were sophisticated enough to use a mobile phone to interrupt the alarm circuit, then I wonder if they had stolen artefacts before *The Bull*, or if this had been a one-off?

I climb back in the car and thump the steering wheel with my fist.

What if I'd woken Eduardo and he'd gone downstairs to get some cheese and olives for me?

Would they have hurt him?

Killed him?

A dull ache spreads through my stomach to my ribcage, and I lean over the steering wheel and wait until it passes. Then, very slowly, I continue to drive through the gates, past the main entrance of the villa on the right and to the back of the estate. I park outside the stables, beside Josephine's hired car, and I'm instantly fired up with anger.

How dare she send the inspector to warn me off?

I squint into the sunshine. In the distance, meandering between the vines on the back of horses, Bruno is riding with Dominique, the estate manager. They seem to be checking the grapes, probably discussing the harvest, wine output, and export.

Ever since I've known Bruno, he's always been a handsome playboy, but I'd never imagined him to be such an excellent businessman and connoisseur of wines. He's turning this estate into a success.

I reach for a bottle of water from my bag and swallow some painkillers as I contemplate the vineyard. When we arrived, Bruno had guided us around the bodega and down to the cellar, where Eduardo had sampled the wine, but now, while everyone else's lives are continuing as normal, mine has been irrevocably destroyed: my baby, my partner, my life. Gone.

I screw the lid back on the water bottle and toss it on the seat. That's when my mobile rings. There is no caller ID, but I answer it anyway.

'Hola.'

'Mikky? It's Olivia.'

'Hi.' I sit up in the seat.

'I've found him,' she says, sounding happy and upbeat. 'He will look at the tape for you. You'll have to take it to him.'

'Okay, where?'

'Poland.'

'You're joking! Why can't I send it electronically?'

'He's very cautious and secretive. He's ex-Royal Marines. He used to fly Chinooks in Afghanistan. I think he could be a great help to you.'

'Used to?'

'Yes. He's started up a hi-tech, surveillance sort of business. He does number-plate recognition and ... well, I don't understand technology, but that sort of thing. So, if you need his help, I can text you his address.'

Poland?

I watch Bruno trotting on his grey mare, winding his way between the vines toward the stable. The horse's hooves clop hollowly on the forecourt, and as Bruno leads it to the water fountain, he smiles and waves.

There's nothing for me here. My baby is gone. My relationship is over. It's time to move on.

'Text me his address. What's the nearest airport?'

It's time to take revenge for the past.

I will keep my promise.

* * *

I sneak into the villa. I don't want Josephine to know I'm back. I don't want her forty million questions, and I don't need her look of concern, making me feel guilty. I stop in the deserted kitchen and pause to look at the spot where I stood just two nights ago.

Another me – another time.

I had stared out of the window, talking to my baby and thinking about our future together while Eduardo, her caring, loving father, was asleep upstairs. I'd made plans for the home that we would have. We were going to move out of Eduardo's apartment and find a villa near Palma, convenient for travelling to and from the hospital, and with a photographic studio for me. We were going to live together – a proper family – until it had all changed.

Eduardo's anger, frustration, and the blame he has placed firmly on me has saddened me more than I could ever have imagined.

Not only have I lost my daughter – I've lost him, as well.

There's no point in standing wondering what might have been. My life is on a new track. I take the same pathway down the corridor as I'd taken that fateful night, and pause to look at the table where *The Bull* had been displayed. The empty space would have been haunting, but today someone has thoughtfully placed an array of fresh, colourful flowers in its place; yet the heady aroma of lilies reminds me of funerals and death.

The hidden camera is near the chandelier in the ceiling. The thieves, like me and the other guests who had gathered at different times to gaze at the sculpture, were unaware that they were being filmed. No one could have imagined what would happen later that night.

Did the thieves know the layout of the villa? Did they guess where *The Bull* would be displayed?

Could it have been prevented?

I pause on the step, imagining Eduardo beside me as we climbed the stairs to bed. I did not know it would be the last time we would be together, and that the happiness we shared was about to be shattered, split into minuscule pieces and scattered like confetti blowing in the wind.

Upstairs, in the bedroom, there's still the faint aroma of his familiar aftershave, and I feel his presence even more. I pick up my iPad and check the CCTV. I watch myself over and over, curled in a ball in an effort to protect myself. My assailant had kicked me – a martial arts move like you'd see on TV or in a film, only this time it was real.

Did I create the situation?

Could I have retreated – gone back to the kitchen?

I focus on the assailant. Why did they kick me a second time? It was a quick, professional movement, balanced and perfect.

I toss the iPad aside, lay back on the bed, and close my eyes.

Would I recognise them again?

I don't know how long I lie on the bed, replaying scenes from the past, listening to accusations and a torrent of angry words, and my head is thumping. I've got to find them. Research is the key.

The Bull is one of a collection: *The Bear* was the first, then *The Bee*, and then *The Barn Owl* – and the latest one is *The Fox*.

Who are the owners of the other pieces?

I check the Art Loss Register. None of the pieces by Umberto are registered as stolen, so I check the main auction houses in Madrid, Paris, London, Berlin, and – as a last resort – Moscow.

Unsurprisingly, there's nothing of Umberto's for sale that is cause for concern.

What if the two incidents weren't related?

Does Glorietta have any enemies? If so, why steal *The Bull*? Why not steal one of the other paintings or some of her other more expensive pieces of art from her home in Lake Como?

Gut instinct tells me that both the incidents are related, but if they are, then there could be more thefts, bombs, and destruction.

Perhaps if the inspector finds out who owns the other sculptures, we might find out who would want to steal *The Bull*. Or perhaps we can find out who could have a vendetta against Umberto.

There's an enormous amount of envy and jealousy between collectors. Maybe someone heard that Umberto has made these sculptures and someone wants to get their hands on one. Or maybe a crime syndicate stole *The Bull* to fund drug smuggling, weapons, or any other illegal activity in the underworld. The bombing of the sculpture could be a political statement by an activist wanting to make a point.

Methodically, I go through my options. The list seems endless and overwhelming. There's no point in me interviewing birthday party guests, interns at Umberto's studio, or searching the Internet for random research – it would take too much man-power and too much time.

Instinct tells me that the bombing of the sculpture, and the theft of *The Bull*, are related, and unless I'm told otherwise, I intend to prove it.

My phone pings. It's Olivia, with a name and address in Poland. I book a seat on a morning flight to Wrocław and pack a small bag. They have a two-day head start, but I'm excited to now have a plan.

* * *

Over a dinner of succulent roast lamb baked with baby shallots in red wine, garlic, and rosemary, washed down with chilled wine from Bruno's vineyard, I tell him, Simon, and Josephine about my encounter with Joachin – the inspector from Europol – and of my visit to Olivia's home and her subsequent message with the contact details of the man in Poland.

'You went to see Olivia?' Josephine pauses with her glass raised to her lips. 'Did you tell Joachin?'

I ignore her.

'Who's the guy in Poland?' asks Simon.

'Peter Brzezicki. Ex-SAS – Royal Marines. He's supposed to be able to trace number plates.'

'Why can't the police do it?' Josephine asks.

'They told me that there's very little cross border cooperation,' says Bruno.

'Is this dangerous?' Josephine insists.

I glare at Bruno. During my visit to Olivia and Umberto this morning, Josephine had stayed at the villa and badgered Bruno for information. She'd been determined to find out what I was doing, and Bruno had eventually caved in and shown her the CCTV.

Josephine is a very determined woman, and when he'd told her my intention of helping to find *The Bull*, she'd been furious.

'What if it's been stolen to fund a drug or illegal trafficking cartel? Then what? Mikky could be in terrible danger.' Josephine glares at Bruno, so I reach for the wine bottle and top up his glass, giving him a cheeky wink.

'Who is this Peter fellow?' she asks.

'Someone that Olivia knows,' I reply.

'You can't go to Poland on your own. You don't even know him. I'm going with you.'

I wipe my mouth with the napkin and toss it onto the table. 'No, you're not. I'm going alone.'

'That's ridiculous.'

'I want to be on my own.'

Simon and Bruno watch our exchange in diplomatic silence.

'It's too far,' she insists. 'It's too tiring – especially after what you've been through. Bruno, stop her – please say something!'

'Don't go, Mikky,' Bruno says unconvincingly.

'Please – I implore you. Talk some sense into her.' Josephine leans across the table and takes Simon's arm. 'Don't let her go.'

'Stop it, Josephine,' I say, raising my voice. 'It's not dangerous. I'm going to meet a guy who might help us. I'm not going to do anything dangerous.' I refill my wine glass. Now that I'm not pregnant, I feel like drinking alcohol again. It deadens the pain.

'It's ridiculous,' Josephine says. 'Why do you have to go all that way just to give him a copy of the tape?'

'It's the only thing we can do – it's been two days. *The Bull* could be anywhere in the world by now. We must find them.' I stare defiantly at Josephine.

'He probably wants to know who he's dealing with to make sure it's legit,' replies Bruno.

'If he's ex-SAS, he may have some ideas or contacts,' adds Simon.

'For heaven's sake, stop encouraging her.'

'I'll cover your costs,' Bruno says, ignoring Josephine.

'I'm on the early flight to Geneva; we can drive to the airport together,' Simon says.

'Stop!' Josephine stands up. She waits until we give her our full attention. 'Is no one listening? Why does no one care what I think?'

'Maybe Mikky just needs to be on her own for a while,' Simon says quietly. 'It's perfectly normal after what she's been through. It will give her time to think.'

Josephine stares at him as if he's said something outrageous, but undeterred he continues, 'She's like you, Josephine. She needs to do things her own way, and sometimes she needs to be alone.'

'This is unbelievable. I can't believe you're not supporting me. You know how worried I am. I'll never forgive you – either of you – if anything happens ...'

It's too late. It already has.

'Don't be worried,' I say. 'I'll be fine, Josephine.'

'This is a conspiracy. You're all against me.' Josephine sweeps out of the room, slamming the door in her wake.

We look at each other in silence, and then I burst out laughing. 'You can never take the drama out of a queen ...'

'She's worried about you,' Simon replies.

'I'll be quick. The trail gets colder with each day.'

'Just be careful,' Bruno says. 'Or she'll kill me.'

Chapter 3

"Man cannot remake himself without suffering, for he is both the marble and the sculptor."
Alexis Carrel

I'm awake all night planning.

How will I make the murderers of my baby suffer?

I'm meeting a professionally trained SAS killer, but I won't need help to kill. I'll manage that myself. I watch the dawn crack open, splitting the vineyard in light and shade, and I imagine my revenge. By the time I drag my tired and aching body through the airport and onto the plane, I'm wired but exhausted. In the window seat, I close my eyes, letting the aircraft lift me into the sky and toward my unknown destiny.

At last, I'm on their trail. I'm not running away – not this time. I'm chasing. I'm chasing those responsible for ruining my life and for killing my unborn daughter. I'll hunt them down, and I won't rest until I find them.

In my experience, thieves are paid to steal and loot stolen artefacts. They're often stolen to order. They're also sold on the black market to unscrupulous collectors, and I can't take the risk that the thieves – and murderers – will disappear without a trace.

I'm a day and a half behind them, but I've made my promise, and I place my hand on my tummy and pretend she's still there. I whisper and tell her what Mummy is doing.

Out of the window, the ground is growing closer. Wrocław is about 250 kilometres from the Polish and German border, and it lies on the River Oder. It's the fourth-largest city in Poland, and dates back over a thousand years. Strategically situated, it had once been commandeered and invaded, and had been included as part of many European kingdoms. More recently, it had been part of the German Empire. However, after the war in 1945, and the border and territorial changes, Germans either fled or returned to their own country. Wrocław had become a part of Poland again. The majority of the population are now Polish.

I take a taxi from the airport to the city centre, and I'm curious as the car negotiates the narrow streets near the historical centre. My senses are suddenly heightened by the cultural changes around me, and the sea of foreign faces in the street. I'm interested in their expressions and mannerisms. It's a photographer's habit, but now I don't know why I bother – that's all in my past. I haven't time for such trivialities.

The taxi halts at the entrance to the pedestrianised historical zone and, after paying the driver, I fling my rucksack over my shoulder, already wondering about the man I am going to meet.

Military, army, disciplined?

I pass an assortment of old buildings, juxtaposed with trendy cafés, bars, and restaurants. There's no sign of the war-torn Poland of the past. Now, I see wealth around me, and I'm exhausted by the assorted food smells – sausage, coffee, stews, and tobacco – that make me suddenly queasy. I lengthen my stride. There's no time to waste. I have to get the CCTV to Olivia's friend. The longer I take, the more chance the thieves have of going underground, and I may never find them.

I check the address of the apartment, tucked down a narrow side street in the exclusive part of town. The polished stone building looks like a renovated, converted mill or granary. It's four storeys high, and I imagine the price or rent for an apartment would be expensive.

SAS – well paid?

I press the buzzer and while I wait, I glance up at the façade of the old building, wondering who could afford to live in a place like this.

'Yes?' A deep voice cuts across my thoughts.

'It's Mikky dos Santos,' I say into the intercom.

'Come up.' The door buzzes and clicks open.

Peter Brzezicki is stocky, broad, and solid. Dark, shoulder-length hair hangs limply over his face, and his square jaw is covered with a massive Viking beard. Curly chest hair sprouts from the top of his grubby T-shirt, covering his neck and forearms. His dark eyes regard me coldly as he opens the front door warily and glances over my shoulder.

'Come in.' His voice is gravelly and raw, as if he hasn't spoken for a while.

We don't shake hands. Instead, he turns away, so I close the front door and follow him down a corridor. My boots are noisy on the wooden floor, but it's his heavy limp and prosthetic left foot that makes the thumping sound.

He leads me into a cluttered room, where long purple curtains are currently closed, covering the far wall. Only the dull overhead ceiling light, and a small atrium from the hallway, provide enough light to prevent me from knocking my shins on the furniture. I survey the room with distaste, conscious of the vile stale smell. On the wall to the right, a pine bookshelf is heaving with books in different languages. In the centre of the room are two massive leather black sofas, sporting an array of cushions, rugs, papers, and discarded magazines. On a low, square coffee table, stale food lies untouched in takeaway boxes, which explains the putrid and fetid aroma. A glass-topped dining table, ringed with brown mug stains, is covered with an assortment of computers, monitors, laptops, and several TV screens. One is currently showing CNN – it's on mute.

'What do you want?'

'I was told you could help me,' I reply.

'I doubt that.' His accent is public-school British, and it's out of place in this skanky apartment.

'I can pay you.'

'I don't need money.'

'I've come from Spain.'

'You've wasted your time.'

'I don't believe you.' Anger begins to rise in me. 'Why agree to see the CCTV?'

He stands a head taller than me, a few metres away, with his hands dug into his pockets. His eyes are cold and hard. I want to hit him, but I say softly, 'Why? Look, I've no one else who can help.' A swelling of nausea overtakes me; alcohol from last night, a lack of sleep, and travelling, all make me feel as if my baby is alive and kicking inside me. I hold onto the table, hoping I won't collapse, and perspiration breaks out across my forehead and trickles down my spine. I lick my lips. 'Can I have some water?'

Reluctantly, he leaves the room and returns with a grubby

glass, but I drink thirstily.

'What do you want me to look at?' He scratches his beard.

I place the empty glass beside the TV, pull out the USB from my pocket, and hand it to him before he changes his mind. He's missing two fingers on his left hand.

'It's urgent,' I whisper, fighting the nausea.

'What's on it?' He sits down heavily at the table, as if he's pleased to get off his feet.

I breathe shallowly; the lingering smell of rancid food and the lack of fresh air in the room is making me worse.

'It's security camera footage taken from a villa just outside Barcelona.'

He slips the USB into his laptop and clicks the keyboard efficiently with the stubs of his fingers. While he waits for it to load, he scratches his nose absent-mindedly with his thumb. He smells as if he hasn't washed for days – perhaps weeks – but he's my only hope.

'It's the theft of an expensive sculpture,' I add, concentrating and trying to focus. 'Two nights ago.' I can hardly believe it's only been two nights – it seems longer since my life was blown to pieces, but as I stand beside this injured man, I can't imagine the extent of his shattered life. He's probably hiding from the world in this rancid cave of despair.

'This it?' he asks, as the image comes to life on his screen.

I lean over his shoulder, then pull away and cover my nose. 'Yes. I need to identify the white van. You'll see it in a minute.'

'This the robbery?'

'Yes. It's a private birthday party.' I don't elaborate, and we watch the scene play out in silence. We get to the point when we are all standing admiring *The Bull*.

Peter whispers, 'What the hell is that?'

'It's a sculpture – made of paper, sheet music from the opera of *Carmen*.'

'They call that art?'

'Presumably.'

'People actually pay to have that shit in their house?'

'They do.' He reminds me of Eduardo.

We watch in silence as the evening progresses and the various couples head upstairs to bed, and when I appear with Eduardo, I have to turn away. When the two thieves enter the villa through the front door, I stroke the scar on the back of my hand and Peter leans forward to study the screen. 'Easy access?'

'Bruno, the owner, set the alarm, but they bypassed it somehow – we think they used a mobile phone to block the circuit.'

'Um. It's easy if you know how.'

'Really?'

'Any idea who they are?' He doesn't take his eyes from the screen.

'Not yet.'

They walk cautiously into the villa. They don't waste time. They see *The Bull* immediately, and the taller of the two intruders sinks to his knees and places the bag on the ground. In the bottom-left corner, I appear on the screen. I don't want to see this all again. I walk to the sofa – I'm about to sit down, but the debris and crumbs prevent me, so I stand watching Peter's face, gauging his reaction from a dark distance, wondering what he's thinking. I'm overcome with tiredness, and my legs are weak. I give in and perch on the edge of the sofa. My eyes close and I see the murderer before me, his eyes narrowed in a smile, and I'm drifting. Suddenly, my body twitches and I blink awake and sit upright, but Peter seems not to notice. He's still focused on the screen, tapping buttons and concentrating.

I wait for what seems an eternity, enjoying the softness of the sofa at my back, allowing my eyes to rest for seconds at a time, not caring that it's dirty and smelly, or that I feel sick. I wait, hoping the moment will pass and that my forehead will not remain clammy.

'Um,' he mutters. He's tapping the keys, and I imagine him examining their faces, close up, just as I did.

'There was a camera at the front gate?' he asks.

'There are four cameras; two at the gate, one at the front door, and one inside. They spray-painted one at the gate, but they missed the other one, as it's hidden behind a bush. They sprayed the one at the front door, and these images are from the camera inside the reception, which they also missed. The time of their arrival and departure is in the bottom-right corner.' It's probably unnecessary for me to explain, but I can't seem to focus. My voice sounds distant and slurred. 'They were only in the villa for ...'

'Four minutes. Professionals.'

Long enough to kill my baby.

Peter says, 'Not necessarily. It could be anyone.'

'I want to track the van.' I sit up, suddenly feeling hot, and I slide my arms out of my leather jacket. 'Olivia seems to think that you'll be able to find the registration and help me track the van – can you find it?'

He looks up from the screen and stares at me. 'That was you in the villa – trying to stop them?'

'Yes.'

'Gutsy!'

'Stupid,' I mumble. 'Completely stupid – I should have run.'

His focus returns to the screen for what seems an age, so I ask, yawning, 'Can you help me?'

'Why me?'

'Why not?'

He pauses for a long time then says, 'Maybe.'

'How long?'

'It depends ...' He watches the film again from beginning to end, and I close my eyes, drifting, imagining my daughter's face as I thought she'd be when she grew up. All those birthday parties and Christmases we would have spent together, and the presents I would have bought. I force myself to stay awake, but I can't concentrate, and when I open my eyes, I'm conscious that Peter is sitting watching me.

Have I been asleep?

He's staring at me. He's noticed *The Scream* on my arm, and I wonder if he's looked at my cleavage to see St John the Baptist's bloodied head on my breasts. I rub my hand across my forehead. 'So, can you help me?' I struggle to lean forward.

'Did she hurt you?'

I can't reply.

My daughter didn't hurt me.

The words are lodged in my throat.

'I'm in a hurry,' I say eventually. 'I need to find them.'

'The whole world is in a hurry.'

'I know, but—'

'Is it a matter of life and death?'

'It's a bit late for that,' I mumble.

'It was a side kick with a front kick. She's well trained.'

'She?' I sit up. 'She? What do you mean, she?'

'Your assailant was a woman. You didn't know?'

I move quickly and grab his computer, and turn it around to face me. 'Where? Show me,' I hiss. 'How could I have missed that?'

He rewinds it to the part when they come into the villa – the taller one with the small one. I watch her closely as she moves with a lightness and grace that I hadn't noticed before – or had I? She's the smaller of the two. When she sees me, she turns and seems to glide effortlessly to chase me, pulling me back and raising her foot. When she makes contact with me, I fall, but she's ready. She wants to fight. When I try to get up, her second assault is aimed directly and deliberately at my stomach. I crumple and fall.

'Why didn't I notice?' I complain. 'How could I miss something so bloody obviously important? A woman? I can't believe it.' I turn away, angry and frustrated.

'You've been emotionally involved,' Peter explains. 'It's hard to be objective under those circumstances.'

'But no one else noticed her. Do the police know? Could they have seen it?'

Peter doesn't answer me. His stare is penetrating, and I turn away from him.

'I thought I was concentrating, but I wasn't. I've ballsed up. What a bloody mess!' I groan.

'No one who's seen the tape has picked up on it?' he asks.

I shake my head. 'I don't think so. Not until you. What else have I missed?'

'Well, I would say she's in charge. She's the leader of the two.'

'Why?'

'She entered the villa first, and besides, there's something authoritative in her manner. The way the other guy carries the holdall and kneels down to wait for her to put *The Bull* inside the bag.'

'But the other guy spoke. He said something; I'm sure he did.'

'What did he say?'

I have to think. I can't remember, and then I shudder. He said, 'Leave her, leave her alone.' I stare at Peter.

'I remember distinctly now. His voice – he was Spanish – but he spoke in English.'

'So,' Peter replies. 'We're looking for a Spanish male and a female trained in martial arts, but they both speak English as a common language.'

'Wow!' I smile, weakly. 'Well, that's a good start. Will you help me?'

Peter regards me, scratches his beard, and frowns at the screen. He begins looking at the film sequence again, then as an afterthought, without looking up, he says, 'The kitchen is through there. You can make me some black coffee.'

* * *

In the kitchen, the smell is overwhelming. I push open the window and wonder where to begin. The counter and toaster are covered in crumbs; old butter tubs, tins, and yoghurt pots are festering alongside mouldy cheese and stale bread. Searching for something clean, I randomly open cupboards. They're full, with cans of beans, soup, and fruit all turned like soldiers, facing me so that I can read their Polish labels. The rubbish bin is overflowing, and I swat away a fly before finding a dribble of cleaning liquid. I wash two mugs thoroughly, wait for the kettle to boil, and check my phone messages.

There are three from Josephine, urging me to take care and to let her know I've arrived safely. I text her, telling her I'm in Wrocław and that Peter is helping us. I send a similar message to Bruno, who is still in Barcelona, and another one to Simon, who is lecturing in Geneva this morning.

I consider telling Bruno and Simon that a woman killed my baby, but I don't. I'm not sure what contact they have with the police or Inspector Joachin García Abascal, and I'm not taking any chances. With this dirty, unkempt man in the other room, I might stand a better chance of finding her – *her*!

The kettle whistles and I make strong coffee for us both.

'Any luck?' I ask, shoving a dirty cup to one side and placing the mug on a coaster beside him.

He leans back and stretches in the chair. His muscles are ripped in his tight navy T-shirt, and a ripple of body odour washes over me. 'Maybe.'

I take a hard seat at the table opposite him and wait. He resumes his concentration on the screen while I sip my coffee and wonder how Olivia Harrison knows him.

'I'm waiting,' he says eventually. Sipping his coffee, he nods at the computer. 'I've asked a friend to help me; he's trying to decipher the blurred number plate.'

'That's encouraging,' I reply.

He moves around the apartment, stretching the muscles in his neck and chest, as if he's been sitting at the table all night. His limp is more prominent now, and the pain is evident on his face as he moves gingerly toward the curtains. He lifts them to one side and peers down into the street with an intense look of concentration, as if he's studying the faces of the people passing by.

'You can open a window if you like.'

He doesn't reply, and the silence between us grows.

'So, you're ex-military?' I say.

'Royal Marines.' He glances at me and then returns his attention to the street. 'Then Special Air Service – SAS.'

'Is that how you got injured?'

He doesn't reply, so I ask, 'Were you in Afghanistan?' I wait, but again, he doesn't reply. 'Do you mind me asking?'

'It's none of your business.'

'It's hot in here.'

'I like it.'

'When did you last go outside?'

'Don't piss me off.'

This time, I let the silence hang between us for longer than five minutes, which seems an eternity. I don't move, and I don't sip my coffee; I barely breathe. Eventually, he lets the curtain drop back in place, and he stands in the dark, speaking clearly and quietly.

'I was part of the elite force that was sent to the Middle East to train Syrian rebels. Our job was to train them to become the New Syrian Army – the NSA. But it didn't go to plan – well, not to my plan, anyway ...'

'I'm sorry.'

He pulls back the curtain and cracks open the window, and a rush of warm air floods into the stale room. He continues to stare down into the street, unseeing, and he speaks as if he's spoken this script aloud a thousand times.

'We helped the NSA to launch an attack on Al-Bukamal, a town on the Iraqi border. It was occupied by the US, but then it was held by IS. It was a crossing point for foreign jihadists. We needed to take back control, but the mission failed,' he says with a sigh. 'Presumably because of the lack of sufficient air support promised by our allies.' He turns from the window to look at me. 'Our vehicle was blown up. The other three occupants didn't make it.'

'I'm sorry.'

'They tell me I was lucky.'

I don't know what to say, so I wait, allowing the silence to grow between us, studying the proud, injured man standing before me.

Peter is well spoken and probably privately educated, but under the circumstances of war, everyone is an equal target to the enemy – they're all just bodies, adversaries, people to be killed.

'And now you're here,' I whisper.

'Yes.'

'Why Poland?'

'My family are here – well, my uncle lives here. My grand-father was in the Polish Resistance during the war. He saw his father and brother shot by the Germans. He was one of the men who escaped in the tunnels out of Warsaw, and when he got to England, he joined the British Army and fought against the Germans. He married my grandmother, who was a German Jew. She had arrived in England by boat during the war. Her family had perished in Auschwitz. My grandparents fell in love, and so my father and uncle were born. My father married an English woman. My parents live in Shropshire, but my uncle always wanted to live in Poland. He came to live here, and my sister and I grew up visiting him here. I learned to love it. Last year, after I came out of hospital, I didn't want to stay in England, so I visited my uncle, and I decided to stay.'

'You have friends here?'

'No.'

'How did you meet Olivia?'

'I don't know who she is. She contacted me through a friend of a friend, who was on a mission with us a few years back. He does surveillance work in London. You know the sort of thing. He left the military and found he could use his skills in the civilian world.'

'So, do you work with him or with the authorities?'

'I don't work ... with anyone.'

'I can pay you.'

His mobile rings and he picks it up. 'Hello?' He listens intently, then sits down at his computer and begins tapping the keys again with enthusiastic commitment. The loss of his fingers doesn't affect the speed of his typing, and I wait and watch. When Peter hangs up, he turns his computer screen to face me.

'I think we have something. Want to see?' We lean over the screen, and he taps the keys of a second laptop. 'It appears that the van was stolen earlier that evening in the south part of the city. It's a standard white Ford transit van used for removals by builders, by maintenance men, and by just about any tradespeople. It's easy to be inconspicuous in such a vehicle and to drive undetected from one country in Europe to the next. That's one of the reasons why it's been harder to locate. It's been a process of elimination ...'

Neither the police nor Joachin García Abascal – Josephine's friend with Europol – gave us any indication the van had been stolen or that they even had access to this information. I remember my conversation yesterday with Joachin in Barcelona, and his request that I share information with him, and fleetingly, I wonder if Josephine has told him I have come to Poland.

Peter taps the keyboard, and the image of the white van parked outside the gate of Glorietta's villa comes up on the screen. He zooms in on the number plate and with technology far superior to anything I have seen before, incredibly, the blurred letters of the licence plate materialise clearly.

'Wow!'

'Okay, so we've identified the type of van, and I've got the registration. Now, we just have to track where it's gone or where it's going.'

'How will you do that?'

'ANPR, Automatic Number Plate Recognition, is widespread in the UK – that's probably because it was a British invention; cameras are set up to help national security and counter-terrorism. In Europe, it's called LPR – Licence Plate Recognition – and it's a little patchier over here, but that's probably due to its ability to be used as a surveillance tool. There are all sorts of fears over intrusion, privacy, and that sort of thing ...'

'Do they have it in Spain?'

'They have the technology implemented at most border crossings between Spain, France, and Italy. Sometimes static cameras are used, or they can be fitted to police and border patrol vehicles.'

'So, this enables police forces and counter-terrorism units to work together across Europe?'

'In principle, each country installs their own, but they won't share the data openly unless it's a serious international matter or a warrant for an arrest has been issued. Mostly, it's low-level operational stuff like stolen or untaxed vehicles which relate to specific crimes, and databases retained and held by each country.'

'You think you can access this information?'

'I might be able to.'

'Is it difficult to do?'

His eyes are the colour of horse chestnuts. 'Believe me, it's easier here than in the Middle East. Big Brother is watching you all over Europe. There's very little that can't be caught on camera. You just have to know how to access the information.'

'So, why aren't more crimes solved?'

He scratches his beard. 'I don't know. I guess because of the lack of cooperation, bureaucracy, good old politics, and competition. Then there's rivalry and jealousy between police forces and also between countries.' He frowns. 'Luckily, we can get past all that crap. There's something coming through now.'

We wait for something to load on his computer. Then he points at the screen.

'That's the A9 – they took the motorway to Perpignan.'

A white van appears as a snapshot, hurling along the motorway in the early morning traffic, caught on various cameras at different angles. There's no doubt it's the same van, and when we zoom in on the number plate, it matches the one that had been parked outside the villa.

My heart begins racing.

The screen changes and another image of the van appears. The time is registered and located on the bottom right of the screen.

'It's six-thirty in the morning. They've been driving for almost two hours. They didn't stop?' I ask.

'Maybe for petrol or to go to the toilet.'

'Where are they heading?'

'They're in France, near Montpellier.'

'They're not heading to Paris or London – so maybe they're

going to Switzerland or Italy?'

He pauses before tapping more keys and answering, 'I don't know. Let's hope we can keep tracking them.'

'Who helps you?'

'If I told you, I'd have to kill you ...'

'That's not funny,' I say, but I smile.

* * *

'Tea?'

I open my eyes and blink at the sunlight coming in through the window. Peter is standing over me, holding a mug in one hand and a packet of chocolate biscuits in the other.

'What time is it?'

'Two o'clock. You crashed out,' he says. 'I didn't want to wake you until I had something.'

I swing my legs around and sit up on the sofa, remembering how tired I'd suddenly become. It is over seven hours ago that I left Barcelona. It had been early morning, and now it's afternoon. I'd fallen asleep while waiting for more information on the white transit van.

'Thank you.' I take the tea gratefully.

'Nice tattoos,' he says, nodding at *The Scream* on my arm. I'm guessing he can also see down the V in my T-shirt.

'Thanks.'

'Never seen masterpieces like that before – although, to be honest, I've never seen the point of art.'

'I guess the Royal Marines don't breed many artists.'

'Not usually, although we're not all philistines.' He sits beside me on the edge of the sofa and dunks a biscuit in his tea. Watching him eat biscuits reminds me of the crumbs scattered

111

on the floor.

I rub fingers through my matted hair, conscious of his close proximity but not threatened by his presence. His mood seems lighter. His long hair is now tied back and wet from the shower, he's wearing a clean Pink Floyd T-shirt and jeans, he smells of spicy cologne that isn't unpleasant, and his brown eyes regard me thoughtfully.

'Is there any news, then?' I ask.

'There may be a possibility that they changed the number plates, so that they don't look so out of place in each country. We're just checking.'

'Who's we?'

'Just a rogue group of misfits.'

'Hacking?'

'Um ...' He tilts his head and smiles.

'They never ditched the van. Why not?'

'I wondered about that. It's the first thing a professional would do. So, maybe they're not professionals, or maybe they thought no one would have access to road cameras across Europe. Perhaps they're very naive, or they have no money, or they don't want to run the risk of stealing another one?'

'Or they're stupid?'

'I doubt that,' he says, reaching for another biscuit while simultaneously brushing crumbs from his beard.

'Would they not be afraid of being stopped by police – you know, a roadblock?'

'They had a good head start. The villa is only an hour or so from the Spanish border. Did you say it belongs to a well-known opera singer?'

I tell him about Bruno and Glorietta, knowing that he's probably already found all the information he needs, but it keeps us both occupied while we wait. Then I tell him about Umberto Palladino and the bombing of *Los Globos* the day before Glorietta's party, and how I visited his art studio and then bumped into the inspector in the street. I keep the details scant and don't over-elaborate about anyone or my relationships with them.

Peter listens attentively, sipping his tea. He seems to contemplate my account before he asks, 'Could the two incidents be linked – the theft of *The Bull* and the bombing of *Los Globos*?'

'I think they are, but I'm yet to prove it. I have to find a link.'

'So, you're an artist and a photographer?' he says. 'If you'd stolen the sculpture, where would you take it?'

I consider his question. 'I'd either have a buyer lined up, or I'd try and sell it on the black market in a different country.'

'Why?'

'I guess for the same reasons you mentioned. It's about cooperation between countries. Taking it out of Spain slows down the process of tracking from where it originally came. It takes longer to authenticate, but I worry that if it's been stolen to order, it might be gone forever. It could be a dealer or collector from anywhere in the world: America, China, Japan ...' I sip my tea and crunch a biscuit, catching the crumbs in the palm of my hand. 'I must find them before they go underground.'

Peter watches me as I tip the crumbs into my mouth and says, 'So far, we have a stolen white van, a Spanish male, and a female expert in martial arts.'

'We need to work out where they're going. Let's look at a map,' I suggest, 'and try and track their route.'

Twenty minutes later, while Peter is hunched over his computer, I've cleared the lounge, taking the stale food, empty cartons and boxes, and dirty plates and mugs into the kitchen. I dump three waste bags outside in the hallway and hope the neighbours aren't drawn to the vile smell, then I wipe the surfaces in the kitchen clean.

In the living room, I pull back the curtains and crack open the windows, and Peter glances up irritably. 'Christ!' he complains.

'Air is good for your brain,' I announce, and I wipe the tables in the lounge. 'Have you got any Ordnance Survey maps?'

He produces a folded map from a concertina file beside the table, and I smile. He's organised, and I guess he's probably got a stack of maps from every country around the world.

I'm kneeling on the floor with the map of Europe spread across the coffee table, cursing Peter for not hoovering the floor as crumbs and grit grind into my skin. I brush them off, unwilling to be his housekeeper. There's a limit to my domestic skills.

Peter finds it difficult and painful as he sinks to the floor beside me. His prosthetic leg is stretched out under the table.

'If they are heading north, there's Germany, Switzerland, Luxembourg, Belgium, Scandinavia, and beyond,' he says, stabbing at the map with his finger stump.

I grab a piece of paper and make a list of possible destinations. 'And south into Italy, Slovenia, and Croatia.'

'Why are you concentrating on where it's going?' he asks. 'Why don't you think about who would have stolen it?'

'I have, but I don't know the answer. It could be anyone – people I don't even know and for any reason that I might not even be aware of ...'

He tugs his beard. 'It must be someone who knew about it. Someone who knew it was in the villa. Secondly, well, who would want it? And thirdly, if it was related to the previous bombing incident, then who is the common denominator? Why not start with the guest list?' he asks. 'Any martial arts specialists?'

I reach for my bag and pull out a list of guests. 'I've been through the list with Simon and Bruno. Both of them agree that *The Bull* is highly unlikely to have been stolen by any of the guests.' I pull out my iPad. 'Stealing or looting artefacts isn't like any other crime. It's not like nicking a radio or a phone or something.'

'It's not?'

'No, not at all. This is all premeditated – there's greed, jealousy ... all sorts of reasons for looting.'

'So, you don't think any of Glorietta's friends or relatives might be jealous or might want revenge for something?'

'I'd stake my life on it. We're all very close and, well – in a funny sort of way – we're family. We look out for each other.'

'All the guests?'

'The core of us.'

'And the rest?'

He has a point, but I'd covered this back at the villa. 'I did go through the list with Bruno ... he was pretty adamant.'

'Well, humour me. Let's go through them. Show me who they are so that I can build a picture in my mind.' He brings the CCTV up on the iPad screen propped on the coffee table.

I stretch out my legs and explain, 'There were forty-eight guests in total. Plus, the swing-band and the outside caterers.' I point to the images. 'There, look! That's Eduardo and me, Josephine and Simon, Glorietta and Bruno, and her cousin Filippa and husband Antonio – we all stayed in the main house. Their son Lorenzo and Martin – Jeff and Olivia's son – stayed in one of the cottages,' I say. 'And our friend Dolores and her daughter Maria stayed in the second cottage.'

We watch the film in its entirety a few times, fast-forwarding until the party is over and the guests begin to drift up to their rooms; me with Eduardo, and then Lorenzo and Maria appear.

'Who's the girl?'

'Maria, she's Dolores's daughter. Dolores was my old art teacher, and they live in Mallorca.'

'So, where did the other guests stay?'

'In hotels nearby, probably on the coast – some live in the area or have apartments in Barcelona like Olivia and Jeff. You can see footage of the guests leaving.'

'Have you shown this to anyone else?'

'Bruno showed it to me, Simon, and Josephine.'

Peter shifts his artificial leg to look at the paper in my hand with my scribbled notes. He uses the stubs of his left hand to point at the list.

'Why do these names have a line through them?'

'Because those people wouldn't steal it.'

'How do you know?'

'Because Bruno is married to Glorietta and he bought it for her. It was a birthday present. He wouldn't steal his own sculpture. Simon is Josephine's partner. Josephine is my birth mother – so I know they wouldn't steal it. Filippa and Antonio are her cousins, and Olivia and Jeff are good friends – she's ex-Met police and used to be Glorietta's bodyguard. And Eduardo was my partner.'

'Was?'

'He's my ex.'

'Since two nights ago?'

'Yeah.' I stand up. 'But I'm over him. More tea?'

* * *

I wander around the room, stretching my legs, pleased to have some air circulating in the room. 'Okay, so what about Umberto? If someone bombed *Los Globos* and subsequently stole a second sculpture from a villa, then what's the connection and why?'

Peter replies, 'Art?'

'Or maybe someone is pissed off with him?'

'True.'

'Maybe it's a client, another sculptor, or a friend ...'

'Jealousy – didn't you say there was a lot of that in the art world – between collectors?'

'Perhaps, but that's for the police to investigate. I don't have access to that sort of information. All we can do is try and track the van and see where they're taking *The Bull*.'

'Didn't you say that inspector approached you outside Umberto's studio? Why don't you work with the police?'

'Joachin? He told me to stay away and not get involved.' I don't tell him about my previous history of art theft or the fact that my unborn daughter has been killed and taken from me, and is my real reason for tracking the thieves.

I've made a promise.

'I can't work with him,' I add.

'Do you have any contacts in Europe?'

'A few.'

'Why not see if anyone is trying to sell *The Bull*?'

'I called some of them yesterday.'

'Then call some more today.'

I have nothing else to do, and I'm restless with anticipation waiting to hear where the white transit van has gone, so to pass the time I follow his suggestion and make some calls.

'A bull?' mutters Marcos in Amsterdam.

We worked together years ago. I learnt most of my under-world art trade from him, especially art forgery, and I trust him enough to tell him about Glorietta's collection. '*The Bull* is part of a series, but I'm trying to find out who bought the other sculptures; *The Bear*, *The Bee*, and *The Barn Owl*,' I explain.

'I can't think of anyone remotely interested in modern sculptures. There's nothing I've heard of at this end, but I'll keep an ear to the ground, Mikky. Have you tried Miguel in Madrid? Or Mohamed? He's in Israel now.'

He mentions two well-known fences, Janus's in the art world, who through their legitimate galleries, sell fake and forged artworks. It has been a few years since I've spoken to either of them, but after I hang up, I call them both. Fortunately, they remember me from years ago, and I spend another hour or so chatting on the phone, but there's nothing they can help me with.

'They promise they'll call if they hear anything,' I explain to Peter half an hour later.

'Impressive,' he says.

'What?'

'You're bilingual.'

'Bingo!'

'How come?'

'I was born in London, adopted, and brought up in Spain. My name is Michaela – it's an Irish name. My real father was a surgeon from Dublin.'

'Are your parents alive now?'

'Only my birth mother and the man I call Papa – the man who raised me.'

'Do you see them?'

'Why do you ask?'

'It looks like you've had a traumatic past – your tattoos,' he says. 'And the scar on the back of your hand – how did you get that?'

'My adoptive parents weren't kind. But I'm happy now. I'm close to my birth mother – and I don't see Papa at all.'

He nods in understanding, and I'm relieved that he doesn't know much about opera or seem interested in Josephine and Glorietta's famous lives.

'What about you?' I ask.

'I told you what happened to me.'

'You told me how you got injured. What about family? Parents, siblings, girlfriends?'

He sighs. 'Not many girls want a bloke without fingers.' He holds up his hand. 'Let alone a man feeling sorry for himself.'

'Post-traumatic stress disorder isn't about feeling sorry for yourself. Are you getting help?'

'I don't need it. I can cope.'

'It's not about coping; it's about living.'

'Yeah, well most girls want a guy with both of his feet. They want the real thing, not some fake of a man hobbling about with his fingers missing.'

'Only girls who are too vain to think about anything but a man's physical appearance. I'm sure there any many girls who would be proud to be with a veteran.'

'That's not exactly the point of a relationship,' he says tersely, and walks stiffly out of the room.

* * *

It's late afternoon, and I'm lying on the sofa staring at my iPad, researching sculptures and projects designed by Umberto Palladino. I'm scanning auction houses. Still, I'm not learning anything new, nor am I finding any possible buyers for *The Bull*. The only thing I'm learning is a background to Umberto's rise to fame and the extent of his popularity.

He's well known all over Europe, but Google also informs me that collectors as far as China and Russia have made bids at auction houses for his work in the past few months. Although none of them relates to the 'animal' collection, it's significant inasmuch as his work is in demand. Two sculptures were recently purchased by an anonymous telephone bid, one at an auction in Paris and the other in New York, but there's no more information on the animal collection.

'RESULT!' Peter shouts.

'What?' I swing my legs off the sofa.

'We've got a breakthrough. The transit van has headed across Germany,' he says, and I jump up and stand to look at the screen over his shoulder.

'Look, they switched plates at this service station, and here, near Dresden. Look, here she is. She's on her own.'

I can see clearly the dark silhouette of her breasts. Peter was right.

A woman.

A woman killed my baby.

'Christ!' he mutters. 'She's crossed the Polish border.'

'She's here – in Poland?' I gasp.

'This is a service station north of Warsaw.' He pulls images onto the screen, and we both lean forward to make out the grainy images. The scene is a deserted parking area at the back of a service station. The white van is parked slightly out of view of the CCTV, and her back is to the camera.

'Where's the other guy?'

'I think she's flying solo.'

'When was this?'

'Yesterday.'

'What's she doing?'

'Changing the number plates. She's definitely female. I was right,' he says with a smile.

'Where's the other guy?'

'I don't know.'

'Is there a clearer picture of her?'

'She's keeping a baseball cap on. It looks like she stopped for a couple of hours to sleep in the van.'

'Where's she going?' I reach over for the map.

'Wait – I've some more stuff coming through, Mikky.'

Peter clicks a few buttons, and three screens show the progress of the van. The driver is wearing a cap pulled low, and the images show only the lower half of her face. I lean forward to get a closer look at her, but Peter flicks to the other screenshots, focusing on the van's number plate.

'The same van, different countries, different number plates. We're assuming that she's staying on the motorway, travelling at a similar speed, so it will be easier to follow her route. This will take a while – we'll have to check all the cameras.'

I check my watch. It's almost five o'clock. '*The Bull* was stolen two nights ago. She's in a hurry. These are images from late yesterday – we haven't any time to lose, Peter. We must find out where she's going.'

'I may have to ask a few favours from a couple of other guys,' he adds, tapping in codes that look like foreign numbers and letters. 'She's driving through Europe, and she's definitely heading north.'

A sense of urgency descends on me, and I'm desperate to get to her before she sells *The Bull* and disappears. I have no guarantee that she's going to hang around once she's sold it, traded it, or passed it on. Feeling anxious and riddled with nerves, I calm myself by scanning the Internet for collectors, artefacts, and museums in Poland. It's pointless, but it gives me something to do.

Poland? Is that a coincidence?

We're tracking her, we're on her trail, and I sense a shiver of anticipation at confronting her.

Promise.

'Bingo!' Peter whispers, and when he looks up his frown has disappeared, and he's smiling. 'She crossed the border into Lithuania.'

'Where is she going?' I glance at the map. 'Russia?'

'She's staying in the Baltics. Here's a picture, here – the van. Look! She's on the outskirts of Rīga.'

'She's in Latvia?'

'She was. Not anymore.'

'Show me?' I'm tingling. I'm itching to go after her.

'We've been able to track the van using a series of black and white satellite aerial shots. It's not usual to be able to do stuff like this – this is a massive favour ...'

'Is it legal?'

'I told you already; I'd have to kill you ...'

I watch the aerial shot in fascination. She's in a built-up city, and the dark shadow of the van travels down a narrow street.

'What's that?' I point to a dark line on the horizon. 'Where's that?'

'That's the coastline.'

'Rīga?'

Peter shakes his head. The van comes to a stop.

'Is that a house?' I ask.

'It looks like it. She's stopped. There's nowhere else to go.'

A small, dark figure climbs out of the van.

'Where is she?'

'Tallinn.'

'Oh my god,' I whisper, as her location dawns on me. She's across the water from Finland but right beside Russia. 'What the hell is she doing?'

* * *

'Where is she? Who owns the property? Assuming she hasn't dumped it or handed it over to someone on the way. We've found her,' I whisper. It's like a delicious secret, and I'm happy to savour it with Peter – my accomplice and my new friend.

'I'll check the flights,' I say.

I'm not prepared to share this information with anyone; not Bruno, Josephine, Simon, Olivia, nor Joachin.

'Don't be crazy, Mikky. You can't just go chasing off to Tallinn. We need a plan.' He checks his watch. 'We also need to eat dinner – a proper meal. You look ill.'

I ignore him. 'Do you know who owns the property or who lives there?' I insist.

'I think I have an idea. There's someone who might help us.'

'Now you've got me interested.'

'Come on. We need some help.'

Peter leads me out of the apartment. He says nothing about me cleaning his flat, but we carry the rubbish sacks I left in the hallway down to the bins. Although his gait is laboured, he's strong and broad-shouldered. He walks in a stilted fashion, as if he's still not used to his fake leg, and it makes him seem off balance and wobbly, so I slow down and deliberately take his arm to admire the buildings around us.

'I never realised Wrocław was so beautiful. These buildings are amazing.'

'My apartment building was an old granary. It was built in 1565 and renovated in 2009.' We turn to look back up at the renovated façade.

'It's stunning.'

'All of the city is beautiful. We pronounce it Vrots-swaf.' He smiles when I try to say it. 'It was named Breslau before 1945, when the Germans occupied Poland.'

'Vrots-swaf,' I say, practising.

For some reason, I don't have such a sense of urgency now. I'm tired and strangely relaxed, and I'm prepared to listen to Peter's plan. Although I don't know who stole *The Bull*, I've found my baby's killer. I also know where *The Bull* is, and I'm grateful for Peter's help. I couldn't have done it without him.

I trust him.

'Where are we going?'

'Be patient,' he chides.

We walk arm in arm, and he points out places of interest as we stroll through the market square, past the town hall, and across Salt Square, through a beautiful flower market. 'This is ul. Więzienna.'

At the corner of ul. Pilsudskiego and ul. Świdnicka, he beams delightedly and points at a group of life-sized bronze statues descending into the earth. 'You'll love this,' he says, smiling. '*The Anonymous Pedestrians* was unveiled on the twenty-fourth anniversary of the introduction of martial law in Poland. It always reminds me of my grandfather, and others like him, who fought in the underground to undermine the Nazi regime. He's passed away now, but he was extremely courageous.' Peter seems very upbeat, and he limps along beside me.

'You must be very proud of him.'

'It's the reason I joined the forces. I'm against oppression.'

'I think you're a very principled man.' I squeeze his arm. 'I think your grandfather would be very proud of you.'

We walk past numerous popular cafés, restaurants, and historical buildings, and Peter continues his explanation, 'Most of Europe is fake. Did you know that? Most of the cities have been rebuilt since after the war, like Dresden and Warsaw. They've renovated the cities in the same styles as they were originally designed, and it makes the cities look authentically old. Tourists still flock to take pictures of castles, museums, churches, and cathedrals, not realising many of them are not the originals.'

I did know this. I thought about it a lot when I went to Dresden for the first time. When I met my birth mother, and I walked around the city.

'Fakes have always interested me,' I reply, but I don't tell him it's because I spent a lot of time as a child in churches, museums, and galleries studying. Not only were they places of refuge from my violent parents, but fortunately, they were also my schools, where I met many priests, historians, and artists – who taught me more than they would ever know.

'In Wrocław, there's an extraordinary amount of young people,' Peter explains. 'It's because of the university situated on the River Oder, a baroque-style building, designed from the 1700s.' He points out the buildings that survived the war and the newer buildings, including a vast amount of Italian-style cafés that have become so popular all over Europe, telling me which are original and those that are fakes.

He pauses at an imposing wooden door just off the main street. 'Well, here we are.' He takes a deep breath while I read the formal gold plaque on the wall in Polish.

'What does it say?'

'International Lawyers. Come on. You'll like Uncle Korneli.'

* * *

We are shown into a busy room on the third floor. It's bright and airy, with simple modern furniture; desks, chairs, and neat bookshelves line the walls. We walk through a series of open doors to the far office, and enter without knocking or being announced.

A man in his mid-sixties, with a hooked nose, neatly trimmed beard, and grey cropped hair looks up from the papers on his desk. He frowns, removes his glasses, and then smiles before standing up and walking around his desk.

He pulls Peter into a hug and slaps him on the shoulders, speaking rapidly in Polish. Peter replies fluently before introducing me.

Peter's uncle extends his hand and regards me closely.

'Korneli Brzezicki,' he says softly. His handshake is firm, and to my dismay, his smile is forced.

'Mikky dos Santos,' I reply.

He offers me a seat, and I notice Peter staring into the adjoining office, and I follow his gaze. There's a flurry of

126

a floral skirt, then the person is gone, and Peter's attention returns to us. He sits beside me on the hard-backed chairs facing his uncle's desk, and I can't shake the feeling of discomfort under his uncle's scrutiny.

They speak in Polish. Korneli is encouraging Peter to go through into the other office, nodding his head, thrusting his chin, but Peter declines. Under all his facial hair, I'm sure he's blushing, and I suddenly wish I had my camera to take pictures of the two men.

'Your hair has grown,' Korneli eventually says in English. 'And you have a beard.'

'Yes.'

'It's been a long time.'

'Yes.' Peter sucks on his lower lip and appears uneasy.

'It's good to see you ... it's time.' Korneli's gaze settles on me.

'Thank you.'

'Is this a social visit?'

'No.'

Korneli looks at my worn leather jacket, black jeans, and scruffy T-shirt. I must look a mess. I haven't slept properly for two days, and I still have bruising on my cheek from when the woman kicked me. His gaze rests on my scarred hand before our eyes meet, and I stare defiantly back at him.

He speaks in Polish, and I look at Peter, but he doesn't translate for me.

'Can we speak in English?' asks Peter.

'So?' Korneli says with a sigh. 'If we must. What's the problem?' He has a native southern English accent.

As Peter explains, Korneli leans his elbows on the arms of his chair and presses the tips of his fingers together. He taps

127

them rhythmically against his lips, absorbing Peter's words as he explains about the bombing of *Los Globos* and the robbery of *The Bull*. He tells him how I came to ask for help and how he has now found the van and tracked the girl in possession of *The Bull*.

Peter's brief resumé is detailed but concise. Korneli rarely asks a question, but sits in contemplation until Peter's finished. He's still tapping his fingers against his lips as Peter concludes, 'I'm waiting for information on the house owner in Tallinn.'

Korneli waits until Peter's account comes to an end and, after a moment's reflection, he asks, 'So, what do you want from me?'

'We need to set up a buyer for *The Bull*,' Peter replies.

I look sideways at him. We haven't discussed a plan, but Peter ignores me and continues speaking to his uncle.

'We need to lure the girl with *The Bull* into a trap.'

'Why don't you go to the police with this information?' Korneli looks from Peter and then to me, and I have the impression he thinks I'm bad news, and that I'm the one causing problems.

I lean forward in my chair, and this time I reply, 'Bruno insisted that this matter remain private. He wanted Glorietta's name to be kept out of the news.' It's only a small lie, but I warm to the theme. I had seen Korneli's eyes widen at the mention of her name – and the fact that the birthday party was in her villa and *The Bull* belonged to the most famous soprano in the world, I hope, has hooked his interest. 'She doesn't want the public to know,' I conclude.

'Does Glorietta Bareldo know you are here?'

'Of course,' I lie.

He's too tactful to ask about my relationship with the world-famous opera star, but I can see he doubts me, so I pull my mobile from my pocket. I show him photographs of Glorietta's party and, in particular, an image of Josephine, Glorietta, and me. We are all laughing as Eduardo snaps the picture.

He hands me back the phone and turns to Peter. 'So, your plan is ...?'

I reply, forcing Korneli to turn to look at me.

'I'm sure that when I explain to the girl that we have proof she stole *The Bull* and that we tracked her to Tallinn, I will be able to persuade her to hand it back to me. I will tell her that it will be our secret and I can tell her that she won't be prosecuted ...' I lie.

'And if she won't hand it back?' Korneli asks.

'I'll explain that the police will insist on a criminal case, but I want to avoid that. I'll tell her that unless she hands it to me, I will tell the police and give them all the evidence I – we – have.'

'What if she stole it for someone else or if she's sold it?'

'That's what I need to find out,' I reply. 'Look, I want to keep it simple. I can't imagine she'll want to go to prison just for stealing *The Bull*.' I smile, trying to muster sincerity on my face that isn't in my heart.

My real aim is to grab her by the throat and kill her with my bare hands, but I obviously can't reveal this to an international lawyer, nor to Peter.

Korneli leans back in his chair, his hands drop to his side, and he sighs.

Peter says, 'We want to meet the girl on the pretext of planning to buy the sculpture. Once we meet her, we can show her the evidence we have. We can prove to her that we know she was involved in the theft and that we could, if we wanted, prosecute her. I will warn her that if she doesn't return it, then we will inform the authorities.'

I look at Peter. I've barely known him seven hours, and already he's inferring that he's coming with me to Tallinn, and I'm not sure I want him with me.

'Perhaps a lawyer would be in a better place to negotiate on your behalf?' Korneli suggests. 'Perhaps we could approach her with your evidence and suggest she give it back. Is that an option?' Korneli asks, regarding us both.

'No,' I say. 'I have to go to Tallinn.'

'But there would be no need for you to go,' Korneli replies affably. 'It would be safer for you this way. Perhaps she is involved with some, let's say, undesirable people. She may have contacts who are not agreeable – they might even be quite violent.'

'I'm not going to let *The Bull* disappear across the border into Russia. I need to act quickly. It's urgent. We don't have a moment to lose, and we are wasting time.' I glare at Peter. 'I'm going on my own. I'll get on a flight tonight.'

Peter looks at Korneli. 'I think an introduction or some help from you would be appreciated, thank you, Uncle.'

* * *

I'm not sure whether I've been outmanoeuvred, and I glare from one to the other. It's Korneli who replies, 'I think I know of someone who might help us. We have a contact in Estonia who could help. A Russian millionaire who buys artworks – she's a collector. She's one of the wealthy new Russians, and she may be willing to act as a go-between to broker a deal. Aniela can set up a meeting. It's not ideal, but you seem determined to go. It's not the right way to do things, either. I do believe that the police in Estonia—'

'Thank you, Uncle,' Peter replies. 'That would be very helpful if you could arrange a meeting for us.'

Korneli nods. 'Promise me, Peter. You'll take precautions?'

'Of course,' Peter says, nodding his agreement.

'It's good to see you again. I'm pleased you're getting out. It's been a long time.'

'Thank you, Uncle.'

'You look like you need some fresh air and a decent meal.'

'I'm fine.' Peter stands up.

'I'll ask Aniela to set it all up and send you the details.'

Precautions?

I glance up at Peter. *What are they talking about?*

Korneli calls out in Polish, and a tall girl with long, thick blonde hair appears. She is wearing a powder-blue floral skirt and jacket that accentuates her suntan.

'Aniela Kowalski is my secretary,' Korneli explains to me. 'She will make an appointment for you to meet Natasha Morozov.'

Aniela doesn't look at Peter. She keeps her gaze fixed firmly on Korneli as he issues her a set of instructions in Polish. She nods and makes notes on a small pad, and I blurt out, 'Natasha Morozov — a new Russian?'

It's Aniela who replies, 'She's the divorced wife of the wealthy General Morozov and the widow of oligarch Comrade Petrov. She moved from Moscow to Tallinn five years ago after her divorce. We have worked with her before, and I'm sure she will be willing to help.'

'She lives in Tallinn?' I ask.

'Yes. That is why I thought of her.' Aniela stares coldly at me, while Uncle Korneli looks pensively at Peter. 'She's a collector of Fabergé eggs – perhaps we could set something up, you know, pretend you want to sell her a—'

'She doesn't collect artworks or sculptures, then?' I shake my head. This is all going to be a waste of time. I just want to get to Tallinn and bash down the door of the house.

'Once someone is a collector, they can't help themselves. They want to collect many things. Maybe Natasha already has an interest in Umberto Palladino's sculptures,' Korneli replies. 'She may have already been contacted about buying *The Bull*. Who knows?'

I'm wondering if this Russian millionaire could have ordered the theft of *The Bull*, but then I say, 'How will you get the girl to meet this Russian woman? Perhaps the girl has a different buyer?'

Korneli's voice is stern. 'That's Aniela's job. She knows about artworks and has contacts in many galleries and with buyers, thieves, and collectors from all around the world. She will find out who this girl is contacting. Believe me, if she is selling it on the black market – Aniela will find it.'

'Thieves?' I repeat.

Aniela strikes me as a formal businesswoman who wouldn't get her hands grubby in the underworld of looted art, thieves, and danger.

Aniela stares at me. She doesn't like me, and I don't like her. 'I will tell Natasha you have a Fabergé egg to add to her collection ...'

'Whatever,' I say with a sigh, and pick up my rucksack and sling it over my shoulder. 'But hurry up.'

'So, what happens now?' Peter asks, focusing on his uncle

and ignoring Aniela's hostile gaze.

'I'm going to Tallinn,' I reply.

A flicker of intense anger crosses Aniela's face, and when she speaks angrily in Polish, Peter's eyes darken, and he grips his fists at his side.

I think he might argue, but she tilts her chin at a determined angle, as if daring him to challenge her, and Peter remains silent.

'She's right,' Korneli says in English. He slaps Peter on the shoulder. 'It's good to see you on your feet again, but you'll have to ditch that Viking beard and tidy yourself up. You look an absolute mess.'

Chapter 4

"One can easily tell that the creator of the paintings in the Sistine Chapel was above all a sculptor."
Edvard Munch

I believe we're heading back to the apartment, but Peter takes my elbow and escorts me in the opposite direction.

'Come on; first things first, I'll organise new IDs for us, and then we'll book a flight.'

'New identities?'

'And a new look.'

'Why do I have to change my appearance?'

'As a precaution. I don't want this all going belly-up and them coming after you.'

'Them?'

'Come on, Mikky. We don't know who's stolen *The Bull* – the Russian mafia could even be involved. If it's worth as much as you say it is, then that sort of sculpture attracts a serious amount of attention. We need to be careful.'

'Is this what Korneli meant about taking precautions?' He doesn't answer, so I add, 'I'm used to colouring my own hair.'

'I'm not arguing.' Peter guides me straight inside a modern hairdressing salon. 'Look, if we're going to do this, then you have to trust me. We're going to do it properly. You must look the part. You can't pitch up to her place looking like you've spent all night at a rock concert. If Aniela gives us a cover story, you can't arrive looking like you're a thief and the one who's stolen an expensive Fabergé egg. The Russian won't let us inside the place or give us the time of day.'

I gaze at his serious profile and realise he's not joking. He rattles off a stream of Polish to a tall, skinny, purple-headed cutter and promises to collect me a couple of hours later.

'You'd better buy me a decent dinner afterwards,' I call, but he's already gone, limping hurriedly down the busy street as if he's never known me.

I spend the next few hours sitting patiently in front of the mirror. I make suggestions to the hairdresser, and although she nods, I have the impression that Peter has told her exactly how he wants my hair, so I give in, close my eyes, and wonder if we will be able to pull off this crazy plan.

While I'm waiting for the colour to take, I pull out my iPhone and google Natasha Morozov.

By the look of the pictures, she's well groomed and confident. The images show a voluptuous, attractive forty-year-old with heavily made-up deep-blue eyes. Being a photographer and artist, I spend a while gazing at her face, studying her features, memorising the details – the birthmark blemish on her right cheek and the dark circles under her eyes – trying to imagine what sort of woman she is.

Then I close my eyes.

How had I missed the fact that my assailant, the killer of my child, *is a woman?*

Has Inspector Joachin García Abascal noticed?

135

* * *

The man who collects me is not the same man who left me in the salon. The matted beard that covered his neck and cheeks has been styled and trimmed against his strong jaw, and his short hair is gelled into a quiff at the front, revealing intelligent dark eyes. He's also changed into grey jeans, an open-necked cream shirt, and a navy linen jacket. Disconcertingly, he looks extremely handsome and years younger than I had first thought. He's my age.

'Peter? Is that really you?' I joke.

I stare back at the reflection of the two strangers in the mirror of the salon. Gone are my dark curls. My hair is white blonde and spiky in an elegant fashion.

'Very trendy.' He raises the shopping packages in his hands. 'I bought you a few things to go with your new look.'

I grin back at his reflection, but he turns quickly away.

'Come on. We've lots to do. We don't have time for dinner in a restaurant.'

In the street, I catch our reflections in the shop windows, and when he ducks into a supermarket, I follow him, aware that he's quiet and thoughtful. I follow silently, wondering if his uncle's secretary, Aniela, has anything to do with his bad humour.

Catching my reflection in the fridge door of the supermarket, I raise my hand to my hair. I've been used to styling my hair differently, but it's been a while since I experimented. Since I became pregnant with Eduardo's daughter, I'd changed. I'd mellowed, and I was calm and happy. There had been no need to pretend to be someone else. Now, I'm returning to the old me, the bitter, angry, calculating rebel. When I want something, I get it, and right now, *I want the killer of my child.*

We buy a couple of pizzas and a bottle of white wine, and we're heading back across the square when Peter says, 'Death is the gateway to life.'

'What?' I reach for his arm, suddenly worried he's more anxious than I thought, but he points to two houses linked by a baroque archway. 'These are called Hansel and Gretel's houses. The pathway between them used to lead to the cemetery.'

I take my hand away from his arm and read the Latin inscription he has just translated on the wall, pleased that he's returned to being my tour guide again.

'What's that?' I point to a small statue on the ground a few metres away, and he smiles.

'That's a gnome, a dwarf, or a Polish leprechaun. They're dotted all around the city; there's about three hundred of them. There's even a museum for them.'

'Why do they have them?'

It's not without irony in his voice when he says, 'It began as part of the Polish anti-Communist movement. Now there are figurines for the deaf and disabled – there's even one in a wheelchair – to draw attention to the disabled.'

'That's good, isn't it?' I walk quickly to keep up with his loping gait.

'You can get a dwarf-map from the tourist office next time you're in Wrocław,' he calls over his shoulder, oblivious of the other people in the street, and he marches through a group of tourists who are obviously dwarf-hunting with maps in their hands. They're taking photographs, pointing, and laughing in delight at a dwarf discovery, but Peter isn't hanging around.

I wonder why he is so angry.

Back in the apartment, Peter won't remain still. He throws

the pizzas in the oven and makes me stand against the white wall while he takes a photograph of my unsmiling face.

'Our background,' he explains, 'is that we're a couple who invest in Fabergé eggs. We're collectors, and we work for ourselves. We're very wealthy, having made our money buying and selling artefacts.'

'Legally?'

'Most of the time.'

'Did Aniela give you this information?'

'She emailed me.'

Now isn't the time to ask him about their relationship, so I ask, 'How did we meet?'

He looks strangely at me, and I realise that although I'm comfortable with him, we barely know each other. He places a glass of white wine on the table. Things are looking up.

'Cheers,' I say with a smile, but he still looks glum.

He sits beside me, sips his drink slowly, and then absorbs himself tapping keys on the computer. A frown crosses his forehead, so I say, 'If this new look of yours is making you miserable, you'd better start growing that beard back, or is there a deeper cause? What's wrong?'

He scowls. 'Nothing.'

'You're lying.'

'Aniela messaged me. We're having lunch at Natasha's house tomorrow.'

'That was quick!'

'Aniela told her we're only in the country for a few hours, as we're on our way to see a collector in Sweden.'

He stands up and disappears back into the kitchen, leaving me to think about our trip to Tallinn. I can't believe we're meeting Natasha so quickly. Meeting Peter has been a game-changer. He's managed to track the van and its destination. Now he's even managed to secure an appointment for us with the person who might help us recover *The Bull*. I'm seriously impressed.

'Should we tell Bruno?' I ask, when he returns with our pizzas.

'Let's wait,' he suggests, topping up my wine glass. 'I'd hate to jinx our good fortune.'

Over dinner, we discuss our plans and outline our reasons for contacting Natasha.

'We'll play it innocently and let's be as honest as we can. I'll tell her that we went to the lawyers to find a reputable collector, and I'll say our real interest lies in one of Umberto Palladino's sculptures. We'll keep it as close to the truth as possible. It may be that she already knows the sculpture is in Estonia.'

'At what point will we tell her the truth?' I ask, but the doorbell buzzes and Peter stands up to open it.

I wait in the lounge, straining to listen to the voices in the corridor. After a whispered conversation at the front door, Peter reappears tugging open a reinforced envelope.

'Here's your new identity.' He tosses an English passport onto the table, and I pick it up.

'Maria Rodriguez-Smith?'

'Yes.'

'And you?'

'Peter Bannon.'

'Is this necessary?'

'Yes.'

'Now what?'

He checks his watch. 'It's time to go. We'll have to wing

it, Mikky. I've booked the late flight to Tallinn and the Hotel Schlossle in the Old Town.'

* * *

The flight between Wrocław and Tallinn is under an hour, and we land just before midnight.

I'm wearing my expensive new brown linen suit, which fortunately covers my tattoos, and with my short hair dyed blonde, I have adopted a different persona. Although I look like a successful businesswoman – strong, determined, and confident – at this moment in time, I'm exhausted. The cat-nap I had on the flight this morning from Barcelona and on Peter's sofa this afternoon had refreshed me, but now I need to sleep properly.

I deliberately take Peter's arm as we walk through the airport, in case we are being watched, but also to make his limp appear less pronounced.

We take a taxi to the Old Town, and in the Hotel Schlossle reception we check in as a couple, signing in with our new identities. The aroma of fresh-scented orange candles is relaxing and welcoming, and had it been another time and place, it might even have been romantic. We follow the porter to an old-fashioned and luxurious bedroom, with a large king-sized bed and spa bath. While I check out the minibar, Peter looks down into the street from our first-floor window.

'That's a real habit you have,' I say, handing him a miniature bottle of scotch. 'Staring out of windows.'

'Just checking.'

'Old habits?'

'Probably. You look exhausted, Mikky. You take the bed, and

I'll have the floor.' Peter breaks the seal of the small scotch and takes a deep gulp without pouring it into a glass.

'I need a bath.' I carry a small bottle of brandy into the bathroom and close the door.

I don't tell Peter that my stomach is heaving with pain, and that my heart is aching with nervous anxiety. The thought of being in the same city as the girl who killed my baby makes me impatient and angry. I feel sick.

Behind the closed bathroom door, I stare at my new face in the mirror and the lifeless and tired eyes that stare back at me.

I made a promise.

I will find her. She has *The Bull.*

I imagine grabbing her neck. Her eyes will bulge while she chokes on her own vomit, then I will cut her slowly, dissecting her body into tiny parts – any punishment will not be severe enough.

* * *

Peter knocks on the door. 'Are you alright?' he calls.

The bathwater has turned cold. I dry my body, wrap a towel around me, and climb into bed.

Peter closes the bathroom door, and I hear him showering. Briefly, I allow myself to imagine I'm staying here with Eduardo and that it's not over between us. But you can't pretend things are alright when they're not. You can't pretend there's nothing wrong when someone is at fault – when there is clearly blame.

I am the accused. I was at fault.

Eduardo was right.

What sort of woman am I?

Who would risk their baby's life as I had done?
I wasn't worthy enough to be a mother.

I'm drifting to sleep when Peter opens the bathroom door. He stands with the light behind him, on one foot, one leg. The other is missing at the calf. He's tied a towel around his waist, showing a body that's well muscled, with a six-pack that's turned a little plump. His hair is wet and stands up in spikes, and the scent of the spicy shower gel wafts into the room.

'Don't sleep on the floor. The bed is big enough for both of us,' I mumble. 'I trust you to stay on your side.'

He leans forward and hops to the side of the bed. 'Thanks,' he whispers.

We lie on our backs, and I'm conscious of the tangy shower gel on his skin and his gentle breathing. The sleepy feeling has disappeared, and now my eyes are open, and my mind is whirling.

'So, what's our cover for tomorrow?' I ask. 'How well do I know you?'

'Well enough.'

'I thought we were keeping as near to the truth as possible.'

'I'll tell her that I had a climbing accident, a couple of years ago, and that's when we went into business. You like art, and you like taking pictures, and we found our first Fabergé egg at an auction in London. We paid fifty pounds for it and sold it for fifty-five thousand.'

'Is that possible?'

'I believe so,' he whispers, and he turns on his side to face me. 'It's happened before; Aniela said it's on the Internet.'

'So, it must be true,' I say with a sarcastic smile.

'Of course. It's gospel.'

'Okay. So, are we going to get married?'

'You've asked me, but I'm not interested.' I hear the smile in his voice.

'Let's make it the other way around, can we?'

'No, that works for me. You're lusting after me.'

'Let's tell her you find me irresistible, but I'm a wild spirit,' I suggest.

'Let's stick to the truth. I'm handsome, and I'm good father material.'

I turn to face him. My head is comfortable on the pillow, but my stomach churns.

Father material?

Now would be a good time to tell him the truth. Now would be the time to say that I'm not really interested in *The Bull* – I just want to find the girl who stole it, and kill her – but I don't.

Very gently, Peter places his hand on my cheek and leans toward me. His kiss is soft on my lips.

I close my eyes. Sadness overwhelms me. I need him, but I pull away.

'As much as I'm enjoying this, Peter, I don't think it's me that you want to be kissing. Do you want to tell me about Aniela?'

His deep sigh fills the room, then he turns on his back and gazes up at the ceiling. In the half-light coming through the shutters, his profile is strong, and I imagine the nights he's spent as a soldier, with his life in danger, staring up at the sky. He begins grinding his jaw, so I reach out and take his hand.

'It's always a lot easier if you let it all out,' I say. 'It's just emotion. Nothing to be afraid of.'

He doesn't reply, and I imagine how hard it must be for him. He's bottled up his feelings, and it's difficult to talk, but there's a peaceful calm between us, and I can almost hear his heart thumping with anxiety.

'Night-time and darkness,' I whisper encouragingly. 'Has it been your friend or foe?'

'Both.'

'There's no shame in talking about feelings,' I say. 'It took me a long time to be able to speak.'

'Judging by what you've tattooed over your body, I'm probably a fraud by comparison.'

'I don't know, Peter. At least you've lost a foot in battle, that's more than I've ever done.'

'Careless, wasn't it?' He explodes into laughter, and it makes me giggle; then between us, we can't stop laughing. It gets louder and louder, and then he's shushing me in case our neighbours are asleep, and then my tummy hurts and tears begin to run down my cheeks. Very soon, my face is as wet as his. We are crying, laughing, and gasping for breath, then somehow, we wipe our tears and ease into a comfortable embrace. I place my head on his chest, happy to feel the comfort and warmth of his strong body.

I haven't been in anyone's arms or had a proper hug since my daughter died three nights ago. Although Eduardo had sat on the bed in the hospital with me and had held my hand, he hadn't been like this with me. He hadn't felt comfortable, and I hadn't felt safe.

He blamed me.

I think about my little girl, and my tears trickle silently over Peter's shoulder as his hand caresses my short hair, my neck, and my shoulders.

'Why is this so easy with you?' he asks in the darkness.

I brush away my tears. 'What's easy?'

'This. Us. Hugging.'

'Because we're friends?'

'I hardly know you.'

'It's not the length of time, Peter. It's how someone makes you feel. You're safe with me.'

'God, I just wish life was simpler,' he says with a sigh.

'Tell me about her.'

'Aniela – it means angel. Aniela Kowalski – Angela Kowalski.' Her name rolls off his tongue as if he speaks it every night, making it sound poetic and beautiful. 'She's my uncle's legal secretary.'

I was right. I knew from the way she had looked at him.

He clears his throat. 'We got engaged just before I went on my last tour—'

'How did you meet her?' I interrupt. 'If it's worth telling, you might as well start at the beginning rather than at chapter four.'

He laughs. 'The book isn't that long.'

'Let me be the judge of that.'

His voice is melodic and deep, and although I concentrate, my eyes grow heavy.

'Okay, well, I used to come to Poland on holiday as a child with my parents. She's the daughter of my uncle's friends, and we used to hang out together. She was solitary, and I felt sorry for her, so I used to insist that she come out with my brother and me and our little sister. We'd go swimming in the river, or walking in the forest. We used to talk a lot. I enjoyed her company. Even though she was a few years younger than me, she was mature and sensible. She was also very wise and very well read. She'd always have a book in her hand, and we used to talk about everything. She was fun to be with and probably the only woman I could have a proper conversation with – someone I could trust.'

'Apart from me.'

'Of course.'

'Then what?'

'Then I went into the Royal Marines, and I didn't get to come back to Poland very often. Any leave I had, I went back to England to visit my family. Then, five years ago, Uncle Korneli and Aunt Kaja had their twenty-fifth wedding anniversary. They had a big party with lots of friends and relatives invited, so I flew over. Aniela was there, and we met up again.'

'And you fell in love?'

'I couldn't believe she'd grown up. She was working with my uncle as a legal secretary. She'd become a career woman, and she was beautiful and successful, but she also had a boyfriend.'

'Oh no, disaster! What did you do?'

He rubs his cheek, and I hear the bristles of the short stubble against his nails. 'Nothing.'

'Unfortunate,' I say.

'More than unfortunate. I was gutted. I couldn't believe the feelings I had for her, but what could I do?'

'Beat him up?'

'He was actually a nice guy.'

'Torture him?'

'I was a coward.'

'So, what did you do?'

'I had to keep coming over here, visiting my aunt and uncle, and trying to get her to notice me. I had to impress her with my charm and charisma before she got married.'

I whisper, 'Good plan, Romeo. All's fair in love and war.'

'It took a while. She was annoyed with me for leaving her and for not coming back to Poland to find her. She thought I'd forgotten about her.'

'You had.'

'She'd been a child. I hadn't realised.'

'So, you won her hand?' I ask.

'Not immediately. She wanted me to fight for her and Aniela wasn't letting the other guy go easily.'

We lie in silence, then after a while I say into the darkness, 'But it worked out eventually. You got rid of the other guy?'

'Yes.'

'You won her over with your good looks and wonderful humour.'

'I believe so.'

'So, what happened then?' I prompt.

'I lost my leg.'

'Careless.'

'Um.'

'And, she noticed?'

'Yes, but ... the thing is, she didn't care.'

I sit up and lean on one shoulder, watching him. 'She didn't care?'

'No.'

'What a woman! So, what's the problem?'

'Me.'

'Okay ... so, what's that, self-pity?'

'I suppose so ... I didn't feel I was whole enough for her.'

'But she loves you.'

'She told me to get out.'

'Why?'

'Because she said she didn't care about the foot, she cared about me, and I wasn't behaving like the man she had got engaged to.'

I lie on my stomach, my head on the pillow turned toward him, studying his profile as he stares up at the ceiling.

'How was your behaviour?' I ask.

'I was angry. I was furious with everyone and everything. My friends were dead. I'd had the world at my fingertips and then got my leg blown off. I lived. I felt guilty. I was pissed off and started ...' he sighs.

'Drinking?'

'Yes.' He turns to face me. 'You guessed?'

'I've been there. I've been so angry with the world that I've taken just about everything you can think of. I thought it might numb the pain.'

'Did it?'

'No.'

'So, you tattooed your body?'

'I had to do something ... at least it was artistic.' My voice is sounding sleepy, and I can't keep my eyes open.

'So, what next?'

'Next, we get some sleep, then we go and get what's ours,' I mumble.

Chapter 5

"Moonlight is sculpture; sunlight is painting."
Nathaniel Hawthorne

I never expected Natasha Morozov to live in such peaceful surroundings. Suur-Kloostri is a beautiful location, and we walk down narrow cobbled streets, past the original medieval convent of St Michael's Cistercian Nunnery, and we stand for a few minutes to admire the spire and bell tower of the Russian Orthodox church. Even though it's a warm June morning, it's not difficult to imagine December and the picturesque scenes of the snowy Christmas market. It's a two-minute walk from the Town Hall Square and Freedom Square, ideally situated near the Viru gates and Viru shopping centre. The pink façade of our host's home has been renovated, and Peter tells me the building is probably from the thirteenth century.

He pushes the buzzer, and we wait.

'What if she knows the girl – and the girl is here?' My body is tense, and my palms are sweating. *What if she paid the girl to steal it for her?* I want to add.

'Then we will find out.'

'I think we should break in, all guns blazing,' I mutter.

'That's not how it works, Mikky. That sort of mission takes

a lot of detail to plan so that you don't get killed.'

'Um.'

'Stay calm.' Peter is a man of few words, but I like him. There's something reassuring in his presence. He's solid and reliable. He's the sort of guy you'd want on your side if there was a fight. Well, let's hope it doesn't come to that. A voice calls out, then the door is pulled open, and an attractive woman stands in front of us.

'Natasha Morozov?' Peter asks.

Her eyes narrow in appreciation, then she smiles and extends her hand. 'Peter and Maria? Please, come in.'

Peter places his hand in the middle of my back and guides me up the few steps inside the house and into the Russian's lair.

Natasha's floral designer dress hugs her voluptuous figure tightly. She shakes our hands and casts a glance over us, taking in my high heels, and then her gaze rests on Peter, and she smiles seductively.

'Follow me.'

Long and wavy auburn hair settles on her shoulders, and her slim fingers rest on Peter's arm as she guides us inside the house, through a spacious modern reception room with a wooden spiral staircase in one corner, which I assume leads upstairs to the bedrooms.

I take a quick glance into a gleaming and pristine kitchen with polished worktops, and beyond that past sea-green double doors to a well-lit area, where a dining table is set with three places.

The air conditioning is perfect, and I realise how hot it's been outside on the street.

It doesn't take me long to realise Natasha is a woman who

knows how to appeal to men. She flicks her false eyelashes unashamedly in flirtation.

'Let me make you something refreshing,' she suggests, without offering us a choice. 'Make yourself comfortable.'

She stands at a small bar, turns her back, and mixes drinks, and it gives me the opportunity to further take in the room; refurbished wooden beams cross the ceilings and far wall, animal-skin rugs decorate the floor, and there are deep-set sofas and glass bookshelves.

It's minimalist and stylish.

'Is this your first time to Estonia?' She stirs clinking ice against the glasses.

'Yes,' I reply.

'Yes,' says Peter.

Natasha's back is turned to us, so I wink at him. So far, so good. Our stories check out.

'Isn't Tallinn beautiful?' Her voice is husky and sensuous, and although she has a noticeable accent, her English is very good.

'We haven't had a chance to see much of the city,' he answers truthfully. He's courteous, and he makes sure we are both seated on the sofas with Martini cocktails before he sits down beside me. Natasha smiles approvingly.

'This is a beautiful home,' I say truthfully.

'I love the elegant buildings in the Old Town.' Her smile is practiced and charming. 'Most of them are important state institutions, such as embassies, schools, and museums. When I bought this building, I knocked two apartments into one. We've been here almost five years now. It's where I'm at my happiest. I love to be near the town. Are you like that?' She looks directly at Peter.

'I love to swim,' he says. 'There's an openness at the ocean, something I never feel in a city or town. But it's delightful here. You've chosen a beautiful place.'

'I'm more of a city person,' she admits with a laugh, and crosses her legs in his direction, so that he has a good view of her thighs.

'Do you miss Russia?' I ask.

She seems to consider my question before answering. 'When I lived there, I loved it. But my life has changed. I think the older you get, the more your priorities change. My life has been very different.' She smiles and her voice takes on a teasing tone. 'I've been married to some very unusual men.'

'Really?' I smile back, encouragingly.

According to the Internet, Natasha is in her mid-forties. Remembering her photograph, I see the small birthmark on her right cheek, and the flicker of doubt – or is it uncertainty? – as she glances at Peter for constant reassurance, as if she's been used to pleasing men all her life.

She's certainly attractive, and I imagine it's hard for a man not to fall for a woman like her. From a woman's viewpoint – mine – I think she's manipulative and calculating. She comes across as a simpering female, but she's a tough bitch. I'd stake my life on it.

'I was married to General Morozov for ten years. I was only young when we met, nineteen or so. It was back in the Nineties; it was pre-Putin, when Boris Yeltsin was president. My husband had political ambitions and was very powerful, but there were rivals and loyalists all trying to take him down. They were fighting and jostling for power. They knew he was ill – cancer – but they couldn't wait. One night – on his way home from his office – he was shot dead.'

She stands to mix us more drinks. I blink at Peter, as if to say, *'OMG she's being very open with us!'* but he won't meet my eye, so I resort to tapping his foot (the real one) with my high heel, but he pulls away and ignores me.

Natasha returns with our drinks refreshed and sits on the sofa.

'That must have been devastating for you,' I say.' To lose your husband at a young age. Did you have a family?'

'Not then. You see, he was much older than me ... and we, well ... no. There were no children. It was a marriage of ... how do you say, convenience? I was young and attractive; he was old and powerful. I didn't love him, but we got on, and we had a good life. He took me to concerts and the theatre, and we had a dacha on the Black Sea. It was a good life but then – BANG! It all came to an end,' she says with a smile. 'But I was lucky. I had come to the notice of Boris Petrov, an entrepreneur and friend of Vladimir Putin. He took me out a few times and we travelled a lot. He insisted I get English classes, and he educated me culturally, you know the sort of thing – antiques, artworks, paintings, and things like that. And so, in 2000, when Putin first became president, Boris was in a good position with the government – not politically, you understand, but economically.'

The new Russians accumulated wealth very quickly after the dissolution of the Soviet Union in 1990. They were a group of elitists who profited by the privatisation of the Russia era – otherwise known as Putin's inner circle of friends. They made a shedload of money from trade deals and foreign investments. Boris Petrov was obviously one of the inner circle, who made money from Putin's rise to power.

Natasha continues speaking, 'We travelled all over the world, and we had a very good life. My daughter Olga was born, but unfortunately, Boris wasn't a kind man. He was very jealous and, as a result, how do you say, aggressive and controlling?' She sighs and her eyes harden. 'I'd had a tough life. I was raised in Siberia, and I'd done well to leave there and then to meet men in prominent positions of power. But it was difficult. I'm not ashamed at what I did, but I wanted a better life for my daughter. I wanted to protect her. I didn't – and I still don't – want her to see the awful things I saw or to suffer what I endured. I knew what I had to do. My instinct was born out of survival. I never wanted to go back to poverty or to Siberia. And I wanted my daughter to be better than me. I want to give her the best opportunities to be an independent, strong woman who can make her own decisions and depend on no one. More importantly, I want her to marry for love.'

'That sounds very sensible,' Peter agrees.

'But I had to be very smart to get away. Boris was very violent and, as I said, jealous. He controlled me. He monitored what I did and where I went. So, I had to be careful and clever. It wasn't easy, but I managed to escape, and I survived.' She raises her chin defiantly. 'It's important for me that Olga is a good person. I want her to grow up with confidence. She must be independent and make her own decisions, and have a good life, and not be held back with the chains of her past – or rather my past.'

'How old is she?' I ask.

'Almost ten.' Her face breaks out into a broad smile. 'She's adorable, and I hope you get to meet her. She will be back after lunch.'

'Was it easy to divorce your husband?' Peter asks.

'No,' she says with a laugh, and leans over to place a hand

on his knee. 'Not at all easy. But I had learned a thing or two in Moscow – principally, how to look after myself. Boris had no real appreciation of art. All he could see was money, money, money. Business – one deal after the next – a property or a company. So, I knew I had to be smart and I began to collect things. You know, I'd buy a painting or a piece of jewellery or a sculpture – and I never told him the true value of anything, and managed to fake receipts. And that came in very handy when I wanted a divorce. I was able to negotiate my separation and take the artworks I'd carefully collected.'

'I'm impressed,' says Peter, smiling in appreciation, and his eyes linger on her cleavage.

'If Boris was jealous, why did he let you leave him?' I interject.

'Of course, Boris didn't *want* us to leave. I mean, he'd had so many mistresses and women he paid for, but he still wouldn't let us go, so I had to speak to Vladimir directly. I told him the truth and how I was frightened for our lives.' She obviously means Putin and I almost choke on my drink. 'He's a good man and a good president. He spoke to him, and eventually, Boris agreed to let me go – that was five years ago.' She drains her glass, and her lipstick is still in place on her enhanced lips before when she adds, 'And, in return, I agreed to the conditions he laid down.'

'Conditions?' I repeat.

'To move out of Russia and to never return.'

'And Tallinn was your preferred choice of destination?' Peter asks.

She shrugs. 'It was a choice. I didn't want to run the risk of bumping into Boris in Paris or London. Even now, I have to be careful.' She stands up and wriggles down the hem of her tight skirt. 'Boris was very unpleasant, and I don't want him near Olga. That was my main condition, and as long as Putin is in power, we shall be safe,' she says with a smile.

'I admire you,' Peter says.

She gives him the benefit of her smile and her cleavage as she bends down to pick up his glass. 'Thank you, Peter. Now, I hope you're hungry? I've made us a light lunch.'

I imagine Natasha's false nails and the pristine cooking facilities in the kitchen and wonder what she has possibly made.

'So, now you know my story. I want to hear all about you both. I can never do business with people I don't know – only friends. I can only buy things from people I like.'

Peter slips off his jacket and smiles at me. I have a sinking feeling that this lunch is going to be far harder and much more difficult than I'd imagined. We'll have to keep our wits about us, and as I stand up, I realise I'm already light-headed.

* * *

As we're shown into the dining room, I ask, 'May I freshen up before lunch?'

Natasha points to the door along the corridor. 'Second door on the left.'

She seems very happy to have Peter all to herself, so I take my time. The bathroom has a sunken bath, and there's a door that leads to a massage room, sauna, and storage area.

I wash my hands and venture into the corridor. Natasha is speaking, but I can't hear what she's saying, and I pause at the foot of the wooden staircase. Is it too risky to go upstairs? There's a double-fronted, sea-green door to my left, and I'm about to investigate when I hear Natasha laugh loudly. I don't want to create suspicion, so I wander back to the dining room, where she has her elbow resting over Peter's shoulder, and they are looking at a book or an album of some sort.

A chilled bottle of wine stands cooling in an ice bucket on the table, and Natasha reaches out and pours me a glass.

'You'll like this, Maria,' Peter says, holding up the book in his hands. 'Natasha has a fabulous collection of artworks.'

'Really?'

'Apart from Fabergé eggs, she is quite a collector,' he says pointedly.

'I'll show you after lunch, Maria,' she says, smiling suggestively at Peter as she removes the book from his hands. 'Come, let's eat. I want to hear all about you both. You've told me nothing about yourselves, and I'm doing all the talking.'

'Go on, my darling,' I say to Peter, as I place a napkin in my lap. 'You tell Natasha how we met. I know how you love to speak about it and how I made you feel. You know, the bit when you brought me flowers and told me you weren't complete without me.'

He laughs, and I help myself to green salad, cold potatoes, smoked salmon, prawns, and herrings.

'Maria was – um ...' he stutters, and to recover himself, he smiles shyly.

I interject. 'It was love at first sight,' I say to Natasha. 'I was on assignment. I'm a photographer and—'

'She found me handsome and wanted to take my photograph,' he interrupts.

'Yeah, something like that,' I say with a grin.

'Where was this?' she asks.

'Wrocław,' Peter replies.

'Near the river,' I say.

'It was autumn.'

'The leaves were falling ...' I add.

Natasha smiles at our rapport, and I tell her how Peter and I discovered that we shared a love of old markets and antiquities.

'Our first trip was to London,' I say.

'We walked for miles around the markets looking for second-hand bargains.' Peter swallows a mouthful of salmon.

'We found this Fabergé egg, and it was simply ... beautiful,' I say.

'I thought it might be worth something,' interrupts Peter.

I laugh. 'No, darling, that was *my* idea to take it to the auction house.'

'I had a hunch it might be a Fabergé,' he says.

'I *knew* it was a Fabergé,' I counter with a smile.

'We were lucky,' Peter says.

'Would you believe how much we got for it?' I say.

'Fifty-five thousand thousand pounds,' Peter answers. He's like an excited schoolboy. 'And we only paid twenty-five pounds.'

I join in with his excitement, speaking quickly, caught in the web of my own fictional story. 'You can imagine, we thought we'd found a way to make real money. So, little by little, we started to invest in more items, and we started to buy and sell ...'

'I must admit,' Peter says, 'Maria does have a knack for this sort of thing.'

'It's probably why you love me,' I say with a smile.

Fortunately, because of my background, I can talk about artworks, paintings, and even the black market with confidence and ease. Natasha's eyes narrow. She is alert, calculating prices and comparing markets with the artworks I talk about, and then I speak about sculptures and how my real love lies with work by sculptors like Antony Gormley, Anish Kapoor, and Umberto Palladino, and I drop in the information that we'd been at the opening exhibition of *Los Globos*.

'Such a shame,' Natasha agrees. 'An amazingly talented man. I can't understand anyone doing that.'

'It was a shock,' I reply.

Peter seems contented to let me speak. Even though I say so myself, I come across as someone who knows a lot, and Natasha asks me questions about my artistic career. I fudge the facts, but we speak about forgeries and fakes, and how a collector must be careful and always insist on the provenance.

'And what if there is no provenance?'

'Then it's probably a fake or stolen,' I announce.

After lunch, Natasha disappears into the kitchen. 'I'll make coffee, and then you can show me the Fabergé egg that you have for sale.'

I glance at Peter, and he smiles at me. We're definitely on the right track, and we are both smiling when Natasha reappears carrying a tray with coffee, bone china cups, and fresh milk, plus three brandy glasses.

'Now, before you show me yours, there's something I want to show you,' she says. 'Not many people know about it, but I think you'll really like it.' She leaves the room and I take the opportunity to whisper to Peter.

'Shall we get down to business? We can't sit here all day and drink.'

He nods. 'I'll handle it.'

Natasha appears in the doorway. 'Come with me,' she says, and she turns on her heels and disappears.

* * *

We follow her down the corridor to the room that I had not entered. She stands aside and allows us to enter in front of her through the sea-green double doors I saw earlier. In the centre of the room, on top of a glass table, is an Umberto Palladino sculpture, *The Bear.*

It's probably one third of the size of a real bear – almost a metre tall. It's raised on its haunches, and its open mouth is snarling in greeting. Natasha mistakes our silence for awe, and she smiles.

'Isn't it beautiful?'

'Oh my goodness!' I exclaim.

Peter limps over to look more closely. I can see that he's amazed by its beauty. He didn't see *The Bull* in person, but now this magnificent, towering sculpture is before us. He frowns, as if angry with me that I'd neglected to tell him the sheer beauty of Umberto's works.

'Where did you get it?' Peter asks.

'I've had it for some time,' she replies.

'It's made of three colours of paper: gold, silver, and red,' Peter says.

'It's an Umberto Palladino sculpture,' I say, playing along with the role. 'Did he make it especially for you?'

Is she one of the collectors?

'Let's just say that it was offered to me,' she replies. 'And leave it at that. I couldn't resist it.'

Offered?

Stolen?

As if reading my mind, Peter glances at me, and I blink to keep myself from speaking. I keep staring at *The Bear,* and

I realise that like *The Bull*, it's probably stolen. If Natasha has stolen or bought *The Bear* on the black market, then the chances are that she might be interested or involved in the theft of *The Bull*. It seems increasingly likely she had Glorietta's sculpture stolen for her collection, and I begin to see her in a new light.

She's responsible.

She sent the thieves to steal it, and they killed my unborn child. Not only did I lose my baby, but I also lost Eduardo and my life. All my dreams, hopes, loves, and plans were shattered that night.

I'm overcome with a sense of anger and rage. I want to grab *The Bear* and use it to smash her house and shatter her life as she did mine. I want to vent this surge of physical energy and hatred, and destroy everything I see; her perfect life, her perfect face and make-up, and her home. I'm filled with so much hate I scarcely know where to look. As if feeling my emotion, Peter moves to stand beside me.

In the corridor, the front door bangs.

Beside me, Peter tenses and his hand squeezes my arm.

There's an excited squeal and running footsteps. Peter holds my hand and his grip is reassuring. The door flings open and staring at us with frank curiosity is a pale oval face with pale blue eyes. It's a beautiful child – unmistakably Natasha's daughter, Olga.

'Mama?' she says.

'Olga, my darling. Come and meet my two friends, Maria and Peter.'

Olga is calm and self-contained. Now she waits obediently, shoulders straight with a rearranged smile on her lips, as her mother beckons her to come forward into the room. She walks like a ballet dancer. Gone is the free euphoria of arriving home and running into her mother's arms with wild enthusiasm.

'This is my daughter,' Natasha announces proudly.

I try to smile, but my mouth doesn't move. Beside me, Peter grips my hand and overcompensates with warmth.

'You look just like your mother, what a beautiful little girl you are. It's a pleasure to meet you, Olga.'

She wears a simple summer dress, and her arms and legs are tanned.

'She's been to her swimming club.' Natasha smiles proudly as Olga stands beside her.

Natasha places her arm protectively around her daughter's waist. It's a beautiful pose, with Olga's arm resting around her mother's waist and her head almost on her shoulder. I wish I could capture the expressions on their faces; their love, joy, and happiness.

If only I had my camera.

But why would I want to take their photographs?

Peter squeezes my hand, but I'm unable to speak.

'And how old are you, Olga?' he asks.

'Almost ten,' she responds.

'You speak very good English. Do you learn it at school?'

'Yes.' She twists her body shyly away and tries to bury her head in her mother's embrace, but Natasha, still smiling, makes her stand straight.

As if sensing my distress, Peter pulls me closer to him, but I cannot stop myself from looking at Olga. She could be my daughter, my child, my family, and an overwhelming sense of unfairness takes over me.

What right has Natasha to be so happy?

She stole *The Bear*, and she's smiling at me as if she's done nothing wrong or illegal. There must be a price to pay. She's responsible for killing my child. If it wasn't for her greed, then my daughter would still be alive.

The Bear's haughty dark eyes are vibrant and hungry; I transfer my gaze to the youthful, innocent beauty of the girl. Life has been unfair.

I have been cheated.

I'm filled with a desire to smash their perfect world, and then I sense another presence standing in the doorway. A young girl drops the child's bag at her feet, and Olga's wet towel drops out. Staring warily at us is a young woman with hair the colour of ink and piercing blue eyes.

It's her.

* * *

My knees buckle, but Peter holds me around the waist to stop me from falling.

'Ah, Nina. These are my friends Peter and Maria. Thank you for bringing Olga home.'

Nina?

The young woman nods at us, replies in Russian, then she raises her hand in a wave to Olga and turns on her heel.

Natasha calls out in Russian, but Nina's footsteps are silent as she walks down the corridor, and there's only a small click as the front door closes behind her.

Nina? She has a name.

Of course, Nina didn't recognise me. My hair is dyed blonde, and I'm dressed in a smart business suit. She didn't expect to see me, especially in Estonia.

I'm overcome with profound emotion and loss that is rip-

163

ping my heart apart. My forehead is clammy and, thinking I may faint, I lean heavily against Peter.

'Are you alright?' he whispers.

I shake my head.

Natasha shares a short exchange and a quick command to Olga, who picks up her bag and tugs at the wet towel.

'Put it in the washing machine,' she says to her daughter, then she turns to me. 'Have some water. Are you sick?' Natasha regards me with dark eyes and holds out a glass. I sip the liquid, unable to reply.

'Perhaps you could call us a taxi?' Peter asks.

'Of course.' Natasha disappears, and Peter holds me around the waist. I lean against his shoulder, needing his strength.

'Are you okay?' he murmurs.

'I'll be fine.' I take a deep breath and pull away.

Peter replies, 'Come on, let's go.'

I push him away, suddenly reluctant to leave, and I move near to study the coloured papers and the black staring eyes of *The Bear*. I am examining it when Natasha appears in the doorway.

'The taxi will be here in a few minutes.' Her smile freezes when she sees me touching its paws, and she looks curiously at Peter.

'What's going on?' She stands near the door, and it's Peter who replies.

'That girl Nina, the one who was here just now, stole an Umberto Palladino sculpture from a villa near Barcelona three nights ago. We followed her here.' Peter's plays our hand without consulting me. He's going on instinct. Like me, he knows that Nina and the girl on camera, is the same one.

'Who are you?!' Natasha demands.

'We want the sculpture she stole.' Peter sounds calm, and his voice is measured.

'I know nothing about it,' Natasha replies.

'It's called *The Bull*. Nina stole it,' he insists.

Natasha's dark eyes widen. 'You're lying.'

'I was in the villa the night she took it.' My voice is hoarse with emotion. 'Nina stole the sculpture, and she beat me. She killed my baby.'

Natasha gasps, 'Impossible.'

I move quickly and lean into her face. 'You talk about your daughter. You spoke about doing the right thing and bringing Olga up to be independent and proud. Yet you behave like a common thief. Stealing for your own selfish, greedy existence. Have you no shame?'

'Mama?' Olga appears at the door and she seems shocked at the tension between us. 'The taxi is here.'

I reach into my bag, pull out a USB stick, and toss it onto the table. 'Take a look at this, then call me a liar.'

* * *

I wait at the kerb while Peter pays the driver, but instead of going into the hotel foyer, I walk away from him and up the cobbled streets in the direction of the Old Town.

'Where are you going?!' he shouts.

'I need a drink,' I call over my shoulder.

He hobbles after me and says tersely, 'We need to talk.'

A few minutes later, we're sitting on the wooden terrace of a busy bar in the Town Hall Square watching people and drinking gin with lots of ice and lime.

'You never told me,' he says, his brown eyes filling with

165

sadness. 'About your baby.'

I shrug and focus on a couple in the middle distance, taking a selfie with the town hall and the fake façade of an old pharmacy in the background. Fake building. Fake emotions. Fake truths. I'm not interested in history – the medieval buildings, museums, and churches, or the old merchant houses. I want to get drunk. I want the pain to go away. I want to feel numb.

'Mikky?' Peter reaches for my hand and says softly, 'Mikky? Why didn't you tell me?'

I pull my fingers away and take a slug of gin. I can see Nina's piercing blue eyes. They haunt me. How could I have forgotten them? The guy with her had said something, but he hadn't spoken in Russian. He'd spoken in English. *Leave her*, he'd said.

She's Russian. He is Spanish.

My memory is a blur. It had happened so quickly, and now my recollection has been re-enforced by constantly watching the CCTV. I've relived the moment of the attack countless times.

'Mikky, I wish you'd told me. I don't know what I would have done – you know, if it had happened to Aniela. I'd be furious. I'd be ...' Peter's voice trails off, and he raises his glass to his lips.

'You don't have to worry – it didn't happen to her,' I reply softly.

'Mikky? Let's try and make sense of this. Two people enter the villa. They knew the sculpture was there. They weren't interested in taking anything else. So, why did they steal it? Were they paid to do it? Did Natasha employ them? Only one drives to Estonia. The other got out somewhere.' I don't say anything and Peter continues his reasoning. 'Did

Natasha want another Umberto Palladino sculpture or is it a coincidence? Or did Nina steal it to sell to Natasha – knowing she already owned *The Bear*?'

'Natasha had it stolen!' I slam my glass on the table. 'She wanted it for her collection.'

'Then where is it?'

I look blankly at him. 'What?'

'Where is *The Bull*?'

'I'm going to find it. And, I'm going to get that bitch Nina. I'm going to rip her eyes out.'

'Mikky, come on. You can't. She's trained in martial arts.'

'I'll buy a gun.'

'Let's concentrate on finding *The Bull*?'

'I don't give a shit about *The Bull*!'

'Mikky, come on,' he says with a sigh. 'I thought you wanted the sculpture back. I thought that's what we were after—'

'Sod the bloody bull. I don't care,' I say, raising my voice.

'You can't change the rules, Mikky. We're supposed to be finding a sculpture – *The Bull* –remember?' Peter sits back and folds his arms, and I'm uncomfortable under his scrutiny. 'Ah, I think I understand now. You came to me pretending you wanted to find *The Bull*, but really you are after the people who hurt you. You want revenge. You want to kill them, is that right?'

'Yeah, bingo!' I signal to the waiter for two more drinks.

'What's more important to you? Finding Nina or finding *The Bull*?'

'I'm going to kill her.'

'I wish you'd told me the truth.'

'I didn't lie.'

'By omission, you have misled me. You've used me.'

Peter has a valid point. I know I wouldn't have got this far without him.

'What would you have done if you were me?' I argue.

He shakes his head. 'Well, you certainly blew it. You even gave her a copy of the CCTV. What were you thinking?'

'How could she let Nina near her daughter?'

The people on the table beside us turn to stare, so I say quietly, 'How could she not know she's a murderer?'

'It's the same the world over, Mikky. Not all people who kill are born murderers. They're married, they have families, and they love. People are a mixture of things – feelings, emotions, reactions – and they behave differently in different circumstances. You can bring out the best or the worst in a person.' He leans his elbows on the table. 'Mikky, look at me. I've killed people. And here I sit in this beautiful square drinking gin with you, like nothing matters ... as if life isn't important. But it is. I know more than most just how precious life is, and it frightens me.'

The waiter places the fresh drinks on the table between us, barely noticing our frenzied exchange. His attention is diverted, and he calls out and waves to someone in the street. All around us, life carries on. Life is normal.

Peter leans back in his chair. 'People aren't bad all the way through, and that's the difficult thing to realise, Mikky. That's why, when you tell someone how awful a person is, they won't believe you. They often haven't experienced that side of the person's character. It's a shock. They don't want to believe it.'

'Well, Natasha will have to believe it. I have it in black and white. It's on film. Nina killed my baby,' I hiss.

'I'm so sorry, Mikky.'

We sip our drinks in silence, and then he asks, 'Is that why you split from your boyfriend?'

I can't look at Peter as I reply, 'He said it was my fault. I should have hidden or walked back into the kitchen. He said I should have pretended I didn't see them. I should have looked after our daughter and put her first. He called me irresponsible.'

'Killing Nina will not bring your daughter back.'

'No, but it will make me feel better. I want justice, Peter.'

I've made a promise.

Chapter 6

"Your life is a sculpture, every day chip away."
J.R. Rim

Compounded by the cocktails at lunch, I'm more than a little drunk when Peter steers me to a small restaurant behind our hotel. I eat tender chicken Kiev and wild rice, and as I rip my chicken apart, I tell him how I hate Nina and how I wanted to kill my mother – the woman who raised me – and how I used to hide from her jealous anger in the quiet sanctuary of churches around Spain. I tell him how there is no justice in the world and how avarice and money have replaced human kindness. Then, just in case he doesn't fully understand, I tell him how corrupt and hypocritical the Church is, with their millions of pounds in the Vatican despite all of the starving people in Africa.

I hate everyone.

Peter listens without comment, and then we stumble back to the hotel. My arm is hanging over his shoulder, and his hand is around my waist. He's almost carrying me, and I'm impressed by his solid body strength.

The receptionist smiles and I lean forward to read his name tag. 'Maksim,' I slur. 'You're very handsome. You should be a film star.' He blushes, and Peter pulls me gently away.

In our room, I collapse head first on the bed, and I wait for it to stop moving, spinning, twisting, and turning, trying to throw me off, but it doesn't. I stagger to the bathroom and throw up in the toilet bowl. Sweat breaks out on my forehead, and I clutch the porcelain as if it's my lifeline.

Peter passes me a damp towel, and after I've emptied the contents of my stomach, he helps me up, and I pass out on the bed.

Game over.

* * *

When I open my eyes, Peter is at the table in the corner of the room, staring intently at his computer. When I groan and roll out of bed, he smiles but doesn't speak.

In the bathroom, I let the water crash down over my short blonde hair, my shoulders, and my neck, cleansing me and my humiliation. I stand in the shower for what seems an eternity, and it dawns on me that I've known Peter barely twenty-four hours. This time yesterday, I'd flown into Wrocław, and now he knows my life's story.

As I apply purple eyeshadow and pink lipstick, I wonder if he's angry with me. I push my spiky blonde hair into some sort of shape, and with my pale face and shaking hands, I venture from the bathroom wrapped in my towel.

Peter is speaking on the hotel phone, and he waves his stumpy fingers to get my attention. 'Yes, of course. We'll be right there. Thank you.' He hangs up and stares silently at me.

'Do I look that bad?' I ask.

'You look awful, Mikky, but now at least I understand you.'

'I'm sorry.'

'You've nothing to be sorry about, and besides, there isn't time. You might want to put on your business suit. We have a meeting with Natasha.'

'Natasha?'

Now he has my full attention.

'She's here, waiting in the reception. She wants to talk to us both.'

* * *

After a stilted greeting, Peter insists that she join us in the conservatory for breakfast.

'Please,' he says, leading the way, 'you were very hospitable yesterday, and we're very grateful you've come here this morning.'

She glances warily at me, then she takes his arm, and I follow behind. Natasha is wearing another floral-print dress, and as we order coffee, I can't help but notice how tired she looks. I hope her night was equally as disturbed as mine.

She glances at our surroundings, appreciating the crystal chandeliers and the grandeur of the hotel, with its impeccably dressed staff, who are attentive and professional.

We order omelettes, and after the waiter serves us coffee, Peter says, 'I'd like to apologise. We don't have a Fabergé egg to sell. We made the appointment with you in the hope that you would help us find the person who stole *The Bull*. We would like to buy it back.'

We are still undercover. He's not telling her the truth.

'Why did you come to me?' she asks.

172

'We tracked Nina and *The Bull* to Estonia. We searched the Internet for collectors, and we found you. So, we asked an international legal firm to act as an intermediary,' Peter lies smoothly, neatly covering Aniela and his uncle's involvement.

'How did you follow Nina?'

Peter holds up his hand. 'I cannot reveal that or our sources of information, but it's true. Nina came to you, didn't she?'

Natasha holds Peter's stare, and then she begins to speak about Umberto Palladino. She describes how she first went to his studio five years ago, in Milan.

'I'd decided to invest in one of his sculptures. Boris would never have guessed the value of his artwork, and I needed to hide my investment.' Our omelettes arrive, and over our second coffees, Natasha leans her elbow on the table and contemplates her cup's contents before raising her eyes to stare at me.

'I looked at the CCTV,' she says.

'Nina stole *The Bull* for you?' I say, leaning across the table.

Natasha sighs. 'Yes – and no.'

'Don't lie,' I hiss, and Peter kicks me, with his good foot, under the table.

'I'll tell you the truth,' she says. 'I'd bought *The Bear* as an investment when I was leaving Boris – five years ago. I commissioned Umberto to make it for me, that was my reason for visiting Milan. It represented all of my life: Russia, paper, truth, and lies. It's my most precious and treasured gift. I say gift, because it was the last thing my husband paid for – although he didn't know it. And, apart from Olga, it was the best thing to come out of my marriage.'

'So, how do you know Nina?' I ask.

'I met her in Milan at Umberto's studio.'

'She's a student of Umberto's?'

'Yes. She's originally from Russia, and we spoke together. She was just a young student, and she told me her sister lived in Tallinn, and somehow, we stayed in touch – the occasional email, and when I moved here, she visited me from time to time. We would speak together in Russian, and she got on well with Olga. She also appreciated art.'

'What did she do in Umberto's studio?' I ask.

'She's a sculptor,' Natasha replies. 'I thought you knew.'

Peter shakes his head and answers truthfully, 'We couldn't find a connection between her and the sculpture that was stolen.'

'That's why she knew about *The Bull*,' I say to Peter.

'Has she worked in Umberto's studio in Barcelona?' he asks Natasha.

Natasha shakes her head. 'No, I don't think so. She argued with Umberto a year or two ago, and he threw her out.'

'She was working for Umberto – but in his studio in Milan?' I ask for confirmation.

Natasha nods. 'Nina was one of his brightest students. She's studied in Milan and Florence with some of the most well-known sculptors. She was going to be a big name. She'd had several of her works exhibited, and Umberto had supported her. He mentored her, and he was very proud of the works she did. When I met them, he couldn't speak more highly of her, but then things changed. She'd been working on a project with him. There was a group of them; you know how it works when a big sculpture is designed. It was a special project, but Nina wasn't happy with it. She suggested some changes and Umberto was against any of her ideas. She said he was a control freak and that he had stolen other people's ideas. They had a fight and – he threw her out.'

I sit mulling over this new information, and Peter pours more coffee for us all.

'Do you think she had anything to do with the bombing of *Los Globos?*' I ask.

'No!' Natasha takes a deep breath and sighs. I watch her cleavage sink and settle, but I'm drawn to the expression in her eyes. 'I'm telling you all this, everything I know, because of the CCTV ...'

'We understand that, thank you.' Peter places his hand over mine, and I'm conscious that he's still playing the role of my devoted partner. Natasha must assume the baby I lost belonged to us – to both of us, Peter and me.

'So, where did Nina go after he threw her out?' I ask, desperate for more information. I'm beginning to think now, more than ever, that the two incidents – the theft of *The Bull* and the bombing of *Los Globos* – are definitely related. If Umberto threw her out of his studio, then Nina certainly had a motive.

'I lost touch with Nina for a while, but that happens with creative people, doesn't it? They disappear and do their own thing ...'

'So, what do you know about *The Bull?*' My tone isn't friendly and Peter removes his hand from mine.

Natasha contemplates her answer, and I begin to wonder how much we can trust her. Is she setting us up? Is she in cohorts with Nina?

'Nina was furious with Umberto. She thought he'd stolen her ideas. She had been experimenting with new techniques, working with paper. She'd made smaller experimental objects, like a sunflower made from seeds packets, and then with

Italian newspapers, she'd made an ice cream cone, and little by little, Umberto started to like her idea. He took it one stage further, and he made *The Bear* for me.'

'So, she was upset?'

'I didn't know at the time, but she found me. That's how we stayed in touch, and she offered to make me another sculpture.'

'But you said no,' I guess.

Natasha shrugs. 'Umberto is the sculptor; besides, he was already making more in the collection. He made *The Bee* and *The Barn Owl* ...'

'Who did he make them for?'

'I think *The Bee* was commissioned by a Japanese philanthropist and I believe it is in a garden somewhere in Tokyo. *The Barn Owl* was made for an American billionaire who has a massive estate somewhere in Montana.'

'Umberto must have sold them for a lot of money,' says Peter.

'He isn't poor, but it takes a lot of money to maintain several studios.'

'And Nina wanted money?' I ask.

'Like all creative people, Nina wants to be praised and recognised for her artistic abilities.'

'And her original ideas,' I add.

'Exactly,' Natasha replies.

'Do you think she had anything to do with the drone bombing of his sculpture in Barcelona?' I insist.

Natasha shakes her head. 'I hate speaking badly about her. Umberto wronged her massively.'

'But what she did doesn't make it right,' counters Peter.

Natasha takes a deep breath. 'She told me she came up with

the idea of *Los Globos*, years ago. She was excited. She dreamed she could have her own exhibition in Milan, Rome, or Moscow. She was always full of great ideas and enthusiasm, but she said Umberto wasn't interested. He would get her to work on other projects, and then he would take her ideas and make them work for him. He had the power and position to do it. So, she went to see him—'

'She went to Barcelona?' I sit up straighter.

'I saw her there.'

'You were in Barcelona?' I ask.

'A few months ago. I had taken Olga to see the Basílica de la Sagrada Família. I'd promised her we'd go for a weekend and I bumped into Nina, quite by accident, near Las Ramblas.'

'Near Umberto's studio,' I say.

'Yes. We chatted for a while. Olga was thrilled to see her, but Nina wasn't herself. She was very withdrawn, and I could tell she wasn't happy.'

'Maybe she was upset. Umberto was getting all the credit for her idea?' I suggest.

'So, why did she steal *The Bull*?' Peter asks Natasha.

'I didn't know it was stolen. She came to me two days ago and said she had *The Bull*. She wanted me to buy it from her.'

I stare at Natasha. I can only hope she is telling us the truth.

'And what did you say?'

Natasha bites her bottom lip. 'I'd heard about the drone bomb, but I didn't know about *The Bull*. I didn't know that Umberto had made it for someone else. There had been nothing in the newspapers about a theft, so I contacted people. I had to be discreet. Obviously. But there was no information about *The Bull* anywhere, so I said to Nina that I would think about it.'

'Did you not think to contact Umberto?' I ask.

'And what do I say to him? That I know who stole *The Bull* and I have the chance to buy it? It doesn't work like that, as you well know.'

'So, Nina wants money?' Peter asks.

'It's not that simple.'

'It never is,' I reply, but the irony is lost on Natasha.

'She wants to have her own studio, so yes, that would take considerable financing.'

'Could you not have financed her?' I ask.

Natasha looks surprised. 'She never asked me. And no, it's not in my interest.'

The waiter clears our empty plates, and we pause our conversation, lost in our own thoughts until he's finished. It all makes sense to me now. Nina worked for Umberto, and she believes he stole her ideas. They had an argument, and out of revenge, she bombed his sculpture, then stole *The Bull* to finance a new career.

'Where did she want her studio?' I ask.

'Here in the Old Town of Tallinn.' Natasha glances at her watch.

'Do you want to buy *The Bull*?' Peter asks.

Natasha looks surprised. 'Not now. I want nothing to do with it.'

'Will you help us?' he asks.

'I don't want to be involved in anything to hurt Nina.'

I bristle at her defence of Nina. 'She isn't all sweet and kind.'

'Perhaps not, but she deserves a chance.'

'A chance at what?' I hiss angrily, and I stop as Peter places his hand on my wrist.

'I'm sorry, Natasha. Maria is upset. We don't want to

cause you any problems. All we want to do is to buy back the sculpture. The money will finance Nina's new career, and everyone will be happy.' His voice is smooth, and I almost believe him. 'We would like your help in finding her. Can you please arrange a meeting for us?'

Natasha reaches for her handbag. 'I told you all this because I don't want to be involved. I do not organise looting or encourage stealing. The theft of *The Bull* is nothing to do with me, and I want nothing to do with any of it—'

'So, why did you come here?' Peter frowns.

Natasha looks directly at me. 'Because of what you said about my daughter. I want Olga to know that her mother always did the right thing, but I will not betray Nina nor help set a trap for her.'

'You just want to clear your guilty conscience because you're a thief. All you do is deceive yourself – and your child. You should be ashamed.' I can't keep the anger from my voice.

Natasha stands up. 'If you want help, then I suggest you find the boy who was with Nina in Barcelona.'

'Nina has a boyfriend?' Peter struggles to his feet.

'She had a boyfriend with her the day I met her.'

'A Spanish boy?' Peter asks.

Natasha doesn't reply. Instead, she turns and marches swiftly across the restaurant and out into the foyer, leaving me staring at Peter. My mind is a whirling mash of ideas, and I'm already wondering what to do next.

* * *

'She saw the CCTV and felt guilty,' Peter replies, sitting back down at the table after Natasha leaves. 'But she's given us a lot

179

to think about. At least we know there is a connection between Nina and Umberto – and Natasha didn't organise the theft.'

'That doesn't exonerate her,' I say. 'Whose idea was it to steal *The Bull*? Natasha didn't say – but what if it was her idea? What if she set Nina up and promised she would buy *The Bull* to finance her career? What if Natasha is lying?'

'Let it go, Mikky. Leave Natasha out of it. If she was involved, she wouldn't have come here today to speak to us.'

'Unless it's a double bluff. She wanted to clear her name and let Nina take the blame—'

He taps the table with the stumps of his fingers. 'Maybe Nina was working for herself. She stole *The Bull* with Natasha in mind. I don't think Natasha lied to us.'

I sigh. I agree with him. I don't think Natasha was involved in the theft.

'Then Nina must still have *The Bull*,' I say.

Peter smiles. 'Exactly.'

'Do you have a plan?' I ask.

'I always have a plan. Come on, I'll tell you on the way. Besides, you could do with some fresh air to clear that head of yours.'

We're walking through the reception when the receptionist calls over.

'Mr Bannon?'

I walk on, not recognising the name, but Peter stops. 'Yes?'

'I've been asked to give you this note by the lady who had breakfast with you.'

I turn and follow Peter to the desk.

It's a different receptionist to the one from last night. This one has short blond hair, and his name tag says his name is Kaspar.

'She left it for you just now. She wrote it here in the reception,' he explains.

Peter opens a folded piece of hotel stationery, and I lean over his shoulder. Natasha's looped handwriting covers the page:
Dear Maria and Peter,

Olga and I are going on holiday. Should you wish to know more about the business we discussed, contact my assistant Nina Ruminov.

Best wishes,

Natasha

Nina's address is written underneath.

* * *

'The Old Town of Tallinn is the best-preserved medieval city in Europe, but more recently it's been known for its cyber technology and security. It was also the birthplace of Skype, and now, after being bought by Microsoft, its sister company is in Silicon Valley in America,' Peter tells me. 'Tallinn is a city of cyber intelligence. Even the NATO Cooperative Cyber Defence Centre of Excellence is located here.'

'Skip the tourist classes. I'm not interested, Peter. Let's just get to Nina's house before she sells *The Bull*.'

I'm annoyed that he can't walk any faster.

'Let's get a taxi,' I suggest.

'I googled it. It's as quick to walk.'

I let go of his arm and lengthen my pace.

'Mikky, wait! Slow down. We need to think of our cover story. We'll stick to the fact that Natasha told us about *The Bull* and we want to buy it from her. Let's keep it simple.'

'Will she believe us? Will it work?'

'As long as you don't kill her first,' Peter says with a smile.

'Where's the white van?' I ask. 'What's she done with it?'

Peter shrugs. 'On the film, we saw Nina arrive here. I looked again, and I think she may have hidden it in a garage or lock-up somewhere.'

I slow down to walk alongside him, still mulling over the information. 'So, Nina knew *The Bull* was in Glorietta's villa. Did she also bomb Umberto's sculpture?'

'Natasha seems to think she had a boyfriend.'

'Do you think he was the guy with her that night in the villa – the one on the CCTV?'

'We have to find out. Perhaps you could contact your policeman friend?'

I don't reply. We're standing at the corner of the road, and I'm staring at Nina's house outside the city centre. A white, two-storey apex, Scandinavian in design, with black roof tiles. A blue Volvo is parked on the driveway. In the garden at the side of the house are a trampoline and a doll's house.

'I'm surrounded by bloody children,' I mutter.

'Come on.' Peter rings the bell, while I survey the neighbourhood.

How will I kill Nina?

The door opens, and a harassed but attractive woman stands, holding a snotty-nosed child on her hip. Her black straight hair is tied back, and her blue eyes are weary and watchful. She's an older version of Nina.

A second, older child, with round-framed reading glasses, clings to her mother's shorts and stares warily at us.

Peter speaks in English.

'Hello, we're looking for Nina Ruminov. Does she live here?' He smiles. 'My name is Peter, and this is Maria. We met her yesterday at Natasha's house.'

The woman's look of insecurity fades at the mention of Natasha's name, and she opens the door wide enough to allow us to peer inside. The house is messy but not dirty, and children's toys are strewn across the floor.

'No, speak English.' Her accent is heavy. She places the toddler on the floor, who runs off with the older child. Behind her, in the lounge, the two children jump and roll on top of a giant teddy bear.

'Is Nina here?' Peter asks again.

She shakes her head.

'Will she be here later today?'

She shrugs. 'Work.'

'Does she go to a studio?'

Again, the woman shakes her head, as if she doesn't understand.

'Is Nina with Olga?' I ask.

'Olga?' She makes motions with her hands, indicating she doesn't understand, then she points to her children – who are now busy pulling a toy truck across the floor – and smiles apologetically. She is about to close the front door, but I glance in the hall mirror. Nina is crouching behind the staircase.

* * *

'Nina?!' I shout. I don't take my eyes off her reflection. 'Nina? We need some help. Natasha gave us your address. She thinks you can help us.'

Peter looks at me like I've gone crazy, but I stand my ground and call again, determined to get her attention.

'It's alright, Nina. We just want to speak to you,' I say;

although my heart is thumping erratically, my voice sounds calm. I nod at Peter to indicate that she's inside.

It takes all my self-restraint not to push past the woman in front of me and grab Nina, but I know that Peter is right. We must get her to trust us.

Then I'll kill her.

Nina straightens up and walks down the short hallway toward us. She moves warily, like a panther.

If only I had a knife.

She speaks brusquely in Russian.

'You're sisters?' I ask.

Their resemblance is striking. Her sister backs away from the front door.

'What do you want?' Nina's voice is quiet, and I'm taken aback by her accent. Her English is accomplished. She is slightly smaller than me, but broader in the shoulders, with black hair that would have been easy to hide under a baseball cap. Her blue eyes are hard and cold. They're the eyes I stared into the night my daughter was murdered.

It's her.

I want to reach out and grab her throat, but she is trained and dangerous. I must be careful and bide my time.

'Can we have a few minutes of your time?' Peter asks politely.

Nina stands with her feet apart, blocking the doorway.

'Perhaps we could come inside and speak more privately?' Peter insists.

Reluctantly, Nina moves aside, and we follow her into a kitchen. The beige Formica table is covered with piles of newspapers, children's toys, and books, and amidst all the mess is a shining black crossbow and four bolts. Thin net curtains cover the window,making the room cooler but also gloomier.

'Your family?' I ask.

'My sister's children,' she replies.

Nina's nieces spill out of the back door and onto the lawn, screaming and shouting. A paved area holds a brick barbecue and a table with four worn chairs. Her sister drags a chair into the shade to watch her children.

Peter sits down at the kitchen table and ignores the crossbow. 'I hope you don't mind. I need to rest.'

Nina glances at his foot.

'The thing is,' he says, taking a plastic folder from his bag, 'we know an Umberto Palladino sculpture has been brought to Tallinn.'

Nina leans forward to study the images of *The Bull* with feigned interest.

'We want to buy it. Money is no object. Natasha said you might know someone who can help us?'

We're taking a risk that Natasha won't betray us, and I'm holding my breath only inches from the woman who murdered my baby.

Peter continues speaking persuasively, 'Natasha seems to think that you might be able to help? And we would be extremely grateful if you would work with us – so we can buy it.'

And that's it! That's all he says. Then he sits and waits calmly, and I can almost hear the mechanics of Nina's mind reasoning, whirling, and clunking into action. She looks at me, but I deliberately glance into the garden. I can't take the chance that she may recognise me, even though I've changed my appearance.

Nina scratches her head.

'How do you know this?'

'It's what we do,' I reply. 'We're collectors – nobody needs to know. Only us.'

'How did you know it's here?'

'Natasha mentioned it after we saw *The Bear*,' I lie, and match her stare. I don't blink.

'We're obviously prepared to pay,' Peter adds. 'But we must be quick. We will be here for the next twenty-four hours, but then we leave, and the offer is over.'

'How much?' she asks.

'What's your usual rate?'

Nina shrugs.

'What did Natasha pay you to get *The Bear*?' I ask.

It's a shot in the dark, and we only have Natasha's word that Umberto made *The Bear* for her.

'I didn't sell her *The Bear*.' Nina stares defiantly at Peter and her eyes darken. 'I'll think about it.'

We need her to commit to a deal, so I say, 'Umberto Palladino sculptures are very rare. Natasha's very happy, and that's why she recommended you to us. We wouldn't normally approach anyone this way—'

'I can leave you a deposit.' Peter stands up, and I feel him wobble against me. He's right. In a fight, we would be useless. We must win through cunning and then she will be mine.

I will kill her.

The children are screaming in the garden, and the toddler is laughing. The mother picks up her daughter and swings her around again, and she shouts happily.

'Let me give you my phone number,' Peter says. 'Put it in your mobile.'

Nina takes her iPhone from her pocket and repeats the number Peter gives her. Then he passes her a thick brown envelope from the inside of his jacket pocket.

'This might persuade you. Call me.' He holds out the money.

Nina pauses before she takes it. They shake hands, but I can't bring myself to touch her, so I walk out of the front door and into the street, where I'm enveloped by the June sun. It's far more preferable and cooler than sitting with the devil herself.

We stop in a small café, near the Old Town, and order coffee. Peter speaks on the phone in Polish for a considerable amount of time, leaving me to ruminate on this morning's events. I'm hungover and feel sick, and when I close my eyes, all I see is Nina's face.

'What now?' I say, after he comes off the phone.

'That was Aniela,' he says, after he hangs up. 'She's renting us a house in the Old Town, and we're going to set up a deal and trap Nina later this evening.'

'You think Nina will call you?'

'She will after Aniela speaks to her.'

'Aniela is going to call her – why?'

'It will make Nina feel safe. If she's speaking to an international lawyer who is neutral, she will feel confident that we're telling the truth and that we will pay for *The Bull*.'

'But we're not going to pay for it, are we?'

The thought of giving the killer money is beyond my comprehension and my tolerance levels. I know when I meet Nina again, I will kill her – with my bare hands, if necessary.

'I have to do a few things, Mikky. You look terrible. Order another coffee and wait here. I'll be back in thirty minutes.' Peter excuses himself and I sit nursing a black coffee, and after ruminating on the events of the past few hours, I decide to return some of my missed calls and messages.

I spend most of the time talking to Bruno and bringing him up to date. At the end of my report, he says, 'I can't believe you're in Tallinn, Mikky. You found the thief – and it's a Russian girl who's a sculptor – a student of Umberto's.'

'I can't believe it, either.'

'You're definitely sure it's the same person from the villa?'

'Yes.'

She killed my baby.

'And Natasha has now left Estonia?'

'Yes.'

'So, what will you do?' he asks.

'I'm waiting for Peter. He had to go somewhere, and we're waiting for Nina to call. We're setting a trap.'

'Won't it be dangerous? Whose idea is that?' I can hear the exasperation in his voice. 'For heaven's sake, Mikky, you shouldn't be doing this. Why don't you phone Joachin and tell him all of this? Why won't you work with the police? Joachin can help you.'

'What has he done, so far?'

'I don't know.'

'Well, then!'

'I appreciate you are going after *The Bull*, Mikky, but Josephine is worried about you. She thinks you're doing it for the wrong reasons. She thinks you just want to get revenge – is that true?'

'Partly.'

'And does Peter know?'

'We've found Nina. We will get *The Bull*.'

'It sounds dangerous. You promised me ...'

'It's not dangerous.'

I see Peter limping across the square toward me with a box tucked under his arm. 'Look, I have to go, Bruno. I'll call you later.'

'Mikky, please call Josephine. She's worried she hasn't heard from you.'

'I will,' I lie, and I'm surprised when it just rolls off my tongue like it always used to.

I'm back to being me – the real Mikky dos Santos – the liar, the thief, and the cheat.

* * *

Peter pulls out a chair and orders a coffee from the waiter.

'What's in the box?' I ask.

He regards me silently for a few minutes before replying.

'Years ago, I went to a funeral – a colleague's, who died in combat. At the service, his wife and their two children went to stand beside the coffin. The little one, who was probably about knee-height, couldn't see anything. He didn't really understand what was going on and he knocked on the side of the coffin and said, "What's in the box?"'

I stare at Peter.

'Sorry! It's something I've never forgotten.' He shakes his head at the memory and holds up the cardboard box. 'This is a box of tricks that might help us later.'

'So, what's the plan?'

'Well, we wait without spooking Nina. My contacts tell me she's got a lock-up on an industrial estate on the outskirts of Tallinn. My guess is the van is stored there. She's regularly driven between Milan and Barcelona with sculptures for the studio ...'

'So, she knows the roads?'

'More importantly, she knows about swapping number plates, where to stop for a break, that sort of thing.'

'How do you know?'

'A friend called me. He managed to look at Umberto's records for the studio – his accounts and that sort of thing.'

'He hacked into his account?'

'It's not difficult.'

'So, what now?'

Peter opens the box and pulls out a small, square tracking device. He switches it on and waits for the Wifi connection on his iPad. A map comes to life, and we see a red flashing light.

'That's her.' Peter smiles.

'How did you do that?'

'The telephone number I gave her tracks her iPhone. So, we can see exactly where she is and where she goes. They don't call Tallinn "Silicon City" for nothing. It's amazing what you can pick up here,' he says with a smile.

'What if she doesn't take the bait and call us?'

'She will. I gave her five thousand euros in cash.'

* * *

Set a thief to catch a thief, but the plan hadn't been mine. It had been Peter's, and I feel growing respect and admiration for the way he plans and executes the tasks given to him. We're making progress. To my dismay, Nina remains at home – her sister's home – and so we wait.

'We could call the police and have them interrogate her.'

I'm thinking of my conversation with Bruno and how

Joachin might help us if I send him a text message.

'If that's what you want to do, that's fine.'

'Really?'

'I'll work with anyone, Mikky. But I can't reveal the identity of anyone who has helped us. I'd have to tell some lies.'

'Let's wait until we see *The Bull* – or at least that we know she definitely has it – or we haven't got a leg to stand on.'

'Story of my life,' he says with a smile. 'What do you think the police, your friend the inspector, will do if you tell them that we tracked *The Bull* to Tallinn?'

'I don't know. I guess it would take a while for them to get the police involved here.'

'That's why we have to move quickly.'

'We need to find the guy in Barcelona who helped her,' I say.

'Her boyfriend – her accomplice?'

'I've texted Joachin and asked for a list of all the students at Umberto's studio in Milan and Barcelona for the past three years.'

'How will we know if she was dating any of them?'

'We won't, but it's a start. We're one step behind Nina, but we need to be one step ahead.'

'It all takes time – and money.'

'I'll get money for you. Bruno has said he'll meet our costs and pay you.'

Peter frowns. 'I thought you knew me better. I'm not doing this for the money.'

Chapter 7

"Painting is so poetic, while sculpture is more logical and scientific and makes you worry about gravity."
Damien Hirst

We walk back to the hotel and eat a late lunch.

'That's an ingenious way to track her,' I say, taking a mouthful of steak and leaning over Peter's shoulder. My sarcasm reflects my frustration. 'Especially as she hasn't gone anywhere.'

Peter is beside the window, picking at his food, checking Nina's non-movements.

'Technology,' he agrees, ignoring my sarcasm. 'There's no privacy anymore.'

He taps keys on his laptop as he eats, then lifts his phone and speaks in Polish. During the conversation, he looks at me and smiles, then he winks, and after a few curt words, he hangs up.

'Aniela has spoken to Nina,' he announces. 'She's agreed to meet us, on her terms but somewhere public.' He taps the keyboard. 'Let's see where she goes now.'

'Do you think she's worried she might be followed?'

'If Aniela has done a good job, then we know Nina fell for our cover story. I wouldn't think it's dawned on her that we can track her through her iPhone. So long as she keeps her phone with her, then we will know her whereabouts.' He drums the fingers of his good hand on the table, then his mobile rings. 'It's her,' he says triumphantly, before answering the call and holding the phone to his ear.

'Hello, Nina. Good, good. I'm pleased to hear it. Maria will be delighted. This evening – at seven o'clock? Yes. Perfect. Thank you – yes, I can arrange the transfer of money. It's good to have you on board. Good. Thank you.' He hangs up and looks at me. 'She wants fifty thousand euros.'

'She's greedy. Where do we meet her?'

'The Botanical Gardens.'

'Do you know where they are?'

'Nope, but we have a couple of hours to find out.'

'We have to isolate her so that she can't escape.'

'That's the plan.'

'Interrogation, army-style,' I suggest.

He frowns. 'You want *The Bull*, and we'll get *The Bull*. That's it. You told me you wanted to find the sculpture.'

He really doesn't understand me or realise how determined I am, but I don't want to spoil his illusion.

'We're not paying her for it,' I say, finishing my meal and placing my knife and fork together.

'Nina believes us. She trusts us – and she has agreed to meet us.'

'Your uncle is an international lawyer; doesn't this go against everything he stands for?'

Peter stares at me. 'He's doing it for me.'

'What if it gets rough?'

'It won't. I'll look after you. It will be fine. There's nothing

193

to worry about.'

'Fantastic!'

'We'll get *The Bull* back, I promise.'

I don't reply. He doesn't get my sarcasm, nor my determination to exact revenge. I wipe the steak knife on my napkin.

'Let's go and check out the Botanical Gardens. We have work to do,' he says, indicating to the waitress that he wants the bill.

But it's not *The Bull* I want, and if he thinks he can stop me from delivering justice, then he has a lot to learn.

I made a promise.

While he's checking the Internet to find out how we get to the Botanical Gardens, I slip the steak knife into my jacket pocket, wondering if Nina will survive the pain of my Guantanamo Bay-type treatment.

* * *

The Botanical Gardens are situated ten kilometres east from the city centre – a twenty-minute ride by taxi.

Lush and beautiful, the landscaped parkland is situated on the River Pirita. Nature trails lead to pine groves, birch groves, and a mixed oak forest. Drained bogs feature as study trails, and I spend a few minutes studying the map of the gardens on the board inside the turnstile.

In the distance, the eye of the TV tower – the tallest building in Tallinn, with a viewing platform 170 metres high – casts a shadow across the brilliant glass of the hothouses arranged in a symmetrical pattern.

'It's not a massively popular tourist spot,' I say, taking a photograph of the map. 'But there's an arboretum, rose garden, and rock garden.'

'It closes at seven,' Peter says, pointing at the signs. 'She probably wants a quiet place.'

'You speak Estonian?'

'Enough to know the closing time,' he says with a smile. 'The outdoor gardens remain open until eight.'

Several families are on the lawn and are already packing away picnics. As we walk, I link my arm through Peter's, feigning interest in the fat and yellow goldfish in the large pond, and the assorted pungent aromas from the rose garden.

The colours around us are breath-taking: plants, foliage, flowers, trees – a sea of colour, an assortment of summer flowers; purples, pinks, lilacs, whites, reds, oranges, and blues, and a heady scent of herbs overwhelms my senses. In the distance, a goat bleats.

Deckchairs, woodcarvings, pathways, and fields of colour match the splendour of the cross-shaped glass conservatory. One glass building is filled with cacti of all shapes and sizes, with fine needles like pin cushions. Another is vibrant, with lush foliage and palm trees with colourful fruit. Perspiration breaks out on my forehead. The tropical glasshouses are filled with colours, and plants and wide fronds stretch over neat pathways. Trees, birds of paradise, lilies, and orchids stretch and reach, and suddenly I'm claustrophobic. The heat and dryness in my throat make me step back outside and into the fresh air, and I take a minute to sit on a bench and regain my control.

'Are you alright?' Peter asks.

I nod and focus on the arboretum in the distance.

Peter checks his phone.

'The cactus house,' he says. 'She wants to meet us inside.'

'I'll wait here.'

Peter gives me an exaggerated look of patience.

'Come on, Mikky. Let's concentrate on the details. She has *The Bull*. Let's assume she will bring it with her in a holdall. Let's keep it simple. You can verify it, and I can arrange payment.'

'But we're not paying her,' I complain. 'We have to stop her, Peter.'

'It's best to let her leave here without confrontation. We will have the sculpture, and I can stop the bank transfer.'

I stare at him. 'We can't let her go.'

'What do you want to do? Tie her to a tree, wind rope around her chest, or toss her into the pond and drown her?'

'If I have to.'

'She's professionally trained in martial arts, Mikky. Besides, did you not see the crossbow in the kitchen? We can't antagonise her.'

How could I forget Nina's talent for martial arts?

'I need to know the name of the second thief,' I say. 'I need her boyfriend's name.'

A promise is a promise.

He pulls a line of coil from his pocket and winds it around his fingers, demonstrating the most effective method to secure a limb.

'I have this if we need it. If she doesn't cooperate, then I could immobilise her. We can send instructions to her sister to free her later. We don't want to do anything illegal or get arrested.'

'I need to know the name of her accomplice,' I insist.

'Why?'

'You hardly think I'm going to let them get away with this?!'

I shout. 'He was there, too.' I bite my lip and turn away.

He is responsible for my baby's death, too.

'Mikky, I'm going to telephone Nina and tell her we're here,' he says calmly. 'You verify the sculpture. I'll make the bank transfer. It will look as though it's instant, but it will be reversed after three minutes. I have a friend who is waiting to falsify the bank process.'

'You seem to have thought of everything. She'll get no payment then?'

'None.'

'Just one last question ...' When he looks up at me, I ask, 'Are you armed?'

* * *

Peter talks to Nina on the phone with the loudspeaker on for my benefit. My hands are shaking, and my heart is beginning to thump to a new tune. I'm excited, and I'm determined.

My promise.

Peter explains the payment process.

'Text your bank details to my phone number. When Maria has seen *The Bull*, I'll make an instant payment of half of the money to your account. You can check it on your phone. I will send the second payment after we agree to the purchase. The money transfer will be instant.'

'How do I know it's not a trap?' Nina's voice is muffled.

'Because you spoke to our lawyer,' replies Peter. 'Besides, you are the one who chose Botanical Gardens – not us. Tell me where you want us to wait.'

'Make your way to the cactus house. You will see me in one hour – precisely – at seven o'clock.'

Peter checks his watch, then hangs up. He sits with me under the shade of the fir tree, checks his computer, and we wait, watching the red dot transmitting from Nina's mobile phone.

'I thought she'd head for the lock-up,' he mumbles. 'To collect *The Bull* and the van.'

'I'd say she has it with her, in her sister's house. She won't let it out of her sight.'

Peter frowns. 'Really?'

I sigh and then angrily shout, 'This is stupid, Peter! We should have just stormed the sister's house with AK-47s!'

'Too noisy,' replies Peter. 'Besides, the crossbow on the table wouldn't take long to assemble.'

Nina texts her bank details to Peter's phone.

'All traceable, if we go to the police,' he says. 'We could nail her with these bank details. We could also look at her financial records later – after this is over.' Peter doesn't look up. He's scamming a scammer. There must be justice in that.

'Don't you worry what your uncle would say if he knew what you were doing?' I ask. 'His international reputation would be destroyed if his nephew was caught doing illegal activities in Estonia. I can imagine the newspaper headlines: *Korneli Brzezicki's Nephew Disgraces International Legal Firm*.'

Peter frowns and has the grace to ignore me, but my nerves are getting the better of me. I pace around, flexing my fingers, pumping the muscles in my arms. I want a fight.

Peter's life has been filled with violence, war, terror, and heroism, and by comparison, all I've done is forge Vermeer's masterpiece *The Concert*, found an illuminated manuscript, and returned a stolen Torah.

I know I should trust Peter, but what if he protects Nina?

He closes his computer and slips it into his bag. 'Twenty-five minutes,' he says. 'She's on her way.'

'Should I wait inside the glasshouse?' My stomach is clenched and my body taut with nerves. I finger the steak knife in my pocket. It's a knife with a jagged blade, one that Eduardo and I might use when we are camping. A knife to fillet meat. *Now, I will use it to silence the killer of my baby.*

* * *

Peter sits beside me, stretching the muscles in his dead leg, and I wonder how strong he'd be against Nina the ninja warrior, when suddenly footsteps click on the pathway behind us.

Jumping up, I turn quickly and pull out the knife.

Standing in front of us is Aniela.

'Oh, Christ!' I moan, 'What do you want?'

'What the hell are you doing here, Aniela?!' Peter shouts.

'I have to be here,' she replies.

I turn away and scan the horizon, looking for Nina, and check my watch.

Fifteen minutes to go.

Peter grabs Aniela's wrist. 'You must go.'

She pulls her arm away. 'Get off me, Peter. Have you gone completely mad?'

'You can't stay here.' He tries to drag her toward the glasshouse door, then seems to change his mind. 'It's not safe.'

Aniela's eyes narrow and her lips snarl. 'I know what you're doing, Peter. I promised Nina I'd be here.'

'You what?' I gasp.

'She didn't trust you. Either of you. So, I gave her my word that this is all legitimate and no harm will come to her.'

'You can't stay!' I shout. 'Peter, do something with her.'

'I'm not leaving.'

'Aniela,' Peter whispers. 'Please, you must trust me. It's dangerous. You must leave now.'

'I don't care what you do, Peter. This is your uncle's idea. He wanted me to oversee things. It's time for you to heal and repair – not to take on some stupid project that will get you into more trouble and send you to a darker place than you've ever been before.'

Peter grabs Aniela around the waist. 'You're leaving whether you want to or not. You can't stay here.'

'Get off me!' She wriggles free from his grasp.

That's when Peter's mobile rings.

'I can see you all,' Nina says, on the loudspeaker. 'I came early.'

We stand grouped together, and I scan the trees and the foliage, and I even glance up at the TV tower, but I can't see Nina anywhere.

'You'll do as I tell you,' she says, 'or the deal is off.'

Peter sighs and glares at Aniela.

'Tell me what you want us to do,' he says.

'Make a bank transfer now.'

'I can't. We haven't seen *The Bull*.'

'Half the payment now or I'm leaving.'

'Okay, okay.' Peter taps the keys of his phone while I stand searching the landscape, but there's no sign of Nina. I look up and study the cloudless sky, but there's no drone flying high above us. 'Maria must see *The Bull*,' he insists.

'Tell her to go to the gazebo in the rose garden.'

Peter looks at me. I nod and glare at Aniela. It's only a few minutes' walk, but I'm scanning the landscape, watching and wondering where Nina is hidden.

In the gazebo, there's a brown bag on the floor. I pause and glance around. Nina is nowhere to be seen.

Peter and Aniela have followed me from a distance and now stand fifty metres away at the edge of the rose garden, watching and waiting. We have been outmanoeuvred, and I wonder what part in all of this Aniela has played.

I bend down, unzip the bag, and reach for the sculpture. It's not heavy, but I balance *The Bull* beside me on the bench and sit looking carefully at the craftsmanship. It doesn't seem to be as impressive as the sculpture in Glorietta's villa, but I attribute this to the fact it's been in a bag for the past five days. I study the sheet music, but something seems different.

'Where's the real sculpture?!' I shout out, standing back up.

Peter moves toward me, but Aniela puts a restraining hand on his arm.

I toss *The Bull* back in the bag and without zipping it closed, I throw it over my shoulder and walk out of the gazebo. I march past Peter and Aniela and say, 'Tell her if she doesn't show her face, this is going straight in the pond.'

* * *

'This is no time for games!' Peter shouts.

I ignore him and walk purposefully toward the pond, convinced Nina is watching our every move. At the edge of the water, I place the bag on the floor and pull out the sculpture.

Peter and Aniela have followed, but it's Aniela who runs down the grassy bank to my side, scattering ducks, geese, and swans.

'Mikky, stop! What are you doing?'

'It's fake. This isn't the real bull. She's tricked us.'

Aniela looks around in disbelief as I lift the paper statue in my arms.

'Nina?' Aniela calls.

I pause as a dark-clad figure appears from behind the trees near the forest.

'What's going on?!' Nina shouts.

'It's a fake!' I reply. 'You're trying to cheat us.'

'No.' Nina moves forward. 'You're doing this deliberately.'

'It's fake. Come and see for yourself,' I call.

Nina moves quickly, and in seconds she's standing a few feet away.

'Look!' I challenge. 'See here, under the paw. Umberto's signature isn't there.'

When I examined *The Bear* in Natasha's house, I knew Umberto had told me the truth. He signs his initials into the burnt paper. There are no initials on *The Bull*.

'This is a fake,' I say. 'It's unfurling. Look! The glue is coming undone.' I pull at a corner of the paper and peel it back.

'Stop!' Nina shouts, and runs toward us, but I continue speaking.

'This is crap. I'm holding a fake.'

Nina blinks in disbelief. 'It can't be.'

Aniela holds up her hand. 'We can sort this out and reach an agreement.'

Nina is clearly agitated, and I can see by the shock in her eyes that it's not her who has faked the sculpture. She is as surprised as me.

'It's a fake!' I shout to antagonise her further. 'There's no signature!'

'What signature?' asks Nina.

'Umberto signs all these sculptures with his initials. He told me himself.'

'You *liar!*' Nina spits.

'Did you think you could fool us?' I take a step closer to her. 'Make a fake so that you could take our money?'

'No, I—'

'You're a killer.' I throw *The Bull* to one side and, clutching my knife, I lunge toward her.

Aniela cries out, and Nina dodges me. Then arms grip me from behind, and Peter has me locked against his body. Having lost my baby, I'm weaker than I used to be, and my grip loosens. The steak knife falls to the ground, and it gleams in the sunlight. I push Peter off me and bend down. Grabbing the knife, I thrust it at Nina, but she twists my wrist and pulls it from my grip. Turning, she plunges it toward my stomach and this time I sidestep, but Peter – who's behind me – gasps. The blade sinks into his skin. Blood spurts from his wound and he slumps to the floor.

I grab Nina's jacket by the collar and I kick out, but I'm not wearing my traditional biker boots and my shoe flies off. I'm angry, and I begin flailing my arms, biting, kicking, thumping, slapping, but Nina smacks me in the face. She holds me by the neck. Her grip is solid, and I'm choking. Sweat breaks out on my forehead, and my throat is burning. Then suddenly, she releases her grip, and she's gone. She is running away, up the bank to the pathway.

Aniela is crouched over Peter, but I'm on my feet and chasing Nina. Although I'm weak, I'm angry. She's not getting away. I'm faster than her, gaining ground along a covered and colourful archway. As we come out the other side, I dive for Nina's feet in a rugby tackle, and we fall down together on the path. She elbows me in the face and follows it with a karate chop to my neck, but I block her arm. She wriggles away, shifts her weight, raises her foot, and kicks me in the face. When I open my eyes, she's holding a gun to my forehead.

'You killed my baby,' I hiss.

Aniela calls out. Nina is distracted, and instinctively I turn. Aniela is dragging Peter's limp body. His arm is draped over her shoulder, and blood is soaking into his shirt. I stumble to my knees just in time to see Nina vaulting over the turnstile to the car park.

The bitch is gone.

Chapter 8

"I think I understand something about space. I think the job of a sculptor is spatial as much as it is to do with form."
Anish Kapoor

'Call an ambulance!' Aniela shouts.

I'm weak and dizzy. I'm fumbling with my phone, my fingers shaking. My throat is sore, and my neck feels as though it's been crushed in an iron vice.

'Call an ambulance!' Aniela shouts again. 'Quick!'

'No, don't, Mikky. It's okay. I'm fine. It's only a flesh wound. Let me sit here,' Peter replies, and Aniela lets him sit with his back against the wall. She pulls his shirt free from his trousers and dabs the wound with a cotton scarf from her neck.

'If you don't call the police, then I will.' She glares at me. 'I have no idea what you two are doing, but Korneli will be very angry.'

'He doesn't have to know,' Peter replies calmly, taking a bunch of tissues from her hand to stem the flow of blood. 'I'll be fine.'

'What were you two thinking?'

Peter's blood is like a painted map of Africa on her skirt. Her hair has come loose and her brown eyes are blazing. Now she knows he's not dying, Aniela's fear turns to anger.

'How can you behave like this? What is wrong with you, Peter? Have you completely lost your mind? I want no part of this – this – whatever it is that you're doing. It can't be right, and it certainly isn't legal.'

I ignore her and walk back to the pond, where I retrieve the fake sculpture and the holdall. When I return, Peter is still being reprimanded.

I take the front leg of *The Bull.*

'Look!' I peel away layers of sheet music and they come apart easily in my hand. 'There are a few sheets of script music from *Carmen*, but underneath there's newspaper, *El Pais*. This has been made in a hurry. The glue hasn't even dried properly!'

Peter leans forward for a closer look, and even Aniela leans nearer.

'Someone made it deliberately to fool us,' I add.

'Nina could have faked it,' Peter suggests.

'She seemed as shocked as me,' I reply. 'None of it makes sense.'

Peter dabs at his bleeding stomach wound.

'You need a doctor,' Aniela says.

'I'm fine,' he replies. 'It's a flesh wound. Not a good steak knife at all.'

I smile wryly. For the past few days, Peter has been my Robin Hood. Now, pain is etched on his face. I can't just walk away from them and let them pick up the pieces of the mess that I instigated.

Aniela kneels at his side, and they whisper in Polish. I'm listening but understanding nothing of their conversation. I feel sick, my head is throbbing, and my body is aching. After my heart has slowed to a normal rhythm, I reach for my phone.

I need a new plan.

* * *

At Peter's insistence, we return to the hotel. While Aniela takes Peter to the bathroom, where she washes and bandages his wound, I make three mugs of tea, spilling some on the pristine marble floor, but it's the least of my worries.

I sit at the table, checking Peter's iPad to see if I can track Nina's movements via her mobile phone. She had been smarter than us. One step ahead. She must be laughing at us now. Or was she?

Has she been duped, too?

Peter and Aniela continue talking and sipping their tea, and although I don't know what he's saying, she reaches forward to hold his hand and to wipe damp hair from his forehead.

It takes a few minutes for the tracking on the computer to fire up, and I find the red bleeping dot on the map.

'Where is she going?' Peter asks.

'She's moving quickly by road. I think she's heading to the airport,' I say. 'I'll check the Internet and the destinations of the flights leaving Tallinn.'

I made a promise.

I have also endangered Peter and Aniela's lives. Two innocent people who are not involved in my personal war. I have behaved irrationally and without responsibility. I have allowed my heart to rule my head, and my emotions have taken over from my common sense. I have made a mess of it all, and I have let everyone down, including my unborn daughter.

Nina escaped.

It's all my fault.

Aniela looks at me, and she smiles sympathetically. 'You need to get some rest, Mikky. You look terrible.'

I shake my head, and I turn angrily away. 'I'm going after her.'

I slip Peter's iPad under my arm and head out into the street, promising to phone them later. It takes me a while to find a taxi but the traffic is not heavy. The route is straightforward and the journey to the airport only takes fifteen minutes. The driver leaves me at Departures and again I check the iPad.

It's bleeping.

Nina is here. I must be cautious.

Inside the terminal, I quickly scan the departures board: Geneva, Vilnius, Stockholm, London Gatwick, Helsinki, Bergamo, Barcelona, Copenhagen, Warsaw ... too many destinations.

The red dot hasn't moved, so assuming she's in a coffee shop or sitting somewhere, I continue with caution, scanning the shop and café. The red dot grows larger, leading me to a quiet area of the terminal, toward the toilets.

The ladies' toilets.

I wait outside for five, ten, and then fifteen seconds. Wary that I might appear suspicious if watched on the airport cameras, I walk inside and check the cubicles. I pretend to dry my hands until there's no one around. The bin is filled with discarded paper towels. Nina is not as stupid as I thought she might be. I've underestimated her.

She's ditched the iPhone.

I pull it out of the bin.

But where has she gone?

I spend a while walking through the airport, listening to the announcements. Then I jump into an airport taxi and get the driver to take me directly to Nina's home. The driveway is empty. There's no sign of a blue Volvo and the house, that had looked splendidly Scandinavian this morning, now appears dishevelled and unkempt in the fading sunlight. There's a light on in the upstairs window, so I ring the doorbell.

Nina's sister peers at me through the crack in the door. Her eyes are large, and she looks frightened.

'Where's Nina?' I ask.

She shakes her head. 'Gone!'

'Where?'

She shrugs. 'Not know.'

'You're lying,' I say, pushing against the door and forcing myself inside the house.

'No, no, my ... children, sleeping. Shush.' She presses a finger to her lips.

I kick my foot against the door and lean into her face, but then I'm shocked, and I pull suddenly away. Her cheek is bruised, and her top lip is thick and caked with dried blood.

'What happened to you?' I whisper.

She doesn't reply, but looks over her shoulder as a child upstairs begins to wail.

'Please,' she whispers. 'My husband is back. Nina ... went. Go!'

'Where did she go?'

She shakes her head.

I want to tell her that Nina killed my child, but there's a sadness in her eyes that I can't add to. I can't add to her misery or make her world a worse place. Nina's sister looks downtrodden and beaten. She doesn't need me to kick her harder and stamp her into the ground.

Is this why Nina needed the money?

209

Words cannot describe the despair I see on Nina's sister's face, and it's a memory that I carry with me as I step back into the street, wondering what sort of man she is married to and what I should do next.

* * *

I return to the hotel and find Peter and Aniela in the bar, and over a few brandies, I tell them what happened. When I'm too tired to sit any longer, I book a separate bedroom for myself at reception.

The young boy, Maksim, who I suggested should be a film star, is suitably astonished when he sees Peter and Aniela heading to their room, so I give him a big grin and wink mischievously.

In my room, I climb into bed. The disastrous attempt to capture Nina, to tie her up and beat a confession from her, and my erratic attempt to follow her to the airport, now seem pathetic. I'm exhausted, but my eyes refuse to close, and I stare at the ceiling, processing the day's events and thinking about Peter and Aniela.

I couldn't help but notice how well matched they are. I was conscious of the silent, unspoken words between the two former lovers. The chemistry between Aniela and Peter is still very much alive.

It's obvious in the gentle way they regard each other, but also in the minute details of their behaviour – the way their touch lingers and how they anticipate each other's needs.

I am not essential to their lives, and it's time for me to move on.

I stare at the ceiling, and I'm suddenly overcome with

loneliness, and a knot of sadness gathers around my heart.

What would I do if I were Nina?

Where would I go?

Did Nina get on a flight or was that a ruse?

Is the blue Volvo hers?

I messed up my chance to get even with Nina, but I'm determined it won't stop me from finding her or *The Bull*.

Who made the fake?

I go back over the events of the night of the theft. I'm thinking of the two thieves: Nina and the taller man – a man who spoke English with a Spanish accent. Her Spanish boyfriend?

He tried to stop Nina from kicking me.

Why?

Could he have swapped The Bull *for a fake?*

I sit up and review the CCTV, hoping I might glean more information about him. *When did the second person – the Spanish guy – get out of the van?*

* * *

It's early in the morning when I knock apologetically on Peter's bedroom door.

'I only want to borrow Peter's computer,' I whisper to Aniela, who is already dressed.

'You'll be lucky! Come in,' she says with a smile.

Peter is already sitting at the table, hunched over the computer screen. The debris on the table shows evidence of room service and a breakfast eaten several hours ago. Aniela disappears, and I see her applying mascara in the bathroom mirror.

'You're up early,' I say.

Peter looks tired, but he smiles brightly.

'We have work to do, Mikky. Nina may have ditched the phone, but we may be able to track her credit card. I'm also checking the flight manifests from last night.'

I slide onto a chair beside him and lean my arm on his shoulder. 'Thank you, Peter, but you should be resting your wound.'

'It's only a scratch.'

'What about Aniela?' I whisper.

'She's happy. No complaints in that department.'

I laugh and hold up my hand.

'Too much information.'

'Thanks, Mikky. She really likes you. You said some very kind things about me last night.'

'It wasn't anything she didn't already know. She just needed to be reminded.'

'It's made me realise, though.'

'Realise what?'

'I'm sorting myself out. I'm not going to lose her again.'

'And what about your Uncle Korneli? What will you say to him about this mess?'

'When Uncle Korneli realises that he's played cupid by sending Aniela to Tallinn, he'll be very happy. This little adventure of yours has brought us back together. I owe you.'

'In that case, can you get me Natasha's mobile number?'

* * *

'I need you to set up a meeting with Nina,' I explain to Natasha, when I finally get through to her. It's taken me three phone calls, six text messages, and two voicemails. I'm not begging her to help – I'm ordering her to.

'I'm not in the country,' she replies.

'You don't need to be. I want to meet Nina – face to face.'

'But I gave you her address.'

'She's gone.'

I'm banking on the fact that Nina hasn't been and won't be in touch with Natasha.

'And I have to find out who did the job with her. I need to know who broke into the villa with Nina.'

'I thought you were just going to pay Nina for *The Bull*.'

'Did you see the sculpture, Natasha?'

She doesn't answer.

'You know, don't you? You knew all along. It's fake.' She doesn't reply, but I know she's listening. She would have let us pay Nina for a fake. She's not to be trusted.

'Maybe Nina switched the sculpture to fool you?' Natasha suggests.

'You know Umberto signs his work and that's why you didn't buy it from her. But you didn't tell her it was a fake, did you? You were just playing her along, and when Peter and I turned up, you couldn't believe your luck. It got you off the hook. You told her to sell it to us. Why?'

'That's how I've survived in business.'

'That's the first honest thing you've said. I think the man who broke into the villa with Nina switched the sculptures. Nina had no idea until yesterday. She was as shocked as me.' Natasha doesn't reply, so I continue, 'I think Nina is going to find him. That's what I would do – especially if he stitched me up.'

'You wouldn't want to cross Nina – she can be ruthless.'

'I already know that, Natasha. So, you'd better tell me who he is before she hurts anyone else. Who is he? Who is the boyfriend?'

Natasha sighs. 'I don't know his name. She told me she was in love. She'd transferred to Umberto's studio in Barcelona on a sabbatical for six months.'

'Who is he?'

'He's a sculptor.'

'You didn't tell us that.'

'I didn't think it was necessary. I thought you'd buy *The Bull* and leave.'

'What's his name?'

'I don't know, but he had access to the sculptures belonging to Umberto Palladino. I think he was bragging – he was another student of Umberto's. I think, like Nina, he was another protégé.'

My spirits are lifting. We know Nina's accomplice worked or is still working in Umberto's studio in Barcelona. I had asked Joachin for a list of students, but he hadn't got back to me.

'Did Nina confide in you?' I ask Natasha.

'Not really. She said a few things about him. Presumably, this boy wanted to earn Umberto's respect, but he was strange. He seemed weird. He had a peculiar sense of fun, as if he had too much money. He's one of the rich kids. He used to do stupid pranks and things, but Nina said that was part of his charm. He made her laugh. But then, after her argument with Umberto, she was kicked out of the studio, and the boyfriend dumped her. He wanted nothing more to do with her.'

'But he broke into the villa with her?'

'If it's him.'

'And he switched *The Bull*, which means he must have made

a fake and swapped it for the real one.'

As I reason aloud, it makes me think that they had plotted the theft of *The Bull* for a long while. It had all been premeditated and planned. He had known what he was going to do. He had known that he was going to cheat Nina.

They had killed my baby.

Natasha says, 'If it is the same guy who was her boyfriend, then he's broken Nina's heart, and he's also scammed her. So, you are right. She won't let him get away with it.'

'No, she won't,' I agree.

The phone goes silent for a while and then Natasha says, 'Mikky, I'm sorry about what happened to you – and your baby.'

'Thank you.'

'Nina was never a bad person. She would not have stolen the sculpture and offered me a fake deliberately. Nina would not do that. This job was too important to her. It was her last chance. She's desperate.' Natasha takes a deep breath. 'She wants to help her sister, Katya. I think Umberto is the father of her children.'

Chapter 9

"I had wanted to be a sculptor throughout life, but to do so, I had to stop painting."
Fernando Botero

After I hang up on Natasha, I tell Peter and Aniela about my conversation.

'Umberto is the father of Katya's children?' Peter says, incredulously. 'The little girl with the glasses and the baby playing in the garden?'

I nod, trying to think things through. 'But we don't have any proof.'

'Okay, then let's focus on the facts,' Peter says, drumming his fingers. 'Nina stole *The Bull* with her boyfriend – or ex-boyfriend – then he switched it after the robbery. This means he must still have Glorietta's original sculpture.'

'I think Nina has gone to find him,' I say.

'So, the sculpture never left Spain,' says Aniela.

'How could he have switched it?' asks Peter, concentrating on his computer screen.

'He must have done it after they left the villa and before Nina left Barcelona for Tallinn,' Aniela says.

'I need a list of students at Umberto's studio. I have to find him before Nina does.'

'Nina's blue Volvo has been filmed leaving Tallinn,' Peter announces, without looking up from his screen. 'And she's heading toward Germany.'

'So, the airport was a ruse. She must have stopped there just to dump the iPhone.'

Aniela asks, 'Do you think she's going back to Spain?'

'I think she's going to find the guy who duped her.' I lean across the table, looking with Peter at the grainy photographs of Nina in the driving seat of the Volvo travelling across Europe. We work backwards on her route – Estonia, Poland, Germany, France – but concentrating is hard work. I yawn loudly and stretch my neck and shoulder muscles. It's been five days since *The Bull* was stolen, and since I lost my baby girl and Eduardo, but I won't give up.

I made a promise.

My face looks like I've been in a fight. My temple is bruised, and my right eye is swollen. My throat is still sore from Nina's grip.

'The longer our search goes on, the less chance we have of finding her,' I mumble.

* * *

Josephine calls my mobile. I've sent her a few text messages, but she's persistent, and when she rings for the third time, I decide to answer it.

'Hello.'

'Mikky? Thank goodness, at last. I've been so worried about you. Where are you?'

'I'm in Tallinn.'

'Estonia? Why? What on earth are you doing? I thought you were coming back to Spain?'

I guess that Bruno has been scant on the information he's given her, and I'm too tired to lie or to play games. It's also good to hear her voice, and I begin to tell her about the events of the past thirty-six hours; my trip to Wrocław, meeting Peter, and our trip to Estonia. I finish by telling her about our encounter with Nina yesterday evening in the Botanical Gardens.

She listens without comment, and when I pause, she says, 'Why don't you speak to Joachin? You could help each other. You're both working toward the same goal but coming at it from different angles. If you pooled your information, then you'd find Nina and, more importantly, you'd probably find the Spanish man who has the original sculpture.'

I know she's right, but the thought of working with a police officer scares me. I've never gone to the police for help. The last time I trusted a policeman – my ex – he killed my best friend, then tried to kill me. It doesn't come naturally to me to trust anyone.

'It wouldn't hurt,' agrees Peter, after I hang up and tell him about the conversation. 'But you must understand that I could no longer be involved. Some of the methods I've used are not legal. It could be compromising.'

'That's funny, especially when you consider an ex-police woman gave me your details.'

He smiles.

'You could contact Joachin, just to see what he says,' suggests Aniela. 'The inspector might give you some information that may help us.'

I note the 'us', and I also note that Aniela hasn't left Peter's

218

side. She sometimes lays her hand on his cheek, against his beard, and they smile together, and I remember she had told him in his Uncle Korneil's office to have a haircut. She was right. He's far more handsome and presentable and, more interestingly, she seems to be in no hurry to leave him and to return to Poland. At least something positive has come from this, if nothing else.

I walk into their bathroom, wondering what to do. As I gaze at my reflection in the mirror, I see dark circles under my eyes and the bruise on my throat. I've lost my baby, my partner, and my life, but more than anything – *I made a promise*. I can't let Nina get away. I mustn't let pride get in my way.

'Pull yourself together. Sort yourself out, Mikky,' I whisper, then I stand tall and straighten my shoulders. I'll leave my hair short and blonde for now. It suits the new single chapter in my life. Whenever your life changes, then your character and appearance must adapt to your new life. Besides, I mustn't waste a minute. It's vital to find Nina, her accomplice – and *The Bull*.

As I come out of the bathroom, I'm conscious Aniela and Peter are both watching me and waiting for a decision.

'What'll I tell him?' I ask.

'Don't mention me,' says Peter.

'The truth,' says Aniela, sounding like a genuine, good, wholesome international lawyer. 'Just tell him the truth, Mikky.'

* * *

'Inspector Joachin García Abascal?' I say.

'Who is this?'

'Soy Mikky dos Santos,' I speak in Spanish. It's easier, and it means that my conversation will not be scrutinised by Peter and Aniela, who are working at the table beside me. They are whispering in Polish, tracking Nina's car as it chases across Europe.

'Mikky? It's good to hear from you.' I hear the smile in his voice.

'How are you getting on? Any luck?' I ask, continuing the conversation in Spanish.

'Well,' he says with a sigh. 'We've been verifying the guests, the band, and the catering crew, and also the students who work with Umberto Palladino, but so far nothing has come to light. They either have no knowledge of, no interest in, or no desire to steal *The Bull*; or they have good alibis on the night. The trail is getting cold.'

'What about the white van?'

'It was stolen and, unfortunately, there are millions of white vans. We're working with the European police. We know the van went into France and we believe they may have changed number plates. We're trying to find out how and when they did this, but it's difficult and it all takes time.'

'What about buyers or collectors for *The Bull*? Have you worked out who would want to buy it?'

'Not yet; I have some colleagues working with specialists on this. We have found out who has the other animals in the collection.'

'Really?' I sit up, wondering if his information will match mine. 'Who?'

'I can't tell you. Where are you? Perhaps we can meet up?'

I take a deep breath. 'I have some information for you.'

'That's good.'

'You'll have to take my word on what has happened, as I can't prove anything – you know, legally, in a court of law.'

I hear a smile in his voice. 'Now, why doesn't that surprise me?'

'I've managed to track *The Bull* to Estonia. I found one of the thieves, the one who kicked me.' I hear his sharp intake of breath, but I continue speaking. 'But the thing is, the sculpture they delivered here to the collector – it's a fake.'

'Did you say a fake?'

'Yes. I didn't tell you, but Umberto showed me how I could tell if his work was authentic. This one was very definitely a fake.' I allow the silence to hang between us for a while, and then I say, 'I believe that a Russian girl and a Spanish boy broke into the villa. Nina, the Russian, is a martial arts expert, but I think the other one switched the sculpture before Nina left for Estonia, without her realising.'

'Madre mia!'

'So, we must find the other person who broke into the villa,' I add. 'Urgently.'

'Do you have any idea who he is?'

'No, and Nina has disappeared—'

'Mikky, I can't do this over the phone. Where are you?'

'I'm in Estonia.'

'Jesus! How long will it take you to get back to Barcelona?'

'I'm not sure.'

Aniela calls out in perfect Spanish, 'If we leave now, there's a flight to Barcelona in two hours.'

* * *

On the plane, I sit in the window seat beside Aniela. Peter is asleep in the aisle seat, his head tilted back and his mouth half-open, and it gives us the opportunity to talk alone.

'It wasn't because he was injured in the war, Mikky, that we broke up. But when he came back to Poland, he rejected me. He told me he wasn't the man for me. He told me to call off our wedding, and when I wouldn't, he became angry. He told me I was marrying him out of pity,' she says. 'Then he started drinking, and he didn't look after himself. I begged him to get help, but he shut us all out, and he wouldn't leave his apartment.'

'He's an incredible guy,' I say.

'Well, thanks to you, we've got him back again. You've given him a sense of purpose. He wouldn't do anything. He wouldn't even take our phone calls or answer the door.'

'It's just as well he has this business.'

'Business?'

'Isn't this what he does, all this surveillance?'

'No. Not at all. He's done nothing for eighteen months. All his friends had given up on him. He had given up on himself, too. He had nothing and no one until you came along.'

'He wasn't doing anything?'

'He was at rock bottom. But you gave him a sense of purpose.' Aniela regards me in silence before adding, 'I'll never be able to thank you enough. I was angry when he came to the office with you. I thought you were having an affair, and I was jealous. I had tried so hard, but I couldn't reach him, and nor could Korneli.' She looks at me and then asks, 'I think you must have said something that made him think about life again. Did you?'

I regard her carefully and, as we chase across the sky in pursuit of the people who destroyed my life, I find myself confiding in Aniela about the loss of my daughter and also about Eduardo, the man I had loved.

'Eduardo thought it was my fault and that I should never have confronted the thieves.'

She glances sideways at me, her face illuminated by sunlight streaming through the window, reflecting the sadness in her eyes. 'I'm sure he doesn't mean it.'

'Eduardo doesn't say what he doesn't mean.'

'It was in the heat of the moment with all the emotion involved. Has he contacted you since?'

'No.'

Peter is quietly snoring when she says, 'Perhaps you should contact Eduardo again?'

'Maybe—' I gaze out of the window at the sleeping scene below us. I see the houses, villages, roads, and mountains. '—Maybe not.'

Barcelona is only a stone's throw from my home in Mallorca – a thirty-minute flight – and I wonder if Eduardo is working, or if his shift at the hospital has changed.

* * *

When we land, I call from the taxi and book two rooms in the five-star Hotel Arts Barcelona. The luxurious, blue-glass hotel, with its Michelin star restaurant, rooftop spa, and outdoor pools, overlooks the sea. I'm not rich, but I'm certainly not poor. My art businesses both legal and illegal have been lucrative over the years and – combined with having received a fee for recovering one of the world's most famous stolen paintings, Vermeer's *The Concert* – it means I have no money worries.

223

We arrive at the hotel tense and exhausted, but the panoramic view of the sweeping bay and glistening sea from our rooms on the twenty-sixth floor is enough to relax any worn soul. It's what we all need.

I phone Inspector Joachin García Abascal and arrange to meet at five o'clock. I need to go shopping, then take a quick siesta, and I'll be ready.

A promise is a promise.

From my window, I watch people on the beach and yachts on the water – people are leading ordinary and happy lives.

Why did my life go so terribly wrong?

* * *

Frank Gehry's golden fish sculpture overlooks the Port Olímpic. It glistens in the early afternoon sunshine, and I take a while to contemplate the intricate fish scales. The sculpture, like those of Umberto Palladino, is exquisite, and I spend a few minutes admiring the process, the level of detail, and the skill involved.

I yawn. My shopping expedition was exhausting but successful, and just as I had finally managed to doze off, my alarm clock was waking me. My short siesta was over.

Now, I'm excited and wired.

Peter and Aniela come out of the lift. They look rested and showered, and they remind me of a newly married couple, with lingering gazes and the slight touch of hands. Together, we walk toward the bar, where we find a table and order coffee.

A few minutes later, I brighten at the sight of Joachin. His confident stride comes to a halt as he stares around at the clusters of small groups before eventually recognising me.

'Rubia! Blondie!' He laughs and kisses my cheeks. 'I hardly recognise you, Mikky!'

'I'm in disguise,' I joke, rubbing my short hair and feeling suddenly self-conscious.

'It suits you.'

'Thank you.' I smile and introduce my two friends from Poland.

Joachin kisses Aniela on both cheeks, and the men shake hands. I'm aware of them sizing each other up, not from a position of physical strength as you would an enemy, but as colleagues and friends.

'So, Mikky dos Santos ...' Joachin rubs his hands together and sits down. 'It looks like you've had a busy few days, and I see you've added a few bruises to your collection.'

'Umm. It's been pretty hectic: Barcelona, Wrocław, Tallinn, and now back to Barcelona. I'm lucky to have had help.' I nod at my friends.

'Where do we start?' asks Joachin.

It's Peter who speaks first.

'Can we assume that what Mikky tells you is true? I cannot reveal my sources or how or where I get my information. Can you please trust us?'

Joachin casts his eyes over Peter's missing fingers, and I'm in no doubt he recognises an injured veteran.

'I'll probably ask, as it's in my nature, but feel free to deflect any questions that aren't relevant.' He nods his head in respect.

I spend the first hour bringing Joachin up to date, telling him how I went to Wrocław and how we tracked Nina to Tallinn, and then of our visit to Natasha's house and how she produced *The Bear*. I tell Joachin how Nina walked in with Olga, and

225

how she sometimes looks after Natasha's daughter, and his eyebrows lift in surprise, but he says nothing.

Then Peter explains how Aniela set up the meeting with Nina to buy back *The Bull*.

Joachin blinks, and to his credit, he doesn't ask for more details or proof of our story. He appears to believe us, and occasionally his brown eyes crinkle in concern. Still, it shows me that he's listening to every detail of our account, especially when I tell him the information I learned after my phone call to Natasha.

'She filled in the missing gaps,' I explain. 'She told me that Nina worked as an intern in Umberto's studio in Milan before moving to Barcelona. They argued, and he threw her out. Nina believed that he stole her ideas – especially the one using paper, like in the technique he used for *Los Globos* and his animal collection.'

As I speak, I find myself warming to Joachin. There's a gentleness to his demeanour that isn't weak, but on the contrary, adds strength to his character. Having thought he was fifty the first time we met, I begin to think he's probably older – perhaps nearer sixty. He wears navy chinos and an open-necked checked shirt, and an expensive watch glistens on his wrist. He toys with a gold wedding band on his slim finger and as I reach the end of our story, I conclude, 'I believe Nina and her Spanish boyfriend stole *The Bull*, but he made a fake and swapped it without Nina knowing.'

'When?'

'He knew what he was doing in advance. He planned it. Supposing he had another bag with the fake already inside the van. All he had to do was climb out of the van and make sure Nina took the bag with the fake sculpture. If Nina was driving, as I suspect she was, he probably climbed out of the van somewhere on the outskirts of the city.'

'You mean, he never went to Tallinn?'

'I don't think he even left Spain,' I reply.

Joachin scratches his cheek and takes the opportunity to study Aniela and Peter, who have remained silent. The work that Peter has done has been invaluable, and Joachin knows it.

'Well, Nina certainly has a motive,' he says, 'if she wants to get even with Umberto. But would she be so obvious as to bomb *Los Globos*?'

'We don't know that the two incidents are related. I can only assume they are,' I reply.

'If her partner or her boyfriend is a student working in the studio here in Barcelona, then he would have known Umberto was making the sculpture for Glorietta ...' Joachin's voice trails off as he gazes across the terrace and out to sea, as if looking for answers to the pieces of the puzzle.

'It wouldn't be difficult to find Glorietta's villa. He may have followed Bruno after a visit to the studio.'

Joachin nods thoughtfully. 'It does make sense. If what you say is true, then it's possible.'

'If this boy – the thief – works in Umberto's studio, then it's obvious he will have seen Umberto working on *The Bull*. He might also have learned the art himself. He might have found it easy to replicate it,' I suggest.

Joachin nods, agreeing with my logic, and so I continue, 'We need to check out the students or employees who had access to the studio during the time it took Umberto to design and make the sculpture of *The Bull*.'

'I have a list.' Joachin scratches his chin. 'But we've already checked out Umberto's students and visitors.'

'Can I see the list?' I ask.

Joachin shrugs and reaches for his iPhone. 'Why not?'

I take his phone and glance through the names. There have been about thirty students and eight visitors to the studio in the past six months, but none of the names mean anything to me.

'Nina's name is not on the list,' Joachin says.

'She must have been fired by then. You must check the dates further back.'

'Will do.'

'Can you send me this list?' I hand him back his phone.

'I'll email it to you.' He taps a few buttons, and it pings onto my iPhone.

'So, you think Nina's boyfriend made a replica of *The Bull* and substituted the real one for a fake, and now she's found out, she's come back to Barcelona to confront him?' Joachin asks.

'She wants *The Bull* and I believe she will stop at nothing to get it. I've been on the wrong end of her martial arts skills twice, and that's too many times for my liking. She won't get away from me the next time.'

'Where do you think she is now?'

'We have reason to believe,' I reply, not looking at Peter, 'that Nina may already be in the city.'

'Then we must find her.'

'We must find them both,' I say. 'See if you can find out where Nina is staying. Can you check all the small hostels?'

'You don't think she'll stay with the boyfriend?'

'Not if he's done this to her. She'll be exhausted after driving, and she'll need to rest. Meantime, I'll start checking and find out who dated Nina Ruminov.'

'How?'

'There's someone I need to talk to.'

* * *

Outside in the street, I eye my new purchase with eager antici-pation. My earlier shopping trip proved more successful than I could have imagined. Parked at the side of the kerb is my new red Triumph Street Scrambler. With its 900cc twin Bonneville engine, it has more power than anything I've bought before. The salesman told me that it has a higher rev range by an extra 500rpm. Although it's technically a scrambler, it's built for more control and comfort; more importantly, it's versatile, easy to handle, and quite beautifully classical. The silver chrome glistens, beckoning me to it like a moth to firelight.

I strap on my helmet and swing my leg over the black seat, pleased to be back in my uniform: a faded Rolling Stones concert tour T-shirt, leather jacket, black biker boots, and jeans.

Eduardo had made me promise never to get back on a motorcycle. He'd said I was too precious, but I think he'd really been worried about our daughter. Under the circumstances, it's too late. That promise belonged to my last life and to a different woman – not me.

The engine purrs, and I feel the throbbing power beneath me as I glide into the busy Barcelona traffic. It's been a while since I've ridden a bike, but I haven't forgotten the love and freedom it gives me.

I would love to have shared this experience with my daugh-ter. Not all motorbike riders are crazy as Eduardo believes; most of us are respectful of roads, with a love of power and speed.

I'm certain that my daughter would have loved it, and I can almost hear her excited laughter as she squeals for me to go faster. Winding my way north of the city, I head for the Basílica de la Sagrada Família, the Gaudí-designed, familiar landscape, and then to the Parc Güell, Gaudí's mosaic masterpiece and museum. I'm exploring. Familiarising myself with one-way streets and roadworks, and dodging rented cars, getting used to my bike. I head back via the Plaça Catalunya to my destination in the Gothic Quarter.

I park, unhook my helmet, and lock the bike. I'm pleased with my purchase. This bike is a dream. It's a positive step in the right direction.

Mikky dos Santos is back.

* * *

When I buzz on the door of Umberto Palladino's studio, my heart is thumping. I'm suddenly reminded I was here in another life. Five days ago, I'd been exhausted after losing my daughter. Since then, I'd travelled to Poland and Estonia, putting my past firmly behind me. I'm after Nina and nothing and no one will stop me.

The door buzzes open.

I made a promise.

I push open the door.

As on my previous visit, the vast studio appears in disarray, with various shapes and pieces of work in progress; wood, metal, timber. Larger models and more complicated art pieces stand on the ground, all sizes and shapes, that mean nothing to me but will at some stage, in the future, come together in amazing designs. The process of design is complicated. Sculptures often involve many people. Unlike painting, creating sculptures often involves a team; designers, artists, and sculptors, who work together to prepare rough drafts, drawings, and sketches; and assistants, who make smaller models, replicating the bigger design. It all takes time, manpower, management, and energy.

I glance at the variety of work in progress on the tables across the untidy room and imagine Nina working here. I wander between the various benches, waiting for Umberto to pay me attention.

Is this what Nina would have done?

He works in isolation, concentrating and unconcerned I'm behind him. Once again, he's dressed in a grubby grey boiler suit, and this time he's welding a giant iron arm to a solid base of copper. Sparks fly. While he works, I walk toward the spiral staircase, and I have my hand on the rail and my foot on the bottom step when Umberto's voice rings out.

'What are you doing?'

'As you're busy, I was going to take a look upstairs.'

'Why?'

'Curiosity.'

He stares at me with undisguised annoyance. 'You've changed your hair.'

'I'm flattered you noticed.'

He doesn't reply, but instead, wipes his hands on a soiled cloth and coughs loudly. His features crease into an angry frown and he appears worn out, weary, and resigned.

El Pais, or any of the national or international press, haven't been kind or flattering in their account of the drone bomb. The general opinion is that, if Umberto was willing to make a creative political statement, then he must also accept the consequences of the risk that was always present. He's been criticised and slated just as much as some critics have been sympathetic and shocked.

'This is inconvenient, and it's not doing my reputation any good,' he grumbles. He doesn't offer me his hand in greeting, but continues to stare at me with bad humour.

'Are you referring to the bombing of *Los Globos* or the theft of Glorietta's sculpture?'

'It's nothing to do with me. I told you.'

'Well, that's the main thing, Umberto. At least you still got your money.' He doesn't bristle at my sarcasm, so I continue, 'Glorietta doesn't want any publicity. The theft of *The Bull* hasn't got into the newspapers, so what are you so afraid of?'

'My students and my clients are being interviewed by the police. It's an invasion of our privacy, and it affects my creativity. This is not good. I don't want you, the police, or anyone else nosing around my studio.'

'Are you frightened your ideas might be stolen?' I challenge, but he turns his back and covers up a few sketches with a cloth.

Why hadn't he told the police he'd fired Nina? They could have started their investigation with anyone who had a grudge against him, and Nina's professional anger and resentment would be more than a good enough reason for her to be investigated first. Had he kept her out of the picture for a reason?

Did he really steal her ideas?

'I'd have thought that you would want to find the culprit. Don't you want to know who bombed your precious sculpture?'

'I've already told the police everything I know.'

'Then why are you being so defensive?'

He sighs theatrically, reminding me of a blustering pantomime caricature, and I smile.

'What if I told you I found the sculpture that was stolen from the villa?'

Now I have his attention, and his frown deepens.

'But it was a fake,' I add.

'A fake?'

'I went to Tallinn, and I met your friend, Natasha. Did she buy *The Bear* from you?'

I watch the expression change on his face to one of curiosity.

'I don't divulge that type of information.'

'You don't have to. But, anyway, she was offered *The Bull*.'

'*The Bull*?'

'The thief who stole it from Glorietta's villa tried to sell *The Bull* to Natasha. Does that surprise you?'

'Did Natasha buy it?'

'I already told you – it was a fake.'

He continues to look confused.

'I checked the sculpture, Umberto. You showed me, remember? By looking under the hoof or the paw. *The Bear* had your initials, but they weren't on *The Bull*.'

'So, you haven't found *The Bull*?'

'Not the original, not the one you made for Glorietta. The one I saw came away in my hands. It was created quite recently. The glue hadn't dried, and it was made with newspaper from *El Pais*.'

'How is that possible?'

'I think someone made a fake – then swapped it. How long would it take to make a replica?'

He shrugs. 'Maybe a few weeks – months ... I don't know ... are you sure it wasn't *The Bull*?'

'Could your sculpture come apart and unravel?'

He shakes his head. 'I use a special glue, and there's a certain amount of drying time needed.'

'Perhaps they couldn't wait for it to dry?' I suggest. 'Maybe there wasn't time. Who would know about these techniques?'

'I have studio assistants. Anyone who studies and works here could find out this method – it's a creation that only I use.'

'It was a good copy but it wasn't as technically perfect as the one you made for Glorietta.'

'Then it definitely wasn't mine.' He turns away, as if I'm dismissed.

'No, but it was almost good enough for a Russian millionaire to – almost – pay for it,' I lie.

Umberto seems to consider what I've said, then he picks up tools randomly from the bench – a scalpel, a chisel, and a twisted piece of wire – and then places them back down on the bench again. He straightens them into a neat line, then messes up their alignment as he speaks.

'This is why I make my sculptures special, so that they cannot be copied. Do you understand nothing about art or originality?'

'Are there any students – a particular student – who would know how to use this technique?'

He shrugs. 'They learn here all the time. Great masters have great students. They are taken from the best universities because they show the most promise and talent. They are creative and eager to learn. They have youth and vigour on their side and an energy that is passionate and all-consuming. They're hungry for knowledge and greedy to learn. They often become better than us – better than the original, better than their own teachers, and that's how life is. I have spent years learning, experimenting, working hard, discovering new techniques, but then someone younger can come along, and they can do everything immediately – things that I have taken years to perfect. They haven't had to experiment and spend time learning the hard way. They haven't pondered for long enough to find solutions themselves. They are thieves and robbers who steal our knowledge. They're already learning from the masters at the top of the ladder.'

'It must be difficult – and a little annoying?'

'It's like the cycle of life – each generation must be more innovative, push more boundaries, and make a difference.'

'So, they think they're better than you?' I say, and he glares at me sharply before replying, 'There are some students who would make you think you have lost your touch, but not in my case.'

'An ego war?'

He ignores me.

'Do you think your collections make a difference?' I ask.

'To certain collectors – definitely.'

'You create for collectors?'

'I create for me. If they want to buy my work, then that's fine. I'm wealthy enough. I have a reputation. My work is mine – and mine alone.'

His arrogance, belligerence, and self-regard for his own greatness runs alongside his lack of sympathy and his denial at having any responsibility or culpability for anything. It makes me wonder what it takes to make someone that way.

'Do you feel angry when people make copies of your work?' I ask.

'It's not the same – it's like owning a Monet or owning a

fake Monet. The collector or the buyer knows the difference. They are the true appreciators of work, not the journalists or critics who write reviews, or the thieves that work in the auction houses. It's the individual. That special person who is prepared to pay the price for an original. It's only cheapskates – people who have no regard for true art and creativity – who are happy to settle for fakes or copies.'

'Obviously, money has nothing to do with it?'

As an art forger, I know how it works – I forged one of the greatest masterpieces of all time, and sometimes not even experts can tell the difference.

He doesn't reply, so I fold my arms, lean back against the bench, and wait. It must be equally as frustrating for a teacher; you show your students how to achieve new talents and new techniques, and then they come up with a more brilliant idea.

Did he copy from Nina or did she copy from him?

'Just supposing one of your students decided to make a copy of *The Bull*. Could they do that here in the studio without you realising?'

'I'm sure someone would notice. You'd need an extraordinary amount of paper, whatever you decided to use – even if it wasn't sheet music. You would have to source it from somewhere.'

'Do students take an interest in each other's work?'

'Sometimes. Students come and go all the time – sometimes they work upstairs, day and night. They have projects, and I have projects, and some of my work includes their help. We work as a team. I design, and someone else can physically do some of the work. That's why I have studio assistants. If we're working to a schedule or a strict timetable, then we all pull together.'

'I have a list of students.' I pull out my phone. 'Can you go through the list with me and tell me which ones would have the talent to make a replica of *The Bull*?'

'There's no point. I could say this one could or that one couldn't, but I would never know for sure.'

'Which students knew you were making *The Bull* for Glorietta?'

'None.'

'Really?'

He looks surprised. 'I create art, but the students don't always know my clients.'

'Could they have seen Bruno, here in your studio?'

He asks angrily, 'Why are you so convinced it's one of my students? It could be anyone.'

'It's definitely someone from here.'

I haven't played my ace card yet. I haven't confronted him with the complete truth, but I will if he isn't honest with me. I scan the names of the students and begin reading them aloud.

He scratches his head.

'Maybe someone made a fake copy, but a different person broke into the villa? Artists are thieves for ideas, but they don't steal tangible objects. Look, as far as I know, the students aren't even aware that *The Bull* has been stolen.' He picks up a hammer and weighs it, tossing it skilfully between his hands.

'And what about *Los Globos*? Who do you think sabotaged that?'

He slams the hammer on the worktop, and I jump.

'Enough!' he shouts. 'Enough of your pathetic attempts to play detective. The Guardia Civil are looking into it, so I suggest you stay out of it.' He tosses the work tool across the bench. 'I'm sick of you all.'

I put my boot on the bottom step, determined to see upstairs, and this time Umberto doesn't stop me. Instead, he
turns and walks away with determined strides. For him, our
conversation is finished.

* * *

I'm standing on the second step when I call out, 'What if it
was a prank? What if it was a joke – would someone want to
upset you or damage your reputation?'

'My students are serious. They're artists. I don't allow them
in here on a whim. They've worked hard to gain a place in this
studio. They must achieve certain criteria at university and
have the necessary recommendations, and even then, I choose
them with care. They're individually chosen by me. There's
not much to see upstairs, so hurry up and then get out.'

I continue up the circle of stairs to the brighter and lighter
studio space, where three students are working quietly, and I
wonder if they heard our exchange.

A dark-haired Japanese girl is sculpting an animal from
wood that resembles an owl. She glances up but doesn't take
any notice of me. Her long hair falls like a curtain over her
inscrutable face.

An older man, probably in his fifties, is leaning over a
concoction of melted tin. He appears old to be a student, unless
Umberto has older interns that work for him. His boots make
an indent in the warm metal at his feet, and he seems obsessed
with the shape and size of his achievement.

The third man is younger – in his early twenties – and
athletically built. He wears headphones, and he peers at me
from behind protective glasses. He's crafting something so

small I can't see it.

I sigh. It's all been a waste of time. None of them seems remotely interested in my presence, and I'm not sure what I had expected.

Who is Nina's boyfriend?

I trail my hands along the empty work stations, where absent students have left works in progress, and wonder where the fake bull was crafted. There doesn't seem to be anything resembling a mass of paper.

Natasha said Nina's boyfriend was weird?

Was it made as a deception to extract money, a prank, revenge, a game, a challenge?

Could Umberto have staged the drone bomb?

I walk around, but there is nothing else to be learned here. *I could ask the students questions, but what could I ask them that the police haven't already covered?*

I return downstairs to Umberto's studio, determined to get a result from my visit. I haven't finished with him yet. I still have my ace card to play. He is clearly surprised to see me again and his eyebrows knit together in a puzzled frown.

'What now?'

'Why didn't you tell the police about Nina?' I ask.

'Nina?'

'Nina Ruminov – the student you fired.'

The colour drains from his face.

'Bingo!' I say, hardly being able to keep the sarcasm from my voice. 'A reaction at last.'

'Nina isn't important.'

'Have you spoken to her?'

'No.'

'Why?' I fold my arms.

'There's no need.'

'How do you know?'

'She's not important.' He tosses a soiled rag onto the workbench. 'I need to work. I want you to go.'

'I can either ask you these questions now or tell the police. Believe me, they'll ask the same pertinent questions, so this is the easiest option. The quicker you tell me, the faster I will leave here. How long have you known Nina?'

'She worked in my studio in Milan,' he replies.

'But she came here to Barcelona, didn't she?'

'Only for a month, but that was last year. Why would she ...?' He pauses, as if working things out, and clarity appears in his eyes. He shakes his head.

'Nina has nothing to do with this.'

'Nina broke into Glorietta's villa and stole *The Bull*.'

'I don't believe you.'

'She took it to Estonia. She thought that because Natasha has *The Bear*, then she would buy it.'

'She tried to sell it to Natasha?' Umberto sits heavily on a stool and holds his forehead in his hands. 'I can't believe she would do something so stupid.'

'What can't you believe? That Nina would steal *The Bull* or that she would try and sell it to Natasha?'

He looks at me, considering my question.

'Nina's a complicated girl. She has problems. Severe problems.'

'Like what?'

He shakes his head. 'Have you proof she did this?'

'She tried to kill me.'

Umberto passes a hand over his face and rubs his head.

'She has a temper, and she can't always control her emotions.'

'She's also qualified in martial arts.'

'Yes.'

'How long did she work for you?'

He thinks back, calculating. 'She must have started six years ago with me in Milan. I can't remember all the details, but she was an exceptional student, and her work came to my attention. She worked on several projects. There was a commission by a gallery in London, the Tate or something, I can't remember the details, and then another in Athens, but she wasn't easy to work with. Some of the other students complained about her. She wanted to take short cuts, and she was always in a hurry.'

'Greedy for knowledge or greedy for fame?'

'She was a taker. You know the sort ... one that sucks you dry. No matter what you give, it's never enough. They want more. The fountain of knowledge. The elixir of life. The reason to be. The meaning of everything. She was intelligent but insatiable, and the problem was, she never digested anything properly. She was always onto the next step ... always in a hurry. She lacked the refinement of the thought processes that are integral to creative work – the foundations, the essence of what makes a sculptor original.'

'Did she have good ideas?'

'Of course, she wouldn't have worked with me otherwise. She's clever, intelligent, and creative, but she lacked the gene of a genius. She believed all her ideas were original, but they weren't. She chased fame. She wanted her work to be recognised and appreciated and, like most creative people, she couldn't hide her jealousy or her ambition.'

'Did she accuse you of stealing her ideas?'

'Is that what she told you?'

This time it's me who doesn't reply, and I stare at him for what seems a long time before he says, 'Look, she got things wrong. She said she'd submitted a project for an award to an art gallery many years ago in Milan. It was a coincidence that I was on the Board. I was one of the artists judging the award. She believed I stole her idea – yes.'

'Which one? The one using paper to create art—'

'Yes.'

'And, did you steal her idea?'

He sighs. 'Don't be ridiculous. Paper has been used in art for centuries.'

'But this sculpture was her idea?'

'*Los Globos* was my idea and my creation!' he shouts.

'You did it all alone?'

'It's normal to use a team on a project of this size. We make designs, and discuss weights, shapes, and the logistics for hanging and display.'

'Maybe her project was on a smaller scale, and you used her idea to create something bigger?'

'I don't remember her project.'

'That's convenient.'

'Don't call me a liar. She has no proof – and no idea is ever original. People have been pressing paper in Japan for centuries. This idea is mine. It's my trademark and my way of using an idea and extending it – as artists do.' His tone is one of practised patience, as if he's explaining things to a five year old, in a manner that might perhaps annoy his students.

'Did Nina have a boyfriend?'

'I don't know.'

'Was there anyone special? A friend that she worked with

. here, in the studio?'

He frowns. 'I don't remember.'

'Think. Think hard. This is important.'

'There may have been one guy ...'

'Really? Who?'

'I can't remember.'

I find Joachin's email on my phone.

'Look at this list of students. Do you recognise his name? It's important.'

Umberto leans forward and squints at the screen in my hand, and mumbles through the names. Then he points with a childlike finger, and I'm aware of his soft hands as his skin fleetingly touches mine. 'Him.'

'Antonio Gomez, are you sure?'

'Yes, I remember now, it was quite traumatic at the time when they separated.'

'For who?'

Umberto grins for the first time, revealing dirty, yellow-stained molars. 'For him. I think I remember someone saying he was her sex slave.'

'Really? Talking of sex, how well do you know Nina's sister?'

* * *

I let myself out of the studio and walk downstairs and out into the sunshine, remembering the rawness of my last visit and the pain in my stomach. Around the corner is the bar where I sat with Joachin, and I remember seeing Martin – Olivia's son – and his friends.

Umberto has provided me with a name, so I make my way to the bar where I sat before with the same vague idea: to keep an eye on the studio.

I order a beer and wait.

While I wait, I call Peter and give him a brief outline of my meeting with Umberto.

'The boyfriend's name is Antonio Gomez. He's one of the students,' I say.

'I'll get onto it,' Peter replies. 'We're sitting by the pool, but I've got my computer. I've traced Nina's Volvo. She crossed the Spanish border at eight this morning – three hours ahead of us.'

'So, she's here in Barcelona?'

'She should be. I'll check the street cameras. It should be quicker to find her now we know who we're looking for and the car she's driving.'

'I'll speak to Joachin,' I say.

I hang up and call Joachin. I tell him about my meeting with Umberto and Nina's boyfriend.

'Nina certainly has a motive,' I say. 'She'll probably stay somewhere cheap and near the city centre.'

'We'll keep checking. I'll get someone to check on Antonio Gomez and get back to you.'

As the waiter places sparkling water on the table for me, I look up and recognise a familiar face in the street walking past me. I remember him from the night of the party, taking pictures of Lorenzo and Maria.

'Martin?' I call out and wave. 'What a coincidence! It's me, Mikky dos Santos.' I laugh and run my fingers through my hair. 'Mikky – from Glorietta's party – I've dyed my hair.'

Olivia's son's face lights up in recognition. 'I didn't recognise you, Mikky. That's a new look.'

'You like it?'

'Very much.'

'Do you have time for a drink?'

'I'm meeting friends, and we're going to play football.'

'How's your mother?'

'She's good. She's at home.' His laughter is light and friendly. 'Dad's had to return to England for a few days on business, but he'll be back tomorrow night.'

'And Lorenzo – tell me, has he heard from Maria? Is he going to see her in Mallorca?'

He grins. 'I think they send text messages. They'll probably meet up at some stage later in the summer.' His face turns serious, and he tilts his head to one side. 'And how are you, Mikky?'

'I'm okay.'

'I thought you had gone – you know, back to Mallorca.'

'Not yet. I'm still trying to work out who could have stolen *The Bull*.'

'It was such a shocking thing to happen. Is there any progress?'

I shrug. 'Not really.'

'Well, I'd best be going. They can't manage without their goalkeeper.'

'Good luck!'

'Call in and see Mum. I'm sure she'd love to see you.' Martin kisses me on both cheeks. 'Take care, Mikky.'

* * *

I'm paying the bill when my phone rings.

'We've found her,' Joachin says. 'We've found Nina.'

'Where?'

245

'She's staying in a two-star hotel out near the airport. She checked in using her real name.'

'That was careless. When?'

'This morning.' The line goes quiet, then he says, 'I'll meet you in Plaça Cataluyna in fifteen minutes.'

'I'm on my way.'

Chapter 10

"Art-making is not about telling the truth but making the truth felt."
Christian Boltanski

'We're trying to locate Nina's whereabouts,' Joachin explains, sounding like a policeman. He's parked on yellow lines, and he keeps the engine running and the air conditioning on. I sit beside him in the passenger seat and rest my head back against the leather interior. 'She's not at the hotel.'

'Can you search her room?' I ask.

'We're not supposed to, but I managed to get a key from the housekeeper. It looks like she slept there, but probably only for a few hours. There's nothing in her bag, just a few clothes and toiletries.'

'Where are you heading now?' I ask.

'I'll try and get some more information on Antonio Gomez.'

'Are you working alone, Joachin?'

He drums his nails on the steering wheel. 'I have some help, but it's difficult. After the bombing of *Los Globos*, there was a terrorist incident reported in Sitges yesterday, and one this morning north of the city in Calella. Many officers have been redeployed. When there's a higher threat to security, national security is obviously more important.'

'What about the team working on the bombing of Umberto's sculpture?'

'Apart from witness statements, they've drawn a blank. Normally with a drone, there's a controller, but they couldn't find one. Forensics are still examining the bomb and drone, but these things take time – and we both know that we don't have that.'

'That's ridiculous it takes so long.'

'Think of how drones can close airports in minutes – all around Europe. Look at what happened in London. All European forces share the same problem – a lack of resources – but we must defend ourselves against the imminent threat of terrorism.'

'But what about your team?'

'There's a couple of us. I've got one near the hotel in case Nina returns, but now we have to find this Antonio Gomez. My team is spread very thinly. There just isn't the urgency, Mikky.'

'So, you mean it's just us?'

'Basically, it's just you and me. Unless something critical happens, then we might get some backup.'

'Great.' I can't hide my disappointment.

'There are people who want to help us, but their hands are tied unless we can prove it's urgent. You see, at the moment, it's not a matter of life and death.'

'It might be if Nina gets to Antonio,' I reply. 'If he did switch the sculpture for a fake, then I think she'll want to kill him.'

* * *

Plaça Cataluyna occupies an area of about 50,000 square metres and is known for its statues, fountains, and pigeons. It's one of my favourite squares, where avenues and streets come together, joining the different districts of the city, including the Gothic Quarter and Raval. It's where La Rambla, Passeig de Gràcia, and the nineteenth-century Eixample meet. Identified by its long, straight roads and grid-patterned streets, Barcelona is nothing but a heady mixture of art and architecture, a bustling city filled with vibrant life, virtually twenty-four hours a day. On any other occasion, I'd enjoy strolling through the streets, but I can't relax – something is troubling me.

I sit astride my bike and watch Joachin pull his car out into the traffic. Parked under the shade of a palm tree, I gaze at the distorted images reflected in my black helmet. All around me, traffic is flowing, horns blast, and engines whine as cars speed past then brake quickly.

I twist the helmet to catch the sunlight, watching the myriad of colours.

I've missed something.

Something important.

Is it Peter?

Aniela?

Umberto?

What have I missed?

A conversation.

On the plane?

Martin?

Aniela had thanked me for going to find Peter in Tallinn. She said everyone had given up on him. He was living like a recluse. At first, Peter didn't want to help me. Martin thought I'd gone to Mallorca. *Why?*

Olivia.

Why did she send me to a man who was suffering from PTSD and a man who had given up on life?

Why did she send me to Tallinn?

I pull out my phone.

'Peter?' I say. 'Why couldn't I have sent you the CCTV video from the villa electronically?'

'You could have done, but I'm pleased you didn't.'

'You didn't specifically say I had to go to Wrocław in person.'

'No.'

'Who contacted you about helping me? Was it a good friend?'

'No, I barely knew him. He said he'd seen how bad I was in hospital and I guess he wanted to help me.'

'He knew you weren't in great shape?'

'He was the chaplain.'

My bike roars into life, and I strap my helmet under my chin. There's only one way to find out the truth. I slide out into the traffic with a nagging feeling that Olivia sent me deliberately out of the country – to get me out of the way.

But why?

* * *

I ease my bike toward the gated community of Olivia and Jeff's luxury apartment in Diagonal Mar, a vibrant, multicultural area with shopping malls, beaches, restaurants, and bars. It's a cosmopolitan and modern suburb and is one of the best residential areas of the city, with fantastic sea views – an ideal spot to live and only fifteen minutes from the city centre.

But Olivia is not at home.

I park across the road opposite her building and scan the recent call list on my phone to find her number. She called me five days ago to give me Peter's number.

She found him through a chaplain?

I call her mobile number, and when she doesn't pick up, I leave a brief message. I'm wondering where Nina is and if she's found Antonio Gomez when Olivia's car glides past me and stops at the gate.

I recognise her profile immediately.

I replace my helmet and start the engine. I'm about to follow her inside the complex, but she's not alone. She parks her Mercedes and a young man climbs out of the passenger door.

He's like Martin − handsome, with broad shoulders and narrow hips − but it isn't Martin, it isn't Lorenzo, and when he grins at her, he seems vaguely familiar.

Years of being an artist and photographer have given me good facial recognition memory. I watch the boy laughing. He places his arm around her waist, and he lets her enter the communal front door first.

Is he a friend of Martin's?

I recall Martin and Lorenzo, and their friends who played football. Nacho? And who? Antonio?

He seems familiar. There was a boy upstairs in Umberto Palladino's studio wearing headphones and protective glasses.

It couldn't be the same Antonio, could it?

Surely someone would have said that Martin's friend was a student of Umberto Palladino's?

I'm deciding what to do when Bruno calls me, and I continue to stare at Olivia's front door as we speak.

'Mikky,' he says brightly. 'I just spoke to Joachin, and he has brought me up to date. He also tells me you're staying at the Hotel Arts. You know you're welcome to stay here at the villa.'

'Thank you, Bruno. It's just that I came back with friends – my friends Peter and Aniela are having a mini-honeymoon.' It's not a complete lie.

'Where are you now?' he asks.

'I went to see Umberto.'

'He called me after you left. He's very upset. You told him a fake sculpture turned up in Estonia.'

'I should have brought it back with me, so that he could see it for himself. How long are you staying in the villa for?' I ask.

'There's not much more I can do. The police don't need me. Glorietta's tour is finishing in Tokyo at the weekend, so I may fly out for a few nights and meet her.'

'I'll call up to the villa and see you before you go.'

'Great.'

'Bruno, your friends – Olivia and Jeff – how well do you know them?'

'There was no better bodyguard than Olivia. Glorietta enjoyed her company. But now she's retired, Olivia and Jeff spend more time with Filippa and Antonio. Their sons are good friends – Martin and Lorenzo. Why?'

'It's not important,' I lie.

'Bring your friends to the villa for dinner, Mikky. Come tomorrow night. I'd like to meet them.'

'I'll let you know.'

After I hang up, I sit thinking about Olivia and the boy inside her apartment. Could Olivia be involved? I'm wondering what to do when Joachin phones me.

'Any new on Nina?' I ask.

'She's waiting outside an apartment near the Parc Güell. I

think she's looking for someone. I'm on my way there.'

'You're watching her?'

'I've got one of my men onto it. We're hoping she will lead us to Antonio Gomez.'

'Who lives in the apartment?'

'We're trying to find out.'

'Do you have an address for Antonio?'

'Not yet. It might be his apartment she's watching.'

'Let me know.' I hang up.

If the boy in Olivia's apartment is the second thief – Antonio Gomez – then I'd swear on my life that Nina is staking out his apartment.

Olivia seems to be the link.

I check my watch and dial her number again. She doesn't pick up, and the answerphone clicks to voicemail.

'Hi, Olivia, it's Mikky. I'd love to chat when you have a few minutes. If you can, call me back – I'm in your area.'

I almost add that I'm sitting outside her front gate, but I don't.

I want to know what she's doing. I could storm her apartment, but how would I get in? I could ring the bell? But then what?

So, I sit astride my bike, on the main street, looking through the railings and watching the front door of Olivia's apartment building. My back aches, so I pace up and down and stretch my legs. Then I sit on the step of a residential building in the shade.

It's almost two hours later when the front door opens and the boy comes out of the building. The door closes automatically behind him and he stops on the steps to adjust the straps on his backpack. It's a large rucksack, as if he's been staying with her or is going on a camping holiday.

I snap his photograph on my iPhone, confident that he's not aware of me amongst the other pedestrians and traffic on the far side of the railings. He walks out of the gate and around the corner.

Do I visit Olivia or follow him?

It takes me a few seconds to decide. I follow him on the opposite side of the tree-lined street, twenty yards away, ready to dodge behind a parked car if he turns around.

He pulls out his phone and slows down as he walks and talks. He doesn't turn around. He doesn't look to see if he's being followed. He turns another corner onto the main road and I run to catch up with him just in time to see him hop on a bus. The door closes behind him, and I'm left watching him head back to the city centre, wondering if he's going back to Umberto Palladino's studio.

I text Joachin and Peter with his picture.

'Is this him?' I text. 'Is this Antonio Gomez?'

* * *

Olivia answers her front door. She's wearing summer trousers and a loose top. She's barefoot, still tanned, and attractive. Gold bangles jingle on her wrists, and there's a gold crucifix at her throat. At first, she doesn't recognise me, but then her mouth turns into an O-shape.

'Mikky?'

'I had to get a new look.' I smile and run my fingers through my short cut. 'But I've grown quite attached to it now.'

'How did you get in ...?'

She looks over my shoulder, into the corridor, as if searching for someone.

'A neighbour was leaving,' I lie, smiling.

It hadn't been hard to press someone else's buzzer and tell them about a fake delivery. 'I hope you don't mind me just calling in?'

'I've only just got home.' This time she is lying to me.

I smile back. 'That's lucky, then.'

'Come in. I love your new hairstyle.'

I follow her along the corridor, glancing in the kitchen. In the lounge, there's a discarded turquoise cushion on the floor. She picks it up, dusts it with her hands, and places it back on the grey, L-shaped sofa, and smiles weakly before guiding me onto the terrace to the same spot where I sat almost a week ago. The glass-topped table has two partially drunk glasses of wine, and the bottle is empty.

'Water? Drink?' She follows my gaze. 'Martin is so untidy. He never clears up.'

'I've been calling you,' I say.

'Have you? Sorry, I haven't checked my phone. I don't even know where my bag is.' She laughs and the bangles on her wrist chime.

'Water would be lovely.'

She picks up the dirty glasses and wine bottle and disappears inside. I lean over the balcony and stare across the shaded gardens to the sea beyond, marvelling at the calm quiet of the apartment and the cool shade of the terrace. I'd guessed correctly. The apartment didn't overlook the road where I had waited.

I follow her down the corridor toward the kitchen, my boots silent on the polished marble floor. Olivia is standing at the central island. She's delved into her handbag, and she's looking at her reflection in a compact mirror and hurriedly applying lipstick.

'I thought I'd come and help,' I say.

She jumps and stuffs the compact back into her handbag, composing herself quickly.

'How have you been?' she asks brightly, ignoring my bruises.

'Fine.'

She pours chilled water from the fridge into a jug and reaches for two glasses. I offer to carry the tray, but she waits for me to go ahead of her, leading the way back outside to the calm solitude of the sea view.

'I bumped into Martin,' I say, as we sit down.

'Really? Where?'

'I was in town, and I called into Umberto's studio.'

'Today?'

'Yes.'

She regards me carefully, and there's a slight narrowing of her eyes.

'Didn't you go to Poland?' she asks. 'What about Peter?'

'He couldn't help me,' I lie. 'It was a bit of a wild goose chase to go all that way to Poland – a waste of time. He was a veteran, handicapped with PTSD, so I'm back.'

'Really? I'm sorry he couldn't help you.'

'But you're not surprised?'

'Well, I didn't know him personally. He was a friend of a friend and you just never know how these things will work out, do you?'

'He'd had a bad time in Afghanistan.' I sip my water. 'He wasn't coping with life very well.'

'Oh,' she says, 'but you were desperate, weren't you, and

we were clutching at straws, weren't we?'

'We? Yes.'

'It's a shame I couldn't help. You look exhausted, Mikky.'

The water is deliciously cold on the back of my bruised throat, and I take my time, forming my words carefully. Olivia is not as relaxed as she had been on my previous visit.

'I haven't had much sleep. I've been chasing around, so it's been a bit crazy.' I place my glass back on the table. 'How's Jeff? Is he playing golf today?'

'Er, no. He's in London. He had to check on some business over there.'

'You must miss him.'

'I'm lucky I have friends, and I lead a busy life. So, what are your plans now, Mikky? Are the police any further forward with their investigation? Is there any news?'

I shrug. 'I'm not sure.'

'They came to speak to me.'

'Did they?'

'I think it was the day after you left. They asked me all the usual things, but of course, I couldn't help them. I don't know anything.' She waves her hand in the air and shrugs. 'I feel so sorry ... if only I could help.'

Her eyes are downcast, and she touches her stomach in sympathy for my loss, which only antagonises me.

'Did you tell the police that you are friends with one of the boys in Umberto's studio?'

'Pardon?'

'Antonio. Did you tell the police about him?'

'Antonio?' she repeats.

'The boy that left here a few minutes before I knocked on the door.'

She pauses before responding. 'Have you been watching me?'

'How do you know him?'

'I think you should leave.' She stands up, and when I don't move, she says, 'I don't have any more to say to you, Mikky. My personal life is not up for scrutiny by you or by anyone else. It's time you left.'

* * *

'Don't you think it's a bit of a coincidence that *The Bull* is stolen and you know a student working in Umberto's studio?'

'No.'

'Did you tell the police when they visited you, how well you know Antonio?'

'It's not relevant.'

'So, how well do you know Antonio?'

'That's none of your business. Get out!'

'If you don't tell me, Olivia, then you will have to tell the police,' I say quietly. 'You've been playing me for a fool.'

'Get out!' She points at the door and shouts. 'Now!'

I cross my legs, fold my arms and lean back. 'You see, when I leave here, I will go straight to the Inspector and tell him that you're involved with the theft of *The Bull*. It was your idea.'

'NO!'

'Then tell me.'

'It's not like that!' She turns away and hugs her body.

'I will prove it, Olivia. Believe me,' I whisper. 'I have nothing to lose. My daughter died.'

'No.' She sinks to the sofa and places her face in her hands and says nothing, so I continue speaking and I pull out my mobile.

'You have one minute to tell me what you know. The Inspector will be very happy with this breakthrough – this new discovery is just what he's looking for. It's not a coincidence that you were at Glorietta's party night. *The Bull* was stolen. You knew Antonio worked in Umberto Palladino's studio where the sculpture was made. You told him about the sculpture. You gave Antonio the information he needed. Did you also give him the alarm code for the front door? You are the link, Olivia. The link that I've been looking for and you deliberately sent me away.'

When she looks up, there are tears in her eyes. 'It's not like that.'

'Then you'd better tell me.'

'Oh, God!'

'Ten seconds.' I wave my mobile in the air.

'Promise you'll tell no one. My family must never find out.'

'You're not in a position to barter Olivia, so get started and keep me interested.'

* * *

'He's a friend of Martin's.'

'What's his name?'

'Antonio Hernandez. His parents are friends of ours. Jeff plays golf with his father.'

'Hernandez?'

'Yes.'

I pull out my phone and scan the list. There are two Antonio's on the list: Antonio Gomez and Antonio Hernandez. Umberto had pointed to Antonio Gomez. Has he sent us chasing the wrong man? Did he do that deliberately?

'Keep talking, Olivia?'

'Antonio comes here sometimes, and we talk.'

'About what?'

'Different things: life, girls, stuff like that. I regard him as my son.'

'How does Martin feel about that?'

'He's fine with it. They all get on well. Martin, Lorenzo, Antonio and Nacho. They all play football together.'

'Did Martin tell the police he knows Antonio Hernandez?'

'I assume so.'

Now there are three people at the party linked to Antonio, and three people who knew about the sculpture: Olivia, Martin and Lorenzo.

'Was Antonio involved in the theft of *The Bull*?'

'Don't be ridiculous. Antonio isn't serious enough to do anything as glamorous at that. He's a playboy. He flirts and plays around. He's his father's son. He's a spoilt rich boy who gets everything he wants.'

'But he's a student?'

'He dabbles …'

'Umberto tells me he only takes on the best.'

'Antonio doesn't take it seriously. He doesn't take anything seriously.'

'But he wanted *The Bull*?'

'You've got the wrong person. He likes to have fun.'

'With you?'

'No!'

'So, why did you bring him back with you this afternoon? What did you do?'

'You have been watching me.'

'I was waiting outside and then, by coincidence, you showed up. He was in here for a couple of hours. What were you talking about?'

She shakes her head. 'It's none of your business.'

'What were you doing?' I insist.

'Look, this is all private and has nothing to do with the theft of *The Bull*.' She slaps the palms of her hands together in frustration, and I wonder what sort of a woman would become a bodyguard.

One who takes risks? One who likes danger?

'What sort of person is Antonio?'

My question appears to take her by surprise.

'He's funny and charming ... but he's not a thief.'

'He could be both.'

She takes a deep breath and seems to consider my question. 'He's mature, interesting, clever and obviously very creative. He's exciting.'

'How did you meet him?'

'I told you, he's a friend of Martin's.'

'With Lorenzo and Nacho – and they all play football to-gether ...' I can't hide the sarcasm, but she ignores me.

'They've been friends for a while now. I've known them years.'

'How long?'

'Martin met Antonio a couple of years ago when they were about eighteen, nineteen.'

'And when did you start seeing him on your own? Please don't lie.'

She stares at me and replies sullenly.

'About six months ago.'

'Does Jeff know?' She doesn't reply so I answer for her. 'Of course, Jeff doesn't know. He doesn't know you're having an affair with Antonio. No one does, and you don't want anyone to find out. Is that the truth?'

'It's not like that—'

I stand up. 'Will we go to your bedroom, Olivia? I'd take a guess you spent the last two hours in bed with Antonio. That's why you didn't answer your phone, and you were hastily applying lipstick in the kitchen.'

'God, Mikky, why do you have to do this?' She rubs her temple.

'Because I need to know the truth.'

'He didn't steal anything.'

'But he knew about the sculpture. He knew Umberto was designing it for Glorietta's birthday.'

'I suppose so, yes.'

'You must have discussed it with him.'

'He knows nothing about it.'

She's lying.

'You set me up, didn't you? You sent me to Poland to meet Peter – a man that you thought couldn't possibly help me. A man you'd been told couldn't help anyone – not even himself. I could have sent him the tape electronically but you said I had to take it personally to Wrocław. Why? I'll tell you why – it was to get me out of the way.'

I can almost hear the mechanisms of her brain whirling and clunking to find the next lie.

'I didn't want anyone to find out about our affair. I was frightened you or someone would start asking too many questions. It would kill Jeff if he found out and besides, I was determined to end it.'

'It didn't look like that this afternoon.'

'I know.'

'So you haven't ended it?'

'No.'

'Why?'

She sighs. 'God, Mikky! You have no idea what's it's like being married to a man who has no interest in you. Jeff plays golf all day, and when he isn't on the golf course he's drinking with his friends, or he's on the phone to a supplier in England. I joke that I'm a golf widow, but it's true! It's seriously awful to wake up and realise that you've retired and your life is over. There's no excitement left.' She reaches for her water. 'It's awful when the man that used to worship and adore you has lost his desire for sex. I used to lead an amazing life. I travelled the world before I retired. I had responsibility, and there was danger, glamour, and I lived a full life, but now, now I do nothing.'

'You screw young boys. It can't be all that bad.'

'It's not a crime,' she shouts. 'And I love him. He's fun. He has a wicked sense of humour, and he's exciting to be with – there. Now you know everything and before you ask – yes – the sex is great. He's inventive and innovative, and I love it. He makes me feel like a woman. He makes me feel loved and wanted. Is that so bad? It certainly isn't a crime, Mikky.'

I see her point of view, but I'm not as emotionally moved as she would like me to be.

'I have CCTV footage from the villa the night of Glorietta's party. I'm going to study the images again and if I find out that Antonio was involved in any way – then I will come back here. I will hold you personally responsible for wasting my time.'

'I haven't wasted your time, I promise.'

I stand up and hitch my bag over my shoulder.

'I took a picture of him leaving your apartment. It should be pretty easy to match the images to the CCTV. There is all sorts of technology now – visual facial recognition – it won't be too difficult.'

She shakes her auburn mane. 'Please, Mikky. Don't do this.'

'I don't suppose the name Nina Ruminov, means anything to you?'

'No.' She shakes her head and pushes her hair behind her ears. I'm about to let myself out of the front door, and I have my hand on the handle when it opens.

I step back in surprise.

Martin is on the threshold, about to let himself in. He laughs and kisses me on both cheeks, genuinely pleased to see me.

'It's great you popped in to see Mum,' he says. 'She's been a bit low lately.'

'Really, why?'

'Probably because Dad is in London.'

I glance over my shoulder. Olivia hasn't followed me. She's still on the terrace.

'Martin, just a quick question. Did you tell the police that you know Antonio Hernandez?'

He gives me a strange look and tilts his head to one side, so I say.

'You know Antonio, the one who works in Umberto Palladino's art studio.'

'Of course, I know him. Why?'

'You never mentioned it to me.'

'Sorry, I must have forgotten.'

'Your mum is outside on the terrace,' I say, and I push past him wondering if they have been deliberately obtrusive, plain stupid or more importantly if they are both lying.

* * *

I walk out of the building and into the sunshine. I fumble in my pocket for my sunglasses and take the path beside the garden to the community gate. I've almost reached my bike when I hear a voice calling me.

'Mikky! Mikky!'

I pause, standing with my helmet in my hand.

'Look, I just want to say that I didn't mention about Antonio working in Umberto's studio as I didn't think it was important.' He's breathless and a little flushed.

'Really?'

'Yes, I mean, just because he works there, it doesn't mean anything, does it?'

'The police would be the best judge of that.'

'He hasn't done anything wrong. I mean, he's not involved with that structure going on fire or the theft. Antonio's not like that.'

'What is he like?'

'Like?'

'Yes – as a person. According to your Mum, he's great fun, intelligent and creative.'

Martin smiles. 'I don't think she knows him that well ...'

'Don't they chat?'

'I don't think so.' He looks baffled.

He obviously has no idea they've spent this afternoon together or any other afternoon – having sex. They've been very careful to keep their relationship and their emotions a secret – up until now.

265

'Where does he live?'

'Over near the Parc Güell.'

Warning bells go off in my head. Joachin said that Nina was waiting and appeared to be staking out an apartment – in that same district.

'Does he live on his own?'

' He shares with Nacho.'

'What does Nacho do?'

'He's an engineering student. Why?'

'Where are Nacho and Antonio now?'

'Nacho is going to the cinema this evening with his girl-friend. They're probably at the beach now, and ... I'm not sure about Antonio.'

'He hasn't played football today?'

'Not today, no. He was supposed to come this afternoon, but he didn't show up. He's been a bit like that lately, but that happens when he goes through a creative spell – he shuts himself away.'

I don't have the heart to tell Martin that Antonio spent the afternoon in bed with his mother. I don't have to because my iPhone rings and Joachin's name comes up and I turn away.

'Hello.'

'Mikky, we've lost Nina.'

'I thought she was under surveillance.'

'She skipped into El Corte Ingles and went out of a different entrance about thirty minutes ago.'

El Corte Ingles is one of Spain's most popular departmental stores. It's a massive building with entrances and exits onto different streets. It would have been my choice of venue if anyone was following me and I wanted to lose them.

'Check out Antonio Hernandez, he's another student of

Umberto's, and I think he lives in the apartment that Nina was watching.'

'It's not Antonio Gomez?' he asks.

'No.'

'Mierda!'

Chapter 11

"The essence of a sculpture must enter on tip-toe, as light as animal footprints on snow."
Jean Arp

'What's Antonio's phone number?' I ask Martin.

'What's going on?'

'Give me his number.' I call Peter and say, 'Can we use that phone number trick to track someone again if I give you a phone number?'

'Whose is it?' Peter asks.

'Antonio Hernandez's – he's a friend of Olivia's son Martin. He studies with Umberto in Barcelona, and he's on the list.'

Peter whistles. 'You've been busy.'

'Can you do it?'

Martin shows me Antonio's number on his phone, and I read out the number to Peter.

'Give me a little time, and I'll call you back.'

'What's going on, Mikky?' Martin asks.

'Is this him?' I hold up my mobile and show Martin the picture of Antonio leaving Olivia's apartment almost an hour ago.

'Yes.'

I gaze at the photograph.

Something's not right.

'Mikky? Who were you talking to on the phone? Was that the police? Do they want to find Antonio?'

I ignore him and begin running across the road, back through the gated residence to the front door of the building. Martin appears beside me.

'What are you doing?' he asks breathlessly.

'Open the door. Hurry up! I need to speak to your mum.'

'Why?'

'Come on, hurry!' I urge him to open the door, then I run up the stairs two at a time. Martin has long legs, and he bounds up effortlessly beside me, fumbling for his front door key.

'Tell me what's going on, Mikky!' he demands.

'Just open the bloody door!'

He pushes it open, and I run down the corridor.

'Olivia!' I shout. 'Olivia?!'

Olivia isn't in the kitchen or the lounge, or on the terrace.

'Where is she?' I ask.

Martin grabs my arm. 'Stop it! Mikky, what are you doing? What's going on?'

I push him off and call out again, 'Olivia!'

She opens a door, and over her shoulder, I can see she is in the middle of making her double bed. She flinches and closes the door quickly, and we stand facing each other in the corridor.

'What's wrong?' she asks.

'Antonio left here with a rucksack this afternoon,' I reply. 'He didn't arrive with it.'

'Antonio?' Martin repeats beside me. 'He was here?'

'What was in it?' I ask.

269

'I don't know what you're talking about.'

'Yes, you do,' I say, raising my voice. 'You've kept it here all along, haven't you? *The Bull* has been in this apartment all the time.'

The bag would easily hold a sculpture the size of *The Bull*. I can't believe I missed it. I have no proof, and it's a wild guess, but when I see the expression on Olivia's face, I know I'm right. I'm fired up with anger and frustration, and I don't care who knows about her sordid affair.

'If you don't tell me where he is, Antonio could get killed,' I say.

'What?!' Martin is more shocked than Olivia. 'Mum? What's going on?'

'Oh, God!' Olivia covers her mouth and looks at her son. She turns as pale as the marble tiles in the hallway, then suddenly she pushes past us.

'Where has Antonio gone?' I demand, following her into the kitchen.

'He's gone to play football.'

'Bullshit!' I say.

'Mum, what are you talking about? There's no football practice this evening,' Martin says. 'It was this afternoon, and Antonio missed it.'

'He had a phone call. I assumed it was something to do with football.' She turns away, unable to meet our combined gaze and my accusations.

'Who called him?' I ask.

'I don't know – maybe it was Nacho.'

'Nacho is with his girlfriend,' Martin says, clearly bewildered. 'They've gone swimming, then they're going to the cinema. Why was Antonio here, Mum? What's going on?'

270

I wait for her to explain, but she doesn't. She can't lie quickly enough. She walks to the fridge and pours a glass of chilled white wine. She doesn't offer us a drink, and as she raises it to her lips, her hands are shaking. She challenges me with a defiant stare, and I see the bravery that she would have shown as a bodyguard. Her face is a mask.

Once Martin knows about her affair with his friend, their mother and son relationship will never be the same. I wonder how Jeff will take the news that his wife has been sleeping with a man the same age as their son.

'All I want to know is where he's gone. The rest of the details I'll leave you to tell Martin,' I say. 'This is your opportunity to get rid of me, but if you lie, I'll be back.'

'What details? What lies?' Martin looks quizzically at his mother, but she doesn't reply. 'What's going on?!' he shouts.

'Antonio stole *The Bull* from Glorietta's villa,' I reply.

'Antonio?' he repeats, completely puzzled.

'I have no loyalty to a woman who has lied, misled me, and sent me to Poland to get me out of the way,' I say, then I add, 'And I believe your mum helped him.'

'I didn't help him!' she cries.

'Did you, Mum?' Martin asks.

'I had nothing to do with it. She's lying.'

'Martin doesn't believe you,' I say.

'He wouldn't steal it,' Olivia says angrily. 'Antonio wouldn't do that!'

'Why not?' I ask.

It's Martin who answers. 'Well, he doesn't need the money. He's not poor. Bloody hell, his parents are rolling in it – although his father is a control freak. Why would he do it?'

In the silence after his question, it's Olivia who replies.

271

'He took it for fun.'

'Fun!' Martin's eyes widen, and he steps away to consider this idea, staring at the floor like he can see an invisible picture reflected in the cool tiles.

Olivia leans against the counter, one arm across her chest, sipping wine.

'He's devilish. He thinks it's a fun thing to do … you know, he likes to live life dangerously.'

'Fun?' Martin repeats. 'Has he gone bloody nuts?'

'So, he did tell you what he'd done?' I move nearer to her. 'He told you. He confessed, didn't he?'

'He was confused. He came to me afterwards. I think he wanted to fool the experts. He wanted to replace the original with a fake. It was a prank – a stupid schoolboy idea – he thought he was better than everyone else. He wanted to pretend it was Umberto's and worth a fortune. It was a social experiment. He wanted to prove that people buy sculptures because of Umberto's name, not because they are great art,' Olivia says with a sigh.

'He stole *The Bull*?' Martin asks, his face a picture of incredulity. 'Are you serious?'

'He wanted to prove that an imitation – a fake – is the same as a real artwork, and that people wouldn't be able to tell the difference. He wanted to prove that if people didn't know the truth, then they would happily accept a fake as a real work of art.'

'So, he stole *The Bull*?' Martin repeats.

'It was a silly, stupid idea.' She looks at me. 'Antonio didn't want to hurt you, and he's gutted that you lost your baby. He blames himself, and he's very sorry.'

'It was all a game to him?' I ask.

'Yes.'

'A stupid prank?' I repeat.

'Yes.'

'I lost my baby because of a spoilt rich kid's prank?'

'He told you this?' Martin asks his mum.

'Yes. He told me today – this afternoon. That's why he came here – to talk to me ...'

She's a clever liar. Almost as good as me.

How far will she go to protect him?

'What did you tell him to do?' I ask.

'I told him to go to the police.'

'You told him that this afternoon?'

'Yes.'

'So, *The Bull* was in the bag?'

'Yes.'

'Will he?' Martin asks. 'Will he go to the police?'

Olivia shakes her head. 'He wants to put it back.'

I look at her. 'Put it back where?'

'He's got an idea that if he puts it back in the villa, then no one will be any the wiser and they won't know that it was him who took it.'

'What an idiot!' Martin says, leaning against the counter. 'What a bloody fool. How could he be so stupid?'

'He's made a mistake. A very stupid mistake,' she agrees.

'He believes he's as good as Umberto Palladino,' Martin whispers. 'God! This will ruin him.'

'His career doesn't have to be over.' Olivia reaches over and clutches Martin's hand. 'It was a silly mistake, but it can be put right. Antonio can sort it out.'

'Putting *The Bull* back in the villa as if nothing has happened will not sort it out.' I grip my fists. 'Any more than you

273

pretending that you haven't been having an affair will sort things out.'

Martin pulls away from his mother.

'Affair?' he repeats. 'You've been having an affair – with him?' Martin backs away, shaking his head.

'Darling, it isn't like that,' she says, reaching out for him, but he takes another pace backwards.

'Before you get into this sentimental crap, I need information, Olivia. You're not off the hook yet. I need to find Antonio.'

Olivia's eyes are burning. I think if she could, right at this moment, she would kill me. The feeling is mutual.

She's endorsed Antonio's bad behaviour, excusing his actions as if this was all just a harmless schoolboy prank, but he's older than that. He's a man, and he has to take responsibility for his actions. His inflated ego has been supported and boosted by Olivia's refusal to stand up to him. She should have told him it was wrong. She's failed him as a lover, as a friend, and as a mother figure. She's allowed him to pretend it was fun – a naughty daredevil stunt, all part of his charm and excitement.

'What about Nina? Where does she fit into your neatly made-up story?'

'Who's Nina, Mum?'

'I don't know what she's talking about!' Olivia slams her glass on the counter. 'I've told you what I know, and now you should go!'

'Oh, I haven't even begun yet. If Martin is going to know the truth, then let's tell him everything – or didn't you know that Nina and Antonio are lovers?'

Olivia's eyes widen, and I continue, 'Didn't he tell you about his Russian girlfriend? They decided to steal *The Bull* together, so that ends your pathetic attempt to cover up for him, or was it your idea to steal *The Bull*? After all, you've kept it hidden here for six days.'

'Mum, did you? How could you do that?'

'I didn't know anything about Nina,' she says quietly.

'Do you mean the Nina – the Russian – who worked in Umberto's studio?' Martin asks.

'Do you know her?'

'I've met her a couple of times. They were besotted with each other.'

'How long ago?'

'Six months ago, longer, maybe. She does kickboxing, martial arts, and stuff like that.'

'She tried to kill me in Tallinn.'

'Tallinn?' he repeats.

I point out the bruise around my neck. 'She was trying to sell a fake copy of *The Bull*. She had no idea that Antonio was one step ahead of her and that he'd swapped it before she drove to Estonia with the fake.'

'No – he wouldn't.' Olivia clutches the crucifix at her throat and places it in her mouth.

'He double-crossed her. He's known exactly what he's doing, and he's played you for a fool, Olivia. When did you last see Nina, Martin?'

He seems surprised, dazed – and has to think.

'A few months ago. It was Nacho's birthday, and she turned up looking for Antonio. I thought she'd left and gone back to Milan or somewhere. Antonio was surprised. He'd moved on; he was with another girl that night – Danish, I think she was ...' Olivia flinches, but Martin keeps speaking. 'Antonio always has a different girl, but he liked Nina a lot.'

'Does she have a hold over him?'

'She gave him a few Es – that sort of thing – and maybe a bit of coke.'

'Drugs?' Olivia asks.

'Ecstasy tablets, Mum. Antonio loves getting a buzz. He loves the thrill. Excitement. He's pretty wild when he gets going. I just never thought he'd do something as stupid as to break into the villa and steal that sodding sculpture.'

'I've got them both on CCTV.'

Martin shakes his head. 'Mum, did you know what he was planning to do?'

'No.'

'But you helped him – you kept *The Bull* here in our home?'

She puts down her glass. She's playing for time; she needs to think, requires longer to make up another lie.

Martin and I wait for her to answer.

'He came to me because he didn't know where else to go.'

'When?'

'A few days afterwards – after the party.'

'But why you?' Martin asks.

'He knows my background – my police experience – and I tried to help him. I told him to tell the truth.' She's a smooth liar, but I'm not sure Martin believes her, either.

'How long did you keep the backpack here for?' I ask.

She shrugs.

'How long?!' I shout.

She flinches. 'A few days. I didn't know what was inside it.'

'Didn't you look?'

'No.'

'You're an ex-cop,' I say.

'He told me he was going to give it back,' Olivia says. 'And I

276

believed him. He's a good boy. He's talented. He has so much to offer the world. He doesn't deserve to have his career or his life ruined because of one silly mistake.'

'Mistake? It was a deliberate, premeditated theft. I came to you for help, and you sent me to Poland to get me out of the way, so that you could join in with his faking game.'

She doesn't reply.

'What about the drone bombing of Umberto's sculpture? You'll be telling me next that he had nothing to do with that, either?'

'He didn't. He promised me.'

'And you believe him?'

'He deserves an opportunity to put everything right.'

'Not like Mikky, then? What about her?!' Martin shouts. 'What about her baby and her life?' He storms toward the door and shouts over his shoulder, 'You disgust me.'

* * *

I also leave the apartment quickly at that point. There's no time to lose. I call Peter. He tells me to text Antonio Hernandez and to give him the phone number, which he reads out to me.

'That way, we can track him. Just like we did with Nina in Estonia,' he explains.

I type:

Antonio – I need to speak to you urgently. I've spoken to Olivia. There's no problem. I can help you. Message me on this number. Mikky dos Santos.

I call Peter. 'Done!'

'Give it a few minutes, and I'll tell you if it works. We need him to open and read the message.'

I imagine Peter hunched over his computer, tapping the keys, his face creased in concentration.

'Where are you?'

'Outside Olivia's apartment. She came home with Antonio Hernandez – he's a friend of her son's and a student of Umberto Palladino's, and they've been having an affair ...'

Peter whistles.

'He and Nina stole *The Bull*, and afterwards, Olivia kept his rucksack with *The Bull* here in her apartment.'

'That's the Olivia who sent you to me?'

'She did it to get rid of me. She thought you'd never be able to help me.'

'Well, she's underestimated both of us.' I can hear the triumph in his voice.

'I saw Antonio this morning when I went to Umberto's studio.'

'He didn't recognise you from the villa that night?'

'My hair is dyed now.'

'Of course,' he says, pausing. 'Olivia is complicit in all of this, then?' he asks.

'I think she's in love with Antonio, or at least besotted with him.' I rub my head, stretch the tension in my shoulders, climb onto my bike, and wait.

'But it doesn't make sense, Peter. Was it all a game – a faking game – to prove he was as good as Umberto, or did he make the fake and swap *The Bull* to deceive Nina?'

'Well, if Nina fell out with Umberto and got fired, then she wanted revenge, so maybe she persuaded Antonio to steal *The Bull*. They broke into the villa, but just before Nina took off to Estonia, he double-crossed her and got out of the van with the original sculpture, leaving her with the fake. But who bombed

Los Globos?'

'I think Nina did that.'

'But you have no proof?' Peter asks.

'No.'

'Did Antonio help her?'

'Probably – he likes to take risks. According to Olivia, he likes excitement.'

'So, then Nina tried to sell *The Bull* to Natasha, who realised it was a fake.'

'It wouldn't have entered Nina's head that it wouldn't be the original.'

'Okay, that makes sense. Then we turned up in Estonia, and we told Nina it was a fake, and she realised there was only one person who could have made a fake and swapped it for the original sculpture.'

'Yes.'

'And now she wants *The Bull* back.'

'I think she phoned Antonio, and he's on his way to meet her.'

'Where?'

'Olivia said he's planning on returning *The Bull* to Bruno and Glorietta's villa.'

* * *

The gates to the villa are open. I roar up to the stables and pull the helmet from my head. There's no sign of anyone. I stride inside, shouting for Bruno, but the villa is empty. His office is vacant.

I stand on the verandah overlooking the pool, squinting at the horizon and the rows of neat vines. It's seven o'clock but the early evening sunshine is still powerful. I shade my eyes, scanning for a sign of life.

'Christ, Bruno, where are you?' I mutter.

I run down the steps to my bike, and I'm about to swing it toward the vines when I hear whinnying from inside the stables. I turn off the engine and walk cautiously toward the enormous barn where Bruno keeps his horses.

It's dark inside, and the shade is cool. Instantly, my senses are alert. A welcome breeze flicks through the dry straw. Over the stable door, a horse with a white nose regards me warily and snorts.

'Bruno?' I call.

The horse whinnies and I wish it could speak. It's not spooked, so I touch its nose and whisper, 'Is anyone around?'

The four-legged creature doesn't reply, so I walk past him, looking into the stalls. It's empty, and there's no sound.

Back out in the sunlight, coming toward me and cantering between the vines, Bruno and another man are riding fast. Bruno raises his hand in greeting and brings his horse to a stop a few metres from where I'm standing.

'Mikky!'

'Bruno!'

To myself, I mutter, 'Thank goodness.'

'Are you alright?' He swings himself from his grey mare and throws the reins over the horse's head.

Dominic, the estate manager, calls a greeting from a black stallion, and I smile as he leads the two horses to the drinking fountain at the ceramic trough against the far wall of the courtyard.

'Has Joachin called you?' I ask.

'No.' Bruno wipes the sweat from his forehead onto his

sleeve.

'Antonio Hernandez − a student of Umberto − is on his way here. He wants to return *The Bull*.'

'That's nice,' Bruno says with a laugh, but then his face turns serious. 'You're not joking?'

'He'll probably tell you that he was forced to steal it or that he was blackmailed or some other lie, but he and his Russian girlfriend Nina stole it.'

'Why?'

'Umberto had fallen out with Nina − she was a student of his, and she accused him of stealing her ideas.'

Bruno scratches his head. 'Did he?'

'I'm not sure. But I think she drone-bombed his sculpture to get even with him − and then she wanted money.' I don't elaborate about Natasha's theory that Umberto is the father of Nina's sister − Katya's children.

She killed my baby.

'And Antonio went along with her idea?'

'He made a replica − a fake − and he swapped it for the real thing, and Nina didn't realise until she tried to sell it to Natasha in Estonia.'

'So, she has come back to Barcelona to get it from Antonio,' Bruno concludes. 'But he wants to give it to us?'

'Yes.'

'What a mess this is. Where is Joachin?' he asks.

'On his way here, and so is Antonio.'

'And the girl?'

'The police were following her, but they lost her. She's dangerous, Bruno.'

He frowns. 'I know. Joachin told me she was the one who kicked you.'

'So, you know everything now.' I sit down, in the shade, on the steps of the villa and Bruno sits beside me. He still carries a whip in his hands, and he slaps it rhythmically against the palm of his hands.

'I don't understand, Mikky. They bombed the sculpture and then took *The Bull*. All because Nina thought Umberto stole her ideas?'

'No!'

Startled, we jump up and turn around to see who is issuing the denial.

Antonio has the look of a supermodel. One you'd find on the cover of an expensive magazine. He's tanned and dressed in aquamarine shorts and a white T-shirt. He lifts his sunglasses onto his head to reveal large brown eyes and extends his hand.

'I took *The Bull*, and I'm really sorry.'

Neither of us takes his proffered hand, and Antonio's smile falters. He shakes his head.

'I want to explain. It was a crazy idea, but I—'

'Where's *The Bull*?' says Bruno angrily, slapping the whip distractedly against his long riding boot.

Antonio pauses, then unslings the holdall from his shoulder and places it at his feet.

'I have it here. It's safe.'

The horses at the water fountain snort and stamp their feet, and I'm distracted by their sudden restlessness.

'You broke into my villa, and you STOLE it. Why?' Bruno asks.

'It wasn't about the money. Nina threatened me,' Antonio claims, his voice soft and smooth.

'With what?'

He shrugs and smiles apologetically.

'She was blackmailing me. I was having an affair with a married woman and if my family—'

'I know you've been screwing Olivia. It's not a secret,' I say. 'I also know that Olivia hid *The Bull* in her apartment, and that she sent me to Poland to get me out of the way.'

Antonio's mouth falls open.

'Is this true?' Bruno asks. 'Olivia hid *The Bull*, for you?'

'Well, yes, but it wasn't her fault. She wasn't involved.' He rubs his hand through his hair. 'I never realised all this would happen. I'm really sorry.'

'Why didn't you give it back the next day? You must have known the damage you did. The hurt you caused?'

'I wanted to. I—'

'It was a game to you, wasn't it?' I raise my voice. My anger is stirred. 'Umberto had fired Nina, and you were going to be next,' I say.

'Me?'

'Yes. You were both trying to undermine Umberto. You wanted to damage his credibility. I don't think Nina planned the drone bomb, after all. I think it was you. I think that you thought you were as good as Umberto, and you wanted to pass his work off as your own. So, you stole *The Bull* and made a fake.' I'm making it up as I speak. I want to antagonise and rattle Antonio.

I want the truth.

'No, that's not true. I had nothing to do with the drone. Nina asked me to take her to the beach and to stay with her as she controlled it, but I said no. I told her she was crazy to pull such a stunt.'

'But you stole *The Bull*.'

Antonio shakes his head. 'It was harmless fun. I wasn't

283

thinking. It was a crazy time ...'

'It was all a game?' I take a step closer to him.

Bruno places his hand on my arm. 'Why make a fake unless YOU planned to keep it. Why?'

'To feed your cocaine habit?' I suggest.

Antonio's face darkens.

'That's what Olivia says,' I continue to rile him, 'your drug habit.'

'Olivia?'

I lie, 'She confessed everything to Martin and Lorenzo. They came back to the apartment after you left this afternoon. I took a picture of you leaving her apartment, and I showed it to them. Then I told Olivia how you were fucking Nina, and she broke down. She's furious with you – you lied to her. And, Martin wants to kill you for screwing his mother.'

Antonio takes a step closer to me.

'What have you said to them?'

Bruno places a hand on his chest and stands between us. Although Bruno is shorter than Antonio, he's broader and stronger.

'Look, I was blackmailed,' he wails. 'It wasn't my fault. I had no idea all this was going to happen.'

'LIAR!'

We all turn around. Nina is standing behind us, legs akimbo, dressed in black, pointing a crossbow at Antonio's chest, and she carries a revolver pushed into the waistband of her jeans.

* * *

'You're a liar, Antonio,' she calls. 'I'll kill you, and then I'll kill Umberto. You're both liars and cheats, and I'm not letting you get away with it.'

I sense Bruno's body tighten, and he steps toward her.

'Throw the whip on the floor,' she orders him, aiming the crossbow in his direction.

'Careful,' I say to Bruno quietly, then loudly, I say, 'The police are on their way.'

'I'll use this. I'm not frightened.' She raises the crossbow to her eye and moves a little closer to Bruno. I'm too far away to charge at her, at least ten metres. 'Last chance. Throw your whip on the floor.'

Bruno tosses it to one side, and it lands close to my feet.

Nina says, 'We were in this together, but you betrayed me, Antonio. You swapped *The Bull* for a crappy fake. Did you think I wouldn't notice?'

He doesn't reply, so she shouts, 'Antonio, answer me. Did you think I wouldn't bloody notice?'

'No.'

'Did you think I wouldn't come back get it?'

He shakes his head.

'Well?!' she shouts.

'No!'

'Did you think I wouldn't come and find you?'

He doesn't answer.

'Well?'

'No.'

'Pass the bag over here. That one at your feet. I take it this is the authentic sculpture, not some piece of garbage you made?'

Antonio bends over to lift the bag.

'Slowly, move very, very slowly, Antonio, or you won't have the *cojones* to fuck anyone anymore. Walk toward me with the bag. Good boy. Leave the bag there. Now step back.'

He does as she tells him. The crossbow is pointing at Antonio, and I glance at Bruno.

'When did you swap it?!' she shouts. 'How did you do it? Tell me!'

'It was in the van. I bought two identical holdalls. When we left the villa, I threw the bag in the back of the van. I made sure that when I climbed out, I took the right one.'

'You must think I'm stupid.'

'No, I don't, Nina. I'm sorry.'

'Were you going to sell it to fund your naughty habit? Your secret addiction to white powder? The one you can't tell your rich mummy and daddy about?'

Nina takes a step forward, and that's when Bruno moves. He runs and leaps like a cat, his arms outstretched, his legs flying out behind his elongated body.

My reflexes are slower. I bend to grab the whip, and I'm on his heels when Nina fires. Bruno takes the shot and collapses at my feet, and I stumble over his body. Nina throws the crossbow to one side and reaches for the gun tucked in her belt, and Antonio shoves me in the back. I fall forward in Nina's path, staggering, crashing into her, and we fall on the floor.

Antonio runs. He reaches the grey tethered horse and leaps onto its back, twisting the beast away in a fast gallop. The rucksack is hooked over his shoulder, and I watch him manoeuvre the horse with professional ease, galloping and gaining speed between the vines.

Nina kicks me off and scrambles to her feet. I reach out and grab her ankle, but she twists her foot, kicks me in the shoulder and then elbows me between my shoulder blades.

I cry out and lose my grip. Standing up, she lands a foot behind my knee, and the pain is excruciating, and I scream.

Nina runs and leaps onto the back of the black stallion and, driving her heels into its flank, she gallops after Antonio.

Bruno groans beside me. His shirt is bloody, and his face contorted in pain. Dominic appears from inside the stables. Looking bewildered, he calls out and runs to Bruno; kneeling on the floor, he pulls his phone from his shirt pocket.

'*Madre mia, qué ha pasado, Bruno?*'

Bruno's shirt is covered in blood. His eyes are closed.

* * *

'Call an ambulance!' I shout, nodding at the discarded weapon. 'He's been shot with a crossbow.'

Dominic is shouting into the phone, and three estate workers arrive from the field. They gather around us, helping Bruno to sit up. One runs to get water, another pulls off Bruno's shirt, and the third presses down on Bruno's shoulder to stem the flow of blood.

'Let me look at the wound,' Dominic says, pocketing his phone.

'She shot him,' I repeat.

'Tranquila guapa!'

Stay calm.

I take the water offered to me by the younger estate worker. My body is riddled with pain. Bruno is bleeding, and I'm covered in his blood.

'I'm okay,' Bruno says, opening his eyes. 'I'll be fine.'

They make a dressing from his shirt.

'We'll get him to the hospital,' Dominic says, and barks instructions for someone to get a vehicle.

I sit on the ground, dialling Joachin's phone, but it goes to voicemail, so I hang up and call Peter.

'Nina just shot Bruno with a crossbow. Get hold of Joachin – urgently. Find him!'

'He's on his way to the villa.'

The discarded crossbow lies at my feet beside the discarded whip. I stare between the vines to see where they might have gone. Nina, in pursuit of Antonio, has disappeared.

'Can you manage?' I ask Dominic, as they lift Bruno gently into his 4x4.

'Sí.'

'Bruno? You'll be okay.' I kiss his cheek.

'I'm fine, Mikky. Stay here at the villa. My men will look after you.'

'The inspector is on his way,' I reply.

I'm conscious that I'm running out of time, so I sprint for my bike, but the pain in my knee is excruciating, and I'm forced to hobble, as it travels up my spine and into my ribs. I'm cursing myself for letting Nina get the better of me again. I throw my leg over the seat and the engine roars into life.

'Mikky!' Bruno calls out from the car passenger seat.

I ignore him. One of the workers attempts to stand in my way, but I weave the bike around him and accelerate. I bounce over the dry earth, heading toward the setting sun, scanning the land around me. The ground is uneven, and it jars my body, but I don't care – I keep riding, as fast as I can.

I call out to a couple of workers in the field, asking if they've seen two horses, but they shake their heads. I turn the bike in another direction, criss-crossing the massive estate. I swerve and skid, squinting into the sunlight over the hills; I'm sweating, and perspiration falls into my eyes. I'm exhausted, but then I see a horse. It's running free, galloping alone. It's

Bruno's grey mare. It's scared by my engine, and it rears up before turning away and cantering back in the direction of the stables.

I follow the path where it came from, over the hills and ridges, until I reach the fence – the perimeter of Bruno's estate. I scan the ground, and it's the white T-shirt that eventually attracts my attention. It's flapping in the evening breeze like it's surrendering, and its soaked with crimson blood.

I stop the bike, switch off the engine, and climb off.

It's eerily quiet.

There's no sign of another horse or of Nina.

Antonio's lifeless body lies on the ground. His beautiful features are rigid in death. His face is a mask, a deathly sculpture of skin and bone. He lies on his back, and as I stand over him, my shadow casts his dead body into the shade.

I sink to his side, exhausted. There's no pulse, only a hole in his forehead and a trickle of blood down his face. Nina must have cornered him against the fence. I sit beside Antonio's motionless body on the barren ground, exhausted and defeated. Before, death would have upset me. It would have made me vomit, wretch, and cry with grief, but now I sit numbly staring at this young boy.

I remember the affection with which Olivia had spoken in her support of him. He'd made her feel young, wanted, and loved. He was a boy who had been carefree and funny, intelligent and creative. He had begun a deadly game – a faking game – resulting in his death. A boy who had it all now had nothing. I sit with my head on my upright knees and close my eyes.

'What was it all for, you stupid, stupid bastard?' I whisper. 'All this death – for nothing.'

I hug my legs closer to my face, leaning my forehead against my jeans. I don't know how long I'm there for or even if I've been crying, and it's not until I feel a hand on my shoulder that I look up to find Inspector Joachin García Abascal staring down into my eyes.

'Mikky? Are you alright?' he asks softly.

I shake my head.

'Come on, come with me.' His soft voice is carried on the wind, and he holds out his hand.

'He's dead,' I cry.

'Yes.'

'Nina shot him, and she took *The Bull*.'

'Yes.'

I take his hand, stand up, and brush the dirt from my jeans. I'm covered in Bruno's blood.

A Guardia Civil officer now stands beside Antonio's motionless body, and another is talking to Dominic beside an estate truck and a police car. They all regard me as I stumble over to my bike.

'Estas bien, Mikky?' asks Dominic, his weathered face full of concern. 'Are you alright?'

'Is Bruno okay?' I ask.

'He's on his way to hospital, but he'll be fine,' Joachin replies.

I throw my leg over my bike and gun the engine.

'Where are you going?' calls Joachin. 'You can't leave. The Guardia Civil need a statement.'

'They'll have to wait. This time I'm going to kill her.'

'What are you going to do?!' he shouts. 'STOP!'

Chapter 12

"Sculpture is like drawing in the air. Filling in space. Finding space. Working with contours, planes, light, and shadows."
Denis Hopking

I weave the bike between the vines, over the hills, and past the villa, driving toward the city of Barcelona. I've lost my helmet, but I don't care. The wind is refreshing on my face, caressing my hair, massaging my scalp. I'm liberated and angry. Each time, Nina has been one step ahead of me – but not this time. My body is rigid with tension, and I'm on a mission.

Where is she?

There will be a police hunt for her now.

She murdered Antonio.

I pull the bike over to the side of the road, and I'm sick on the dry, grassy shrubs. In my mind's eye I see Antonio's lifeless face staring in bewilderment up at the sky, and I spit and wipe my mouth. I pull a bottle of water from my bag and rinse my mouth. I'm hyperventilating, and I calm myself, watching the busy flow of cars along the winding road.

Death is so final.

I dig out my phone and see that Peter has been calling me. It's past nine o'clock, and the sun is yet to set. It's almost mid-summer – the longest day – and there's still evidence of light in the sky and the promise of a beautiful sunset. My breathing returns to normal, and my hands stop shaking, but I'm angry. After three encounters, Nina has beaten me and escaped. I re-screw the cap of the water bottle and place it in my bag, then dial Peter's number.

'Thank Christ, Mikky. Where are you?' he asks.

'Nina shot Bruno!' I wail.

'Joachin told me what happened. Bruno will be alright. We're heading to the hospital now. Meet us there?'

'I've got to find Nina. She's taken *The Bull*.'

'To hell with *The Bull*, your life is more important. She's out of control. The police are after her now – so if anyone can find her, they will.'

'They haven't been successful so far!' I shout.

Feeling suddenly weak, I crouch down beside my bike and sit on the dry earth. 'I hate them all!' I wail.

'Joachin will help.'

'He can't.'

'He can. He's on our side, remember?'

'I know, but he wanted me to wait for questioning – for a statement – but I've got to find her. Peter, help me!' I shout. 'Where has she gone? Help me to reason it out.'

'Hold on.' I hear him speaking to Aniela, then he comes back on the phone and speaks slowly. 'Look, let's take one step at a time and reason things through. Nina shot Bruno, she's killed Antonio, and she's taken *The Bull*. She knows the police are after her and she's not going to get very far. So, what would you do in her shoes?'

'I don't know ...'

I wait and, as the silence between us grows, I suddenly know exactly what she's going to do.

'She's going to kill Umberto,' I whisper.

* * *

I ride manically through the busy streets, weaving and leaning, dodging cars, buses, and even a group of cyclists. I fly along the busy city streets, seeing everything but nothing – only the road in front of me. Nina has a head start, and it takes me over twenty minutes to navigate my way through the city between tourists, hawkers, kiosks, and stalls.

The street door leading to Umberto's studio is open. I take the stairs two at a time and enter cautiously, wondering if Umberto will be working at this time of night.

There's no sound. No voices. Nothing. The studio appears empty. I walk stealthily between the benches, straining and listening for noises, but there's no one. It's quiet, with only the occasional sound from outside; street noises – engines, horns, and a distant siren – nothing unusual. I pick up a hammer and weigh it in my hand. Then I climb the spiral staircase, glancing everywhere.

Upstairs, where previously I saw Antonio, a Japanese girl, and an older man working, the space is now empty. There are no students and no sign of Umberto. There's also no sign of a struggle.

I exhale slowly, not realising that I've been holding my breath, and suddenly there's a noise downstairs. A door creaks opens. I strain to listen, and lean over the staircase. I can't see anything.

Someone is coming inside, downstairs. Gripping the hammer, I move quickly and silently like a cat, making my way rapidly into the corridor and down the stairs, and stealthily I reach the studio door.

I'll catch her from behind. I pause to control my breath, then very gently and very slowly, I push the door open.

I pause and remain standing where I am.

Nothing.

There is no one.

Very quietly, I step inside. The door slams behind me, and an arm wraps tightly around my throat.

I'm choking.

* * *

'Mikky?!' Peter shouts, and suddenly he lets me go.

'Peter? What the f—' I cough and choke, as he lets me go.

'I didn't realise it was you.' He stands with his arms akimbo, and now I've experienced his SAS training.

I rub my neck. 'You almost killed me. I thought you were going to the hospital? What are you doing here?'

'I came to help you.'

'There's no one here.' I lean against the workbench. Exhaustion grips me, and I'm drained of energy.

'Are you alright?'

'I'm fine.'

'I'll call Joachin and let him know you're safe.' Peter turns away, and I hear him speaking into his mobile.

I wander between the benches, gazing idly at Umberto's recent work. There are sketches and drawings, and also statues made of iron, wood, copper, and bronze. I turn one or two of them to the light for a better look. Had Nina really given Umberto the idea for the *Los Globos* exhibit?

Peter finishes his call. 'Joachin wants to meet us. He just telephoned Umberto and his wife said that he left for a meeting thirty minutes ago.'

'At this time of the evening?'

'She said it was quite unusual. He hadn't been expecting to go out.'

'She didn't say who he was meeting?'

'No, but he did leave in a hurry.'

'Nina must have called him and told him she had *The Bull*.'

'Would Umberto be interested?'

'I don't know. Maybe she's got a hold over him – blackmail? Didn't Natasha say she thought he was the father of Katya's children?'

Peter stares at me. 'Do you think that's true?'

I shrug. 'Maybe.'

'So, where would Nina meet Umberto?'

'I thought she would meet him here. This would be the logical place. She said she was going to kill him and I think she meant it.'

Peter rubs a hand over the back of his neck. 'How would she kill him?'

'Who knows? She turned up at Bruno's villa holding a crossbow and with a revolver in her belt – she shot Antonio through his forehead.' I point to the spot on my own head. 'The girl is an enigma. She's trained in martial arts, and now she's a killing machine. Where did she get that sort of training?'

'We checked. Aniela found out that her father had a military background. He was one of the founders of the FSB – the Federal Security Service of the Russian Federation – previously the KGB.'

'Was?'

'He was killed in a domestic accident, then Nina and Katya lived in Milan for a few years until they moved to Estonia.'

'So, her sister could have met Umberto,' I say.

'How is Nina getting around?' Peter is also thinking aloud. 'She used the Volvo to get to and from the villa, but I'd guess by now she's dumped it and got some other form of transport.'

'You think she's stolen a car?'

'She stole the van, didn't she?'

'What is she doing? Where is she?' I mumble.

'What if she's not meeting Umberto? Maybe it's just a coincidence he's gone out. What if she's driving back to Estonia or going to Milan?' he says.

'She can't run forever, Peter.'

'We've underestimated her. We're not dealing with a rational human being. She's a killer, and we have to treat her like one. Come on, let's go and meet Joachin.'

'Can I have a lift?'

'You almost killed me in there.'

'I came to save you.'

'Okay, hop on.'

'Thank you, honourable, kind lady,' he says with a smile. 'How kind you are.'

'If you're going to be sarcastic, you can bloody walk.'

'A little touchy, aren't we?'

* * *

It's almost ten, and we sit outside a small café in the Gothic Quarter, drinking black coffee. The streets are busy, still streaming with people – the nightlife is only just beginning.

Men have switched from their daytime uniform of shorts and T-shirts to cotton slacks and shirts, and smell strongly of popular aftershaves. The women wear skimpy dresses and have their hair fashioned to fall naturally over their shoulders. They belong to another world. They're glossy, groomed, and giggling, and we're beaten and exhausted.

'They found Nina's Volvo in a ditch on the outskirts of the city.' Joachin's eyes are rimmed red with tiredness.

'What about the horse?'

'The estate worker found it by the east fence. She'd abandoned it.'

My phone rings. It's Josephine.

'I just got your message about Bruno. We had been at the Royal Albert Hall, and my phone was switched off.'

I turn away from the table, leaving Joachin and Peter to talk while I bring Josephine up to date on the events. She listens carefully, asking a few questions as I go along, and by the time I've finished speaking, I'm exhausted.

'Glorietta is flying back from Tokyo. Now, you must get some rest, my darling. You've punished yourself for a week, and you can't do this anymore. You'll be ill. This girl Nina is a monster.'

'I know.'

'She's not just a thief. She's a killer.'

'She's been betrayed,' I reply.

'We've all been betrayed, Mikky, but we don't go around killing people. She enjoys the attention. She bombed Umberto's sculpture in the most dramatic fashion – at the opening – without a thought for people's lives. It was all over the newspapers. She probably loves being in the news.'

My mind is whirling.

297

Maybe she does enjoy the publicity.

'Mikky, are you there? Are you listening?'

'If that's true, Josephine, then maybe she's going to kill Umberto in a spectacular fashion.'

'What? Oh my goodness, Mikky. Please be careful. Let me speak to Joachin.'

'Must go, Josephine. Thanks for your help. I'll call you.'

'I don't want you going anywhere near her. Mikky—'

I pocket my mobile and walk back to the table, where Peter and Joachin are talking.

'She's going to kill him somewhere public – maybe an art gallery.'

'The Arte Moderno Museo Barcelona?' asks Peter.

'I don't know, but it's going to be somewhere dramatic.'

Joachin is already lifting his phone, and he begins barking orders.

'Where are you going?' Peter calls after me.

'For a ride.'

'I'll come, too.' He runs behind me in a peculiar hobble with his artificial foot. I swing my leg over the bike and wait for him to climb on the back.

Joachin follows us. 'They've scaled up the threat level. I've managed to convince them that she's dangerous enough to be planning something public.'

'Good.'

'Where are you going?' he asks.

'I'm going for a ride. It's eleven. I bet she's planning something for midnight. The witching hour.' I push the electric button, and the bike's engine roars to life.

'But what will you look for?'

'*Los Globos* was suspended in the air. The balls were tied by invisible wire that made them look as if they were floating. It was effective and original, and I've got a feeling she'll use that method to draw attention to his death.'

'But how will she do that?'

'That's what I have to work out.'

* * *

The streets are illuminated and sparkling with golden lights. Barcelona is a city that never sleeps, and the night-time energy pulsates up through the streets, and music fills the air. Cervecerías, tapas bars, and outdoor restaurants are full, and people spill out onto the streets, drinking fancy cocktails and slugging back shots with names like *The Monica Lewinsky*.

The city is an architectural delight. Aside from the countless museums and galleries, I run through a list of possible dramatic sites in my head, where Nina could potentially take Umberto. There's the Palau de la Música Catalana, in the Catalan Art Nouveau, listed as a World Heritage Site by UNESCO. Then, there is Gaudí's stone quarry – Casa Milà, otherwise known as 'La Pedrera' – that has a fabulous rooftop night show. Or there's Barcelona's largest ornamental fountain, created in 1929 for the International Exhibition, that provides a stunning display of light, music, motion, and colour.

There are any number of bars, clubs, and pubs, including those on Tibidabo Mountain, which has a spectacular view of the city and panoramic views of the skyline.

I cut across La Avenida Diagonal toward the Parc Güell, where Antonio Hernandez lived. I'm drawn to the quieter locations and, as I ride through the streets with Peter behind me, it gives me time to think. Assuming Nina is going to do something dramatic with Umberto, it will have to be somewhere remote, but still viewed by the public. Not the park, so I turn the bike in the direction of The Basílica de la Sagrada Família, hailed as an architectural gem, but the gates are closed.

I stop the bike.

Peter climbs off and stretches his legs. 'Could she be in there?'

'It has the drama,' I reply, gazing up at the towers.

'Will they ever finish it?'

'Antoni Gaudí died in 1926, so they hope to have it finished for the centennial of his death.' I scan the towers, looking for movement, but how would Nina have got Umberto inside there?

'I'm trying to count the towers,' Peter says beside me. 'I can't see anything or anyone, can you?'

'When it's finished, there will be twelve towers for the apostles, four for the evangelists, one for the Virgin Mary, and the tallest one will represent Jesus Christ. I spent a lot of time in there growing up,' I say, by way of explanation. 'Come on. She's not there.'

Peter grabs my arm. 'We can't drive aimlessly around the city, Mikky. Think! We need somewhere impressive, where Nina can get inside easily without drawing attention.'

I go through the list of buildings in my head. 'OH MY GOD!'

'What? You know?'

'Christ! Come on! Quick!'

* * *

It's a ten-minute ride down the Carrer de la Marina to the Hotel Arts. I circle the roundabout and fountain a few times, glancing up at the hotel, checking the bedroom lights, wondering if I've gone insane.

It's the hotel where we checked in earlier this morning. It seems like a lifetime ago that we arrived and I went out and bought this bike.

It's where we met Joachin and filled him in on the events of our trip to Estonia, and now, as I glance up at the forty-four floors, I'm convinced that Nina is in there.

'Why this hotel?' asks Peter, over my shoulder.

'It's the most prestigious hotel in the city. Full of art. Perfectly located. It's a good place to meet Umberto without him feeling threatened, and she could get inside easily without being noticed.'

'Do you want to go inside?'

'I'll drop you off. Can you find out if Nina booked a room?'

'What about you?'

'I'll check the left side of the building, the far side.'

I leave Peter at the entrance to the hotel and gun the engine. I ride past the casino entrance and onto the wide promenade, and stop the bike to gaze up at the imposing building.

On the first floor, near the bar where we sat with Joachin, the tail of Frank Gehry's golden fish is illuminated and glowing spectacularly in the dark.

I turn my attention to the deserted, arc-shaped beach in front of the hotel. Squinting in the night sky, looking at the tower of the building for something, anything – a clue – to tell me I'm right.

The Presidential Penthouse at the top of the building is lit up, and I wonder which distinguished guest is staying there tonight. The hotel has won some of the most prestigious awards and now is a benchmark of achievement for excellence, service, and attention for hotels worldwide. It has been an icon of the city for over twenty years and provides panoramic views across the sea and harbour for its guests. There are five restaurants, a spa, and the walls are adorned with original paintings by Spanish artists, most of them Catalan.

She's got to be here.

I check my watch. It's almost twelve – it's fifteen minutes to midnight.

I don't have binoculars, so I use the zoom on my phone, and I'm shading my tired eyes when I see movement outside the glass, between the steel structure and diagonal bracings.

It's Nina, and she seems to be lifting a package out of the window.

It hangs, swaying gently.

It's a body.

Chapter 13

"When you slow down enough to sculpt, you discover all kinds of things you never noticed before."

Karen Jobe

My hands are shaking as I dial Joachin's number, and he answers on the second ring.

'She's at the Hotel Arts, and she's hanging Umberto's body out of the window,' I say.

'Christ! Stay where you are and don't do anything. I'm five minutes away.'

I call Peter.

'She's on the eighteenth floor. Joachin and the police are on their way.'

I move closer along the promenade to get a better view and keep my eye on the window. Something is protruding outside the window. Is it a rifle, resting on the sill?

I don't know if Umberto is alive. His head hangs on his chest, and there's a bag hanging around his neck.

There's no sign of Nina. I pace up and down, not taking my eyes from the window, waiting for Joachin.

'I haven't seen her. She must be inside,' I say, when he finds me.

Sirens fill the street. Police vans, cars, and uniformed troops block the traffic and secure the roads.

'We're evacuating the hotel,' says Joachin.

He has a radio in one hand and a phone in the other. He speaks simultaneously into both of them, giving information and receiving answers. 'The GEO are on their way.'

Grupo Especial de Operaciones – the police tactical unit of the National Police Force – are responsible for countering terrorist attacks, hijackings, and maritime threats. They gained international recognition when they foiled an attempt by ETA to attack the Summer Olympics in 1992.

'It's a potential hostage situation. We'll get her to talk to us,' Joachin tells me, before walking away to speak to a uniformed officer.

As members of the force prepare their equipment to enter the hotel, I remember reading how they're trained in martial arts, marksmanship, explosives, and scuba diving.

Nina won't escape them. Not this time.

I stay beyond the barrier, near the beach, and Peter phones.

'I'm in the reception. They're evacuating everyone. I have to get out.'

'She must have lassoed the girder, and she's tied Umberto to the steel frame outside the hotel. It's hard to know if he's dead, alive, or just sedated. She's making an exhibit of him,' I reply.

'It's chaos in here,' he says. 'People know there's something wrong, and now that the GEO have turned up, there are rumours it's a terrorist attack.'

'And Aniela?'

'She's still at the hospital with Bruno.'

A crowd, sensing something exciting is about to happen, has

304

begun to form, and although the police have set up a cordon, it's no real deterrent. The public love a spectacle and I hang up the phone and listen to their comments.

'Is it a dummy?'

'It's a stunt.'

'It's not real.'

'Are they going to kill themselves?'

I lean against my bike and stare up at the hotel. In the road, near the fountain at the front of the hotel, television camera crews and radio stations begin recording events to broadcast around the world.

Journalists have been pulled away from less serious news to cover this *live* event, and they're walking through the crowd, asking for witness statements. Some members of the public are already using their phones to broadcast events on social media.

Is this what Nina wanted?

If she had designed *Los Globos* – if it was her idea – then she would be familiar with the logistics of hanging a sculpture – or a body.

Has she used wire, string, or rope? And, more importantly, what is the purpose of dangling Umberto Palladino's inert body from the window?

What does she want to achieve?

The news reporters are saying it's potentially a hostage situation. They film the GEO team entering the hotel.

What is she doing?

'We're going to start some dialogue with her,' Joachin says.

Rumours begin to surface. Interviewers are reporting that it's Umberto Palladino hanging from the eighteenth floor. There's shock and horror as they watch and wait. Giving him a famous name has made it more real, and the crowd and journalists realise the gravity of the situation and give urgency to the proceedings.

Is he alive?

A whirling noise of a helicopter distracts me. It chases low across the marina and rises, circling a discreet distance from the hotel. Inside the chopper, a uniformed man leans from the opened door, assessing the situation with binoculars. As the craft tilts, I get a glimpse of armed men with rifles.

'They're going to attack the hotel,' someone says.

'They'll bomb the building.'

'Stormtroopers are inside.'

'They've got listening devices outside the room.'

'How many are there?'

'Is it ISIS?'

'Terrorist attack!' shouts another.

I look at the expectant, excited faces of the people around me, standing at the barrier and waiting in anticipation. Some people are filming on their mobiles, while others are chattering excitedly, and some are already getting bored and have wandered off in search of a drink.

Is this what she wants?

I realise then that we've underestimated her again. It's five minutes to midnight.

*She isn't inside the hotel.*Suddenly, I know exactly what she's going to do. Panic wells up inside me, and I scan the crowd around me, looking for Joachin, but he's been swallowed up in the group of reporters, the GEO team, the police, and the public.

Joachin has disappeared.

I pull out my phone.

'Peter? Find out what's hanging around Umberto's neck.' I pocket my phone and swing my leg over my bike. The noise of the engine surprises the crowd, and they move aside as I motor between them, finding a way toward the promenade and harbour.

They haven't made the connection.

As a drone controller, you can be kilometres away, but Nina will want to watch this spectacle, just as she watched the drone fly into the *Los Globos* exhibit.

I scan faces, looking for someone alone, remote, and dressed in black. I ride illegally along the marina, past restaurants and bars, but there's no sign of her. At the far end of the marina, I skid and turn quickly.

I've been a fool.

Revving the engine, motioning to the crowd to get out of my way, I accelerate. They curse, shout, and wave their fists, but I haven't time to lose. I retrace my route toward the hotel and head out onto the promenade. The marina is on my left and the beach on my right. The chopper is hovering overhead, and I still can't see Joachin, but that's when I hear it.

The drone is flying up from the beach.

I gun the bike and bounce down the steps to the beach. The scrambler kicks up sand behind me, but I focus on the dark shadows. I skid and slide, aware that the drone is getting higher, nearer to the hotel, and that there is a bomb tied around Umberto's neck.

A gunshot rings out and a bullet pings off the chrome of my bike. Shaken, I slide and slip into the sand. My hands are shaking. A dark figure is running away from me, so I climb back onto the bike.

Nina's fast but the sand makes her feet heavy. She carries a console in one hand and a gun in the other. I'm gaining on her. She turns and fires. I duck and accelerate. She turns her back and I lift my boot and kick her between the shoulder blades. The force lifts her into the air. I brake, skidding to one side, and fall onto the sand. Nina is five metres away. She's dropped the console, and we are face to face.

She raises the gun.

'You killed my baby!' I shout.

To my right, there's a vivid explosion.

A scream rises from the crowd. Overhead, the chopper uses the searchlight to scour the beach in broad sweeping movements. I only have a few seconds to kill her.

Nina turns, and I run, lunging for her, grappling with the gun, wrestling it from her grasp. It falls into the sand. She's strong, but I'm furious. Spurred on by revenge, I fight like a wild cat, screaming, punching, and kicking, but her movements are skilled and professional. She deflects my wild punches, chops me across the shoulder, and I stumble as she dives to gain possession of the revolver. I kick sand into her face, then leap on top of her, tugging the revolver away from her grip. I elbow her skull and in one swift movement I suddenly pull the gun free and I roll away. I'm on my feet, panting heavily, and aiming the gun at her face.

Nina springs forward, a knife blade shining in the glare of the searchlight, and I pull the trigger. She falls, and the blade spins from her hand.

Exhausted, I collapse, breathless and sobbing, as a violent whirlwind of dust and sand whirls around me. I cover my face and my mouth, and turn my back as the chopper lands noisily.

I drop the gun. I want the earth to swallow me up. I want this terrible, powerful force to create a vortex below me that I can slide down and disappear into forever.

I killed her.

* * *

The storm subsides, and armed troops spring from the open door. The sand settles and partially covers Nina's dead body. One of the officers leans over her, touches her neck, and then whispers something into the radio on his lapel, before walking toward me.

'Mikky dos Santos?'

'Sí.'

'Are you alright?'

I raise my arms in surrender.

'I killed her,' I cry.

He nods and speaks into his radio.

What will they say – Peter, Joachin, Josephine, Simon, Bruno, and Glorietta?

I'm a killer.

I wait. I am crying softly in the sand; grief, remorse, relief. Two guards stand near me, silently watching.

Nina's body is between us and the helicopter. More soldiers stand waiting, observant and wired. The blades of the machine rotate slowly to a stop and all the while I wait, crouching in the sand, staring at Nina's lifeless body.

She's dead.

One week ago, she killed my baby, and now she is dead.

I kept my promise.

A police car drives manically across the sand and skids to a halt. Joachin jumps out, addresses one of the two guards briefly, and glances at Nina.

'Mikky?'

'It's become a habit,' I say. 'Finding me with dead bodies. First Antonio, and now Nina.'

'Are you alright?'

'I killed her.'

'Come on, let's get you home.'

'I don't have a home.'

Joachin lifts me to my feet. 'Come on, get in the car.'

'Are you arresting me?'

'No.'

'I killed her.'

'No, you didn't.'

'I did.'

'One of the soldiers killed her.' He nods at the armed man standing behind me. 'They shot her from the helicopter. She had a knife.'

'I fired the gun. I killed her.'

'You might have fired, but you missed.'

'What?'

Joachin takes my hand and guides me to Nina's side. 'If you can face it, come and see.'

We stand, gazing down at her body, at the blood that has seeped into the sand from a bullet wound in the back of her head.

'You couldn't have shot her in the back of the head. That would have been impossible.'

* * *

I sit on the edge of the promenade, dangling my feet over the wall, watching the clean-up process on the beach. The breaking dawn is incredible, the sun stretches its finger-shaped rays across the horizon, and the sky turns crimson hues of pinks and lilacs.

The mayhem of the past few hours is calming down. Journalists and reporters are still looking to eyewitnesses for the story that will make the headlines, and weary-eyed cameramen continue to focus on the window where Umberto's body had been suspended outside.

I think about the events of the past week and about the thieves who broke into the villa. Antonio and Nina are both dead.

If they could have changed things, would they?

Was Nina on a destructive path for revenge?

And Antonio, with his risk-taking humour and overindulgence in drugs – was he caught up in the maelstrom of her indignant anger?

Had Umberto stolen Nina's ideas?

What will happen to the elusive and bad-tempered sculptor? How will his life unfold? With greater fame? Will he milk all the attention for even greater notoriety?

I'm still wired, and my body is tense. I don't want to leave here just yet. Not until Nina's body has been removed.

They slam the doors to the windowless van, and I watch the tyres eat into the sand and the tracks they leave behind. There will be an investigation, forensic evidence, and statements. I've given mine, but Joachin seems to think it's all over.

How will Olivia take the news that her lover was shot?

She will be questioned for her involvement in keeping *The Bull* in her apartment. And her husband Jeff – will he stand beside her? Will their marriage survive?

I'd imagine that her friendship with Glorietta is over. She

had been allowed into the inner sanctum of immediate friends and family, and she had betrayed their trust. Had Antonio been worth it? Had her life really been so empty and vacuous that she filled it with a boy who was a friend of her son?

So many lives have been inextricably changed forever.

Aniela had rushed back to the hotel fearful that Peter, a man she'd recently found again, had fallen foul of some ill-timed and awful fate, but that was not the case.

When I saw him earlier, he was smiling happily. He told me that Umberto was on his way to the hospital, alive but sedated. Now, Peter and Aniela have retired to their room for much-needed sleep, and I've promised to join them for a late breakfast, in about five hours.

I yawn and stretch. In a few hours, this beach will be filled with tourists and holidaymakers. The city will return to normal, and this will be a happy place filled with children's laughter, picnics, families, and lovers.

Such is the nature of the world. Life goes on.

My phone rings.

'I couldn't sleep, Mikky, and when I put on the BBC News, I couldn't believe it. Are you alright?' asks Josephine. 'Where are you?'

'I'm fine. I'm at the beach.'

'But it's five o'clock in the morning there, isn't it?'

'I thought I'd killed her,' I say, and tell her what had happened.

'But you didn't kill her,' she says softly.

'No, but I would have.'

'But you didn't.'

'I fired the gun. I was a rotten shot.'

'But you didn't kill her,' Josephine insists.

'It makes me no better than her, though, doesn't it?'

'But you didn't.'

'I was lucky.'

'But you didn't kill her.'

'We could go on like this all night,' I say with a smile.

'But we won't,' Josephine counters with a laugh. 'I'm just pleased you're safe.'

'Thank you.'

'Get some rest, and we'll talk later.'

'Okay.'

'Remember, I love you.'

'I do.'

'Oh, and Mikky ...'

'Yes?'

'Spare a thought for the man who did kill her and imagine how he must feel.'

'It's his job. He's trained.'

'Exactly.'

I'm not entirely sure of the point she's making, but when I hang up, my heart feels considerably lighter.

Joachin sits down beside me. He's brought coffee and churros.

'How delicious,' I say.

'It's the least I can do.'

'How's it all going?' I munch happily through the sweet donuts, dunking them greedily into my coffee. I know that once I've eaten and the shock has worn off, I'll need to sleep.

'Umberto will make a full recovery. He said Nina had phoned and asked him to meet her in the bar of the hotel.' Joachin speaks with his mouth full. He's as hungry as I am. 'She told him that she was sorry for her part in the destruction of *Los*

Globos and that she wanted to return *The Bull* in person to him as a token of her respect – but only if he didn't call the police. He thought that getting *The Bull* back would help.'

'And add to his positive publicity.'

'Cynic,' Joachin says with a laugh.

I shake my head. 'Nina wanted to kill him. She was frustrated that no one believed her.'

'He drove to the hotel of his own free will. They met in the bar and she must have slipped something in his drink and then helped him upstairs. When he woke up in the room, he was tied securely with wire and rope.'

'The same wire he used for the exhibit?'

Joachin frowns. 'We'll check.'

'Nina was strong to position him dangling outside. What was hanging around his neck?'

'A homemade Molotov cocktail, easily made, and had the drone with the bomb attached to it hit Umberto, he'd have gone up in flames. The guys in the chopper shot down the drone, and it exploded in the air, fortunately without killing or hurting anyone.'

That was the noise that had distracted Nina, allowing me to lunge for her.

'Was he conscious?'

'Yes. Nina wanted to frighten him, but he was tied up and couldn't struggle.' Joachin screws up the empty bag from the churros and drains his plastic cup.

'Poor Umberto,' I say.

'You feel sorry for him?'

'I'm not sure.'

'She'd placed a rifle on the ledge, which made us think she was inside. We could have wasted valuable time trying to get her to talk or to open the door, but the team were amazing. They have fantastic equipment and they soon realised there was no one inside. They stormed the room and pulled Umberto inside just before the drone exploded.'

'Wow! That's a team you need on your side when you've got problems,' I say with a grin, and place the plastic top back on my empty takeaway cup. 'So, it's time to go home and sleep. Your wife must be worried about you, Joachin?'

'She knows where I am. She understands.'

I climb to my feet and brush the sand from my jeans, still covered in Bruno's blood.

'Why do you think she kicked you deliberately that night?' he asks.

'I don't know.'

'Do you still have your room here?' he asks.

'I hope so.'

'Tell me something, Mikky. How did you know that Nina would lure Umberto to the Hotel Arts?'

'I guessed.'

He doesn't look too convinced, and he asks, 'And, how did you know she would be on the beach?'

'It's where I would have been,' I reply. 'It's what I would have done in her situation.'

We walk over to the promenade, where my bike has been left. There are still Guardia Civil officers walking around, and plenty of uniformed men with guns on show. It makes me feel safe.

'What are your plans now, Mikky?'

'Sleep.'

'I mean after you've rested?'

'I haven't decided. I may go to London and see Josephine.

You know, hang out with her for a while, or I may go back to Lake Como with Bruno and Glorietta for a while.'

'What about Eduardo?'

'How do you know about him?'

'Josephine told me. Are you going back to Mallorca?'

'No.'

'Why not?'

'Because my relationship with him is over. We both said and did things that we can't take back. You can't change the past, but I can change my future, Joachin. It's one thing I've learned. You can destroy something very special in a short time, something that might have taken years to build.'

He nods and has the sense not to comment further.

'I've got a proposition for you, Mikky. I want to have my own team working together on cases like this. You know, stolen artworks, looted items, missing artefacts. You'd be a great asset.'

'A police team?'

'Not exactly, more of a sub-team, a team of experts who can assist us with different skills.' Joachin smiles. 'I'd jump at the chance to work with you, Mikky. You're crazy and unpredictable, but you're also brilliant and intuitive. You have great contacts that are not always legitimate, and that's what's also so useful. You're original and unique. I don't want you to walk away without you knowing that we couldn't have done this without you.'

'And Peter.'

'The offer is extended to him, too. Do we have a deal?' He holds out his hand.

I smile. 'Maybe.'

'You won't disappear?'

'I've nothing else to do and nowhere else to go. Besides, your timing is excellent. I'd promised Eduardo that I'd never return to this dangerous life, and now he's no longer around, I can lead the life that has always been my destiny.'

'You're a natural, Mikky,' Joachin says, shaking my hand. 'At least I can keep you on the right side of the law.'

I swing my leg over my bike and switch on the engine. 'You can try.'

'Don't get into trouble for not wearing a helmet,' he comments with a smile.

'You'd bail me out of jail, wouldn't you?' I don't wait for an answer. I'm more than weary; I'm exhausted. The ride to the hotel takes a few seconds, and I secure the bike and walk into the reception, barely able to put one foot in front of the other. I press the lift button, and my eyelids are already closing.

My phone bings a text message:

I can never tell you how sorry I am. Let me spend the rest of my life making it up to you? Eduardo XXX

A laughing couple comes out of the lift, arm in arm, but I've already deleted the message as the door closes.

* * *

One week later, I walk into Umberto's studio. He's wearing the same grubby boiler suit, and he regards me warily before saying, 'I suppose I should thank you.'

'*Los Globos* was an incredible creation,' I reply. 'Three globes – the past, present, and future – representing war and destruction, fake news and money, greed and avarice.'

He doesn't reply; instead, he takes the red bandana from his neck and mops his forehead.

'It's amazing how you thought of such a powerful idea, but then again, it probably wasn't too difficult for you, was it? It's your life.'

He moves away from me, but doesn't take his eyes from my face as I continue.

'The globe of the past reflected the pain of human suffering; the globe of the present represented everything fake; and the globe of the future was made of money and based on greed and avarice. We cease to do anything kind, and our vices take over.'

His eyes darken in mistrust.

'I know the truth,' I say. 'Have you spoken to Katya? Have you told her how sorry you are?'

He doesn't reply.

'You see, Katya is the epitome of human suffering. You pretended she and her daughter were nothing to do with you because your prime concern was yourself; your fake self, that propped up your fame and your greed. It's your vices that have taken over. You have shown no humility and kindness. Your behaviour was represented in your sculpture *Los Globos*.'

He shakes his head in denial. His thick lips are moving without sound.

I say, 'This was never about stealing Nina's ideas, was it? As you said, the art of using paper isn't original. It was all about Katya – Nina's sister – and Katya's daughter – your daughter. A child that you've never recognised or supported. You're letting a stranger raise your child and beat the mother of your child.'

'That's not true.'

'Nina asked for your help, but you wouldn't do anything. You wouldn't admit to what you'd done.'

'It would ruin me. My wife would never forgive me. My boys would be mortified. You can't make me do anything. You can't prove it.'

I hold up an envelope. 'While you were in the hospital, I got them to do a DNA test.'

'That's illegal.'

'Tell it to someone who cares.'

'I'll deny it.'

'It matches with Katya's daughter.'

He rubs his forehead, turns away, and leans on the bench for support. I take a step closer and say, 'The press will have a field day with you when they find out about your daughter in Estonia. They'll dig up all the sordid details of your past and find out the real reason behind Nina's actions.'

'You can't do this.'

'Did you screw all your students? Was that part of the deal?'

He picks up a chisel from the workbench and studies it in his hand while I continue, 'Nina wanted your help to get her sister away from her violent boyfriend, but you wouldn't do anything. She threatened to go public and tell everyone. That's why you fired her. She begged you for your help but you refused. So, she bombed *Los Globos*, but you still wouldn't do anything, would you?'

'It was my creation.'

'Nina stole *The Bull* thinking she'd sell it to Natasha and make money to save Katya from her awful life, but then Antonio double-crossed her, too. He made a fake. Both the men in her life who she had trusted betrayed her.'

'It wasn't my fault.'

'What sort of monster are you?'

His head snaps up, and he replies, 'I'm not one.'

319

'I know the truth. Poor Katya. You used her. You used them both.'

Umberto's voice cracks with emotion. 'Nina wanted to meet me. She said she wanted to talk, but she wouldn't be reasonable. She wanted money. I couldn't let her blackmail me. She was going to hold me to ransom. We argued. I can't acknowledge the child. I have a FAMILY. It was a mistake. There was no love. No commitment. It was sex.'

'Katya said you promised to help her.'

'No.'

'You're hardly an attractive man – what did she see in you? What did you promise?'

'Nothing.'

'You're lying,' I say quietly. 'Katya wanted to leave Estonia. You promised her she could join you here in Barcelona, but you lied.'

He shakes his head. 'She didn't understand.'

'That you wanted sex but no commitment?'

'There's no room here for a Russian whore!' he shouts. He rubs a hand over his bulbous nose, and he won't look at me.

'Or your child?'

'No.'

'I lost my baby because of you.'

The colour drains from his face.

'You see, that night – as I tried to run up the stairs and Nina caught me – I shouted. I shouted at Nina for her not to hurt my baby, but she did so deliberately. She kicked me and killed my child. So, you're responsible.'

'You have no right coming here. You can't prove it. No one will believe you.'

'Actually, they will. I'm wearing a microphone, and this

320

conversation is being recorded. Peter is outside.' I show him the microphone tucked under the lapel of my leather jacket. 'The press will do their own investigations and will probably pay Katya a fortune for her story. Hopefully, it will be enough to get her away from the brute of a man she lives with, and then she can move to Barcelona.'

Umberto's jaw falls open, and he drops the chisel on the workbench.

'Microphone? What about the DNA test?' he stutters.

'I lied.' I screw up the empty envelope and toss it at his feet.

'Can't we come to some agreement? I'll pay you ...' Umberto leans against the workbench, his face contorted in confusion as he thinks over our conversation. The reality of the events of his past and the fallout for his future begin to hit. He shakes his head in disbelief. His eyes screw up upon the full realisation that the truth will come out, and his voice cracks.

'But ... how did you know?'

'I didn't know for sure but I do now. You've just confessed to the whole world.'

The End.

Janet Pywell's Books

Mikky dos Santos Thrillers:
Golden Icon – *The Prequel*
Masterpiece
Book of Hours
Stolen Script
Faking Game
Truthful Lies
Broken Windows

Boxsets
Volume 1 – Masterpiece, Book of Hours & Stolen Script
Volume 2 – Faking Game, Truthful Lies & Broken Windows

Other Books by Janet Pywell:
Red Shoes and Other Short Stories
Bedtime Reads
Ellie Bravo

For more information visit:
website: www.janetpywell.com
blog: janetpywellauthor.wordpress.com

All books are available online and can be ordered through major book stores.

If you enjoy my books then please do leave a review from wherever you purchased the book. Your opinion is important to me. I read them all. It also helps other readers to find my work.

Thank you.

Truthful Lies

SHE SIGNED UP FOR DOWNTON ABBEY. SHE STEPPED INTO THE HOUSE OF USHER.

Family dysfunction turns deadly in this riveting thriller! At first blush, the Chedwell Estate, with its sprawling grounds and sumptuous Tudor architecture, appears to be a tranquil palace tucked away in the English countryside, but appearances deceive – the Manor is more House of Usher than Downton Abbey.

In a toothsome take on a classic set-up, after their father's death and their mother's debilitating stroke, siblings Roberto and Stella, in a last-ditch effort to keep things civil, Stella demands they hire a curator to prevent Roberto from ransacking the estate.

Enter Mikky dos Santos, tenacious artist, forger, and all-around talented criminal. From her first day on the job, Mikky feels like she's being taken for a ride by fancy con artists –most of all by Roberto, who is at once flirtatious and threatening. But he's also promised her **a reward if she gets the job done swiftly while neglecting to account for certain**

high-end items.

As Mikky does recon, she even learns that **Roberto has dirty dealings with the mafia, and they once had a price on his head**. And there's plenty more she isn't saying ...

Author Janet Pywell's storytelling is as mesmerizing and complex as her characters, and you'll find yourself rooting for one character and then turning against them on a dime. As Mikky tries to piece together this puzzle of deception, illicit sex, and thinly-veiled threats, she can't tell anymore which lies are "truthful" and what's just dead wrong. But she'd better hurry—these people are lethal.

And you'd hate to lose Mikky once you've met her. She's a unique – and uniquely lovable –female protagonist: **a tough, tattooed, yet vulnerable badass who'll steal your heart with one hand while pilfering priceless paintings with the other. She's a must-read for devotees of complex female sleuths from Kinsey Millhone to the sly Jennifer Crusie novels, especially those with an international flavor, like THE [equally-inked] GIRL WITH THE DRAGON TATTOO**.

You can download **Truthful Lies** here: https://www.amazon.com/dp/B081Y3LDKV

About the Author

Janet lived in Spain and worked in the travel and tourism industry for over twenty years. She managed her own marketing company in Northern Ireland, where she studied for her MA in Creative Writing at the Seamus Heaney Centre at Queen's University Belfast. She uses her experiences of living and travelling abroad and knowledge of locations as an integral part of the scenes in her novels.

To add authenticity to her novels, Janet has studied a variety of courses including, Shipwrecks and Submerged Worlds, Antiquities Trafficking and Art Crime, and Forensic Psychology. She combines her passion for writing, history, and cultural heritage, and loves to see people maintain deep-rooted traditions. Her exciting international crime thrillers are expertly researched and keep you turning the pages.

As well as working on her next book, Janet is also a lecturer at Canterbury Christ Church University on the Creative and Professional Writing course.

You can connect with me on:

- http://janetpywell.com
- https://twitter.com/JanPywellAuthor
- https://www.facebook.com/JanetPywell7227
- https://payhip.com/JanetPywell
- https://janetpywellauthor.wordpress.com

Subscribe to my newsletter:

- https://www.subscribepage.com/janetpywell

Printed in Great Britain
by Amazon